PANIC

SASHA DAWN

carolrhoda LAB
MINNEAPOLIS

Carolrhoda Lab®
An imprint of Lerner Publishing Group, Inc.
241 First Avenue North
Minneapolis, MN 55401 USA

For reading levels and more information, look up this title at
www.lernerbooks.com.

Image credits: Kaponia Aliaksei/Shutterstock.com (female); Shawn Hempel/
Shutterstock.com (scribbles); exile_artist/Shutterstock.com; (scribble);
P-fotography/Shutterstock.com (paper).

Main body text set in Janson Text LT Std Roman.
Typeface provided by Adobe Systems.

Library of Congress Cataloging-in-Publication Data

Names: Dawn, Sasha, author.
Title: Panic / by Sasha Dawn.
Description: Minneapolis : Carolrhoda Lab, [2019] | Summary: "When aspiring
    performer Madelaine finds a poem that helps her finish a song she is writing, she
    decides to find the author in hopes of starting a collaboration."—Provided by
    publisher.
Identifiers: LCCN 2018056852 (print) | LCCN 2018060254 (ebook) | ISBN
    9781541561021 (eb pdf) | ISBN 9781541535749 (th : alk. paper)
Subjects: | CYAC: Actresses—Fiction. | Musicians—Fiction. | Family problems—
    Fiction. | Dating (Social customs)—Fiction. | Friendship—Fiction. | Chicago
    (Ill.)—Fiction.
Classification: LCC PZ7.D32178 (ebook) | LCC PZ7.D32178 Pan 2020 (print) |
    DDC [Fic]—dc23

LC record available at https://lccn.loc.gov/2018056852

Manufactured in the United States of America
1-44950-35798-4/19/2019

For JMD, SMK, & MJM, the stars and
folds in my every origami moon.
Everything I do, I do for you. XOXOX

Where words fail, music speaks.

—Hans Christian Andersen

CHAPTER 1
Saturday, April 29

Who would leave a purple paper moon behind?

I stare at it. It may as well be a neon sign.

I should leave it there, wedged between the window and the snack counter.

But I can't help it. It's not every day you find an origami moon at your favorite coffee shop, right near your usual seat, where someone carved *I was here* into the weathered and worn counter. (And how existential is *that*? If you're reading it, it applies to you, because *you were here*, too. Brilliant.)

I set down my books and sweep the moon into my pile of weekend homework. But the moon beckons me from atop my statistics text, as if to say: *Unfold me, Madelaine.*

Slowly, I obey.

The paper is thick, and it's a rare shimmery purplish green. If we're talking Crayola, it'd be sort of Thistle woven with Seafoam.

When I catch sight of a typewritten font on the underside—Times New Roman, I think—I nearly gasp. There are words inside. I don't know if I'm more excited to see what message is here, or anxious that I could be invading someone's privacy, which I really hate to do.

The words inside the moon are beautiful. It's a poem of sorts. About the tide, maybe. Or perhaps it's a metaphor, but the words are mesmerizing. Waves of stars, and saves and wars.

Behind me, I hear the hiss of whispering.

I glance over my shoulder.

Great.

The Sophias (yeah, they're both named Sophia) are here. They accompanied me—courtesy of my dad's wallet—to a Vagabonds show a couple years back, way before the band's hiatus. We got along for a while, the Sophias and me. We hung out, talked about the band, stocked up at Sephora together, and binged on coffee and scones. Then one day, on a text they didn't realize was a *group* text, I caught them talking about me.

> Sophia 1: She's kind of weird isn't she?
> Sophia 2: We're all sort of weird.
> Sophia 1: But she's like not a GOOD weird.
> Sophia 1: She thinks she's so cool cuz she's been on stage.
> Sophia 2: She's not even that good.
> Sophia 1: Must be nice to have Daddy hook you up for the rest of your life.
> Sophia 2: And can you say obsessed? Is she capable of talking about anything besides Broadway and bands and sheet music?

Um . . . obviously I'm capable, but what else of importance is there to discuss? Did I complain about their constant chatter about this guy or that guy, or mascara this, or lipliner that? It's not like the Sophias can handle a debate about the economy. What else were we supposed to talk about?

Let me pause for a second here.

You know the Sophias.

Both their profile pictures are close-ups of them together because they do *everything* together. Occasionally, one of them will post a picture with a guy, but the other is always in the frame, too. Their pages are littered with posts about their latest haul—miniskirts, makeup, hair accessories, shoes. Their bios read something like: *If you're looking for the brightest star in the universe, you found me.* Location: *on top of the world.*

After I saw those texts, I realized they probably just wanted me around for Dad's concert connections, anyway. Fool me once. I haven't spoken to them since.

God, I wish I'd never brought them here, to the café at the Factory, when we were all friends. Just their being here makes this place feel mainstream. And I liked that this coffee shop was mine, that it was a little slice of hipster heaven outside the boundaries of queen bees and wannabes.

Sophia 1 cups her hand over Sophia 2's ear. For not more than a third of a second, our glances meet, and just after, the two of them erupt in laughter.

Rationally, I know they're probably not talking about me. And even if they are, it can't be anything of substance. But their secrets, their laughter . . . the situation feels like judgment, like criticism. Because they are what they are—stick thin, gorgeous, cool, as if even the rain can't cramp the style they have by the boatload . . . and I am what I am—weird and alone.

I shrink a bit lower in my seat. Maybe if I duck low enough I can simply disappear.

I yank the sleeve of my too-large sweater over my hand and use it to wipe away the condensation on the window for a clearer view of the street outside.

Minnesota Avenue is awash with pink as a horde of wedding guests hustles past with umbrellas in varying shades of it.

I snap a picture and post it to my Instagram with a caption: *This storm is a downpour of peonies.*

Now that the image is cemented into my stream, I think maybe I should have looked more closely before I posted it. I see my own reflection in the glass in the picture: my black beanie, adorned with the logo of my favorite band and shoved atop my chin-length waves, the smudge of mascara under my left eye . . . not to mention the mirror-image of the coffee shop's name, hand-lettered on the window before me, spanning across my reflection's forehead.

I don't usually post pictures of my whole face.

Maybe if I were one of the Sophias, I wouldn't worry that people might find my image not good enough . . . my hair too frizzy, my eyeliner too thick. But being me, I worry about these things. The last thing I want is for someone, somewhere to dig up an old image of me, an old opinion I once posted, and decide who or what I am.

I open the diary app on my phone and jot down what I'm feeling—on display, judged.

A second later, my phone pings as my usual supporters on Instagram chime in with little heart icons, validating me. It's a great world we live in where one's self-esteem is boosted by something so incredibly unimportant as likes on social media, right?

My older half-sister, Hayley, weighs in with virtual hugs. One good thing about the world's obsession with putting our lives online: it's like Hayley's still involved in my daily routine, even though she's all the way across town at DePaul, a safe distance from the turmoil our family life has become since Mom and Dad ceased all civil communication.

Hayley: Get ready to be fabulous in 5, 4, 3, 2 . . .

Hayley always remembers when I have an audition, and she always makes sure to pump me up beforehand. I've been performing since I was practically a toddler, and Hayley's been there to support me every step of the way.

Hayley's the one person I never feel discombobulated around. Even though we hardly hang out anymore, and she's on to the next phase of her life—which has very little to do with me—she's still my best friend. She's been there for me since I was tiny.

She was there for me when I was being torn in opposite directions by the two entities who vowed to keep me whole. She was there for me while I watched my parents' marriage slowly and angrily disintegrate, and then again as they battled in court for years before the divorce was final. I don't know what I would've done without her. My parents weren't thinking of me unless they were arguing over who'd gain control of the trust that holds my earnings.

Now, my parents don't speak to each other. Ever. They communicate through me, which is to say they throw shade at each other through me, and it's exhausting. Why can't they just get it together and be decent to each other?

Heart palpitations. I can't think about it all right now.

I breathe. Relax. Sink into the music.

The alerts on my phone add to the symphony surrounding me.

The murmur of fifty conversations echoes around the room.

Raindrops spatter against the copper awning outside.

The occasional crash of thunder reverberates through the walls of this old building.

It's all percussion. Drums and cymbals.

The rattle of the elevated train across the street. The screech of its brakes as it jolts to a stop at Division.

And the voices of drenched bridesmaids passing on the sidewalk outside may as well be the woodwinds.

So far, I've counted six maids in varying shades of pink—carnation, salmon, tickle-me-pink, cotton candy . . . all the standards. They're rushing by in bare feet. High-heeled sandals dangle from their fingers, and tuxedo jackets, with pink rose boutonnieres pinned to lapels, are tented over their heads.

They're all confident, even in the midst of the downpour.

Then again, if they're bridesmaids, they obviously have friends. Tonight especially: they're the elite, the chosen ones at the head table, elevated above the other wedding guests. Except maybe that one there.

I fix my gaze on one girl who's hanging back a little. No groomsman cups her under the elbow to guide her around puddles. She's making her own way.

She's the only one not having an absolute ball in the rain, seeming in deep contemplation, as if she doesn't get the punch line of a joke everyone else thinks is hilarious. Maybe she's the obligatory cousin in the lineup. I recognize the way she's lingering just a step or two behind, being present without engaging. Doing so is an art form, and I would know. I feel like the obligatory "cousin" pretty much everywhere I go.

But if I tune out the whispers behind me, if I lift the Sophias out of the equation, I'm riding out this storm in my happy place.

This is one of the oldest buildings in Wicker Park, the Chicago neighborhood where I live. As a whole, this place is called the Factory: art galleries and shops, including the café, on the first floor; studio space on the second; and, on the third, with a separate entrance off Minnesota Avenue, a wide-open event space, chic and lofty, where today someone's obviously hosting a wedding reception.

I pull the beanie off my hair, which would fit right in with the wedding party's color scheme. The box was labeled Rose Gold, but it's basically pastel pink tinting my not-so-natural blonde hair. Although it's subtle, Sister Mary Angela hates it. When she first saw it earlier this month, she remanded me to lunch in the dean's office, which I think is bogus, but I can deal. It's not like I want to eat with my contemporaries anyway.

Last week, my sentence was suddenly lifted. Although I didn't know until Hayley told Mom and me, Dad offered a donation to make the "problem" go away.

Out of principle, and out of respect for my mother, I decided to continue with the dean's office routine.

See, despite what the almighty Sister Mary Angela thinks, I didn't dip my head in pink tint as some act of rebellion. Generally, I like rules. I just also like a little variety. And this color has an underlying purpose: My mom's a breast cancer survivor, and next week is the two-year anniversary of her kicking its ass.

I'm not sure even Mom made the connection, but that's all right. Like I said, I didn't do it to get attention. It's a private tribute to my mother's strength and perseverance.

The barista calls from the counter, "Order for Madelaine." Only she says it more like Made*lynn*, ignoring the long A, so I don't get up right away. There could be two of us waiting out the rain here. It's awfully crowded.

"Mocha roast? Two pumps of peppermint?" she says. "With a butter croissant?"

Yeah, she means me.

I don't bother correcting her when I collect my second cup

of the afternoon. She's not the first person who's mispronounced my name. But she could at least smile and make me feel like my seven-dollar mocha roast is worth the price, couldn't she?

I return to my seat at the window-side counter.

And for a second, I lock gazes with a man on the other side of the window. He's in a black raincoat, hood up, but somehow I know he's looking at me.

Judging.

Spying.

A chill runs up my spine.

Hunting.

CHAPTER 2

I have to calm down.

I go through the process in my mind so that the panic doesn't get out of control.

He's just a man. Just looking at the coffee shop.

Breathe.

Find reality.

Think.

What's perception? What's real?

Where in the Venn diagram of life do perception and reality overlap? Likely, this guy isn't in that weird little overlap.

Okay. I'm okay now.

There's a wrought iron floor register under this barstool, and on a day like today, the heat takes the dampness out of the air just as readily as it dries my canvas high-tops. Cozy. Home away from home, save the giggles of the two girls behind me, who laugh as if they were just inside my head. Ha! I can practically hear them saying. *Imagine being so full of yourself you think everyone's watching you.*

I shake it off.

I pop my earbuds back in, log into Lyrically—a site for music addicts like me—and let the music play. It's my own work, and it's only half done. Won't be complete until I have the perfect lyrics to accompany it.

I stare at the splinters of lyrics I can't seem to write.

Sure, there's a flash of promise in some of these words. But when nothing of brilliance flows from my fingertips, I find myself wandering the internet. Checking Instagram. Everyone's up to something. Hayley's eating cheese puffs.

Funny how posting a pic of your orange-stained fingers amounts to "up to something." But this particular post has already jump-started a conversation. Commiserations. Suggestions. Who knew one could consume such snacks with a plastic fork right out of the bag?

But Hayley's like that. Magnetic. She's comfortable, entertained, and entertaining.

Weird that, of the two of us, I'm the performer.

Yet I wish I had my sister's ease.

It's the hypercritical world we live in that gives me pause every time I'm about to put myself out there. It's bad enough to get a barrage of criticism from professional reviewers after a run on stage, but to hear the clunky opinions of *everyone in the world* who just wants to run down *everyone else in the world* . . . jeez. Even when those reviews are sloppy and self-centered—this insert-art-form-here didn't meet my individual needs and maybe it was because *nothing* would have met my individual needs at the time—they still affect me. Still have me questioning my worth, my talent, my goals.

I take a deep breath. Just thinking about it makes my heart seize.

Yet at the same time I feel an urge, a determination deep inside me, to actually *make* something of myself. I want to be known—and not for just what my dad can do for gossip girls.

I want to be able to say I did well, I have a future, I was here.

I trace the carving on the countertop with my fingertip.

It might happen. If I keep auditioning. If I keep honing my skills. If I spend my senior year amongst people who understand me, I can make it. And maybe I'll even manage to do more than bring other people's music to life—maybe I'll find the creativity and the courage to share my own creations with the world.

Lots of people from this neighborhood paved the way. They could have been sitting at this counter, once upon a time, or maybe they've ridden in the same L cars that take me to school, which absolutely blows my mind. Wicker Park gave the world numerous musical geniuses, not to mention a slew of comedians from The Second City. And someday, maybe, some other girl sitting on this stool, looking out at a rainy day is going to say *Yeah, Madelaine Joseph wrote her first song here. #LifeGoals.*

The rain against the windows is nearly hypnotic when paired with the music piping through my earbuds. I can shut the whole world out on days like today.

I draw inspiration from the sounds resonating in my ears and watch the people around me. They migrate like birds—a flock crosses the street en masse, heads of umbrellas dripping raindrops, and people inside the cafe fall in line, taking turns at the apex of the V when their names and coffee orders are called out.

Each of them embodies a note in a song, showing up here and there, fading, and popping up again moments later.

I hear music by just looking at the black dots and circles positioned on the staff. My sister rolled her eyes when I first told her that. But it's true.

I pick at my croissant. Sip my peppermint mocha.

I jot down lovely phrases when they come to me, things like *he bridges the gap with smiles*. Then I think it sounds like dental work, so I cross it out.

Beneath a folded moon.
Moon of folded parchment.
Folded moon.
Paper moon.
Origami moon.

I read the poem I found in the origami moon again. A few lines repeat twice on the page. It reads like a chorus:

Something in the breeze
Freed
East coast memories
I hide
Beside me.
Deep inside
Abiding like the tide.
Somewhere in the ocean
Rose
Golden tones
Bellowed notes
I hide
Beside me.
Deep inside
Abiding like the tide.

Wait.
I rewind my track. Play it again. It *fits*.

Oh. My. God. It fits!

I glance around the room, aching for a look of acknowledgment, a nod, a *Yeah, that's my moon.*

The activity around me carries on as if I'm not even here, as if I could lift right out of this scene and no one would notice. No one's looking at me, no one's worried about me or this origami moon.

I'm not usually one for collaboration, but . . .

I have to find whoever wrote this poem.

My phone buzzes with a text.

Dad: Car arriving shortly.
Dad: Got caught up in a meeting so I'll see you
    afterward for dinner.
Dad: Knock 'em dead!

My heart sinks. Dad was supposed to pick me up himself. Ever since Mom started working full time, getting me to auditions and rehearsals has been his responsibility. I mean, Giorgio may be a kick-ass driver, but a pep-talk guru he's not.

I get that Dad manages other talent, though. I'm not his only client. And he knows I rarely get stage fright anymore, so it's not the end of the world if I have to go to an audition by myself. Even an audition of this magnitude.

I look out at Minnesota Avenue just as Dad's business limo pulls up to the curb.

Ugh. I'd much rather have hopped on the L if he couldn't make it.

I mean, the bridal party walked in the rain, but I get my dad's car?

Pushing down my frustration, I gather my things, purple

moon included. Beanie on head, hoodie zipped up, backpack slung over my right shoulder.

"Must be nice," I think I hear one of the Sophias say as I head toward the exit.

Maybe she's not even talking about me. Maybe it was my imagination.

But I know it wasn't.

I take a deep breath. It's okay. I'd rather be me than be a Sophia.

CHAPTER 3

I'm sitting in a room with eight other girls just like me: all five-five to five-eight, fifteen to eighteen years old, with a bag full of necessities—dance shoes, sheet music—and a pocketful of dreams.

I pull out the brown bob wig from my bag and secure it over the rose-gold waves atop my head. I'm not sure how they're going to feel about my pink hair, and I don't want to give them any reason not to consider me.

"Madelaine Joseph?"

She said my name correctly. Good sign. "Yes." I stand.

My fingertips go numb for not more than a breath before my mother's voice filters into my head to calm me: *Shut out the world. Just perform out there.*

I smile and follow the casting director down a hallway.

"Any relation to Jesse Joseph?"

Sigh. "He's my father."

She jots a note and turns over my headshot, I assume to read my bio.

"And Ella Norini's your mother." A smile. "Is she still working?"

"She is." It's not exactly true, not in the sense the casting director means—unless she wants to know if Mom is still an executive assistant splitting time between two large corporations in the Loop—but it's not a lie.

For a second, I fully register the fact that my talented mother is making copies and filing paperwork. Such a waste.

"Well, with parents like yours, I'm excited to see what you can do."

"They've been wonderful sources of influence." It's what I'm supposed to say, and it pleases her.

I enter the audition room.

"Mezzo-soprano?" she asks.

"Yes."

"Dance experience?"

"Twelve years instruction in ballet, jazz, tap—"

"You tap?"

"Very well." If I do say so myself.

"No one taps anymore."

"I think it's making a comeback," I say.

"From your lips to God's ears."

"I studied tap under Andrew Tomlinson. And I have seven years lyrical and contemporary, ma'am."

"Professional productions?"

"Yes, ma'am. I've been performing since I was about four, and my career launched with *Mary Poppins* when I was six."

Her finger traces words on the back of my headshot. She raises a brow and looks at me over her glasses. "I see you've had a busy few years."

I smile and nod.

"Let's get started."

I sing my heart out. I tap by request. I read for the part of Pepper.

It's nothing I haven't done dozens of times in the past year, nothing I won't do hundreds of times in the years to come.

But *this* audition could very well cement my future. A production of this size, under this director, just might put me in line for acceptance to NYU—my dream school. It could open doors to work outside the city, across the country, and maybe even light the path to the almighty Broadway.

You might think it's strange that I'm comfortable on stage or in front of a panel of judges or on camera, when having a simple face-to-face conversation terrifies me some days. But it's a pretty common phenomenon for people like me. When I'm performing, I'm allowed a break from the mess I usually am. I fit myself snugly into whatever character the stage demands, and I thrive under those lights.

I perform till my heart's about to burst . . . only to have the casting team stare at me blankly throughout the whole process.

Once it's over, Pepper dissipates, and Madelaine slowly filters back in. I pull the wig from my head. Hello, old boring self.

Now that I'm no longer in character, I'm agonizingly conscious of every raised eyebrow, every downturned lip, every dismissive grunt that the casting team directed at me. They were all smiles at first, but they painted the entire room a shade of doom once the door closed.

Trying to breathe steadily, I check my phone.

Hayley sent her usual break a leg. I adore my sister, despite the obvious animosity between her and my mom lately.

Mom sent the expected string of hearts and this audition's version of *you-were-tap-dancing-in-utero* to encourage me.

Even my Nana Adie texted a goofy-yet-inspirational meme.

And the latest text from my father.

Dad: You got this. See you soon. Morton's tonight?

I was really hoping we'd get to hang out at his place. I haven't been there in forever. Quality time with my dad these days has started to feel like a series of business meetings. And I never know how to respond when he changes our plans. At least he didn't cancel outright this time. The only thing more awkward than sitting through a rushed dinner out with him would be an evening at home listening to Mom rant about his parenting style.

I have to find a way to make my way onto a stage. I have to find a decent escape in a character—any character—so I can cease being me for hours of rehearsal, for weeks of runs, while my parents sink back into another string of useless arguments.

I imagine the Sophias rolling their eyes at this thought—*yeah, like it's so tough riding in limos and jet-setting off to Broadway to take in a show whenever Daddy offers*—but they don't understand. They don't understand the exhaustion I feel in being the rope in the constant game of tug-of-war between my mother and father.

Sure, maybe the world is at my fingertips when I'm riding around with Dad, but the majority of the time, I'm with my mom, who sighs heavily and checks the balance in her checking account if I tell her I'm out of mascara.

I take a selfie, this time ensuring only one of my eyes is visible in the frame, and post it to Instagram: *Audition = wars of Scarlet and Razzmatazz in my nerves.*

"Hey, Lainey."

I look up from shoving my dance shoes back into my bag. The familiar voice belongs to another girl who frequents the Chicagoland audition circuit. "McKenna. Hi." I hope she doesn't mistake my tone as my being less than friendly. She's never been anything but ridiculously nice to me, but she's also mega-talented. If she auditioned for Pepper, I'm screwed.

"A bunch of us are heading out for smoothies. Sort of a celebratory thank-god-that-audition's-over. Brutal in there, weren't they?"

"Yeah. If ever a casting team could take the most talented people in the city and make them feel clumsy and idiotic, it's this one." Ugh, I'm babbling. I either freeze up or blurt out way too much when I stumble into a conversation with someone I don't know well.

McKenna smiles. "You wanna join us? Brendon's coming—you know my brother, Brendon, right?"

Pause.

If the Sophias are attached at the hip, Brendon and McKenna Weekes—twins—are attached at the umbilical cord, but they're a hell of a lot more pleasant. Their collective bio might read something like *Never fully dressed without a smile*, or maybe *All the world's a stage*. Their social media is packed with group pictures, declarations about the world's best performances, and Tony-award predictions.

"And Brendon's all about this new guy he's dating—"

"A guy this time?"

"You know Brendon. If someone's hot, they're hot."

I nod. "Agreed." I don't actually know Brendon that well, but he's super open about being pan, and I respect that. I wonder what it's like to be so confident, so sure of who you are and what you want. I have enough trouble approaching someone of one gender, let alone *any* gender.

"Should be pretty entertaining," McKenna's saying.

If I could conjure even a fraction of her brother's animation,

I might actually find a place I fit. I'm half-tempted to blow off my dinner plans with Dad and tag along. But that'll piss Dad off, and I don't think I have the energy for one of his freeze-outs. "Thanks, but I gotta meet my dad."

"Some other time, maybe?"

The truth is I'd really love to hang out with more people who understand theater life, but I tense up a little at the thought of it. For one thing, we're constantly in competition with each other, and I think that'd be hard to overcome. I mean, how do you enjoy and support someone who just stole your future? At least I never had to worry about *that* with the Sophias.

Second, it's always a hassle to start hanging out with a new crowd. Once Dad catches wind of it, he'll be buying up tickets to the hottest Broadway show du jour to ensure things go well with my new friends.

Sounds great, right? I suppose it is—in theory. But that's how the Sophias happened.

Still, I nod. "Sounds good."

"Great." Her phone is out of her pocket now. "Still have the same number?"

"Yeah." My heart lifts a little to know that she hasn't deleted my number from years ago, when we were both ensemble in *Peter Pan.*

"I'm adding you to the group chat. God, can you believe the call-back list will be posted by morning?"

Once again, the weight of all we've just done hits me like a brick wall. My immediate, and in some respects long-term, future is simmered down to a ten-minute slice of my day. "It'll be tough to sleep tonight."

"We'll be in it together, sister. Commiserating. Seriously, if you can't sleep, reach out."

My phone pings with a *hello* text from McKenna, part of a group message, which McKenna has inexplicably named "Raspberry Beret."

I text back the same and, just for fun, switch the alert for the text group to the Prince song for which it's named.

A few seconds later, His Royal Purpleness sings through my phone when McKenna's brother chimes in on the message.

Brendon: Dream it, be it, do it.

"Ha!" McKenna points to my phone. "Fast work! That's *great!*"

I like this about McKenna: it wasn't exactly edgy of me to pair the song with the text group, but she's enthusiastic about it anyway.

"You ever going to come to our high school?" McKenna shoves her phone into the waistband of her dance pants.

"Actually, I'm going to be talking to my dad about it again tonight."

She crosses fingers on both her hands and lets out a little squee.

"I know, right?" And for just a second, I again consider blowing off my dinner plans to join her and Brendon.

But like the dutiful daughter I am, I text Dad's driver, then go out to meet the car at the corner.

While I'm waiting, I catch a glimpse again: a figure on the corner across the street.

Black raincoat. Hood up.

I hold my breath.

Is it the same guy I thought was looking at me earlier at the Factory?

Giorgio pulls up, and I exhale.

Probably not the same guy. Black raincoats are very common, after all.

Giorgio drives me to Morton's. Dad and I sit down to dinner. Dad's on his phone, so I stay on mine, checking my favorite band's website. No one's heard from Vagabonds since last July. God, how I've missed witnessing the band's banter online. I've missed watching their a cappella snippets performed with the ukulele, their reluctant interviews . . . They were an escape in my otherwise harried existence.

Hayley's texting again.

Hayley: How'd it go today?
Me: Eh.
Hayley: Psh
Hayley: I'm sure you were fabulous.
Me: Ehhh
Hayley: You're awesome. You'll get it.
Me: Here's to hoping.
Me: Found something interesting at the coffee shop.

I fish the origami moon from my backpack and unfold it. Snap a picture of it. Text it to my sister.

Me: And the weird thing is that it actually fits with the piece I'm working on.
Hayley: Who wrote it?
Me: Don't know.

Dad clears his throat. "Uh-huh," he's saying into his phone. "Yeah. Me, too."

I try not to roll my eyes. I know he's talking to his girl-friend, whom he refers to as Miss Karissa, like she's my kinder-garten teacher. They've been together for . . . God, it must be years now, but for some reason he hardly ever talks about her or their relationship.

"Yeah, okay." He shifts in his seat and practically turns his back to me. "Tomorrow night. Sure. Get Jennica and the boys ready, and we'll all take a trip out there. Yeah. Me too. I do, I do."

God. He can't even tell her he loves her in front of me.

I wonder if this is how Hayley felt when Dad left her mom to pursue a future with mine. I wonder how long it took for her to feel as if she were part of his new adventures . . . because more often than not, I feel like a visitor with a limited day pass. Then again, Hayley was only about four when it all happened to her, and her mother isn't super involved in anything but sedatives—in fact I don't even know if Hayley's even still in touch with her mom. So her experience was probably very different than what I'm going through.

I shoot her another text.

Me: Talk later?
Hayley: At study group tonight. Big test Monday.
    Tomorrow morning?
Me: OK
Hayley: <3
Me: <3 <3 <3

Dad finally gets off the phone.

"So you're taking Jennica and the boys someplace?" I ask, copying his phrasing, like the boys are a single entity. "Where are you going?"

"Hey, let's talk about you," he says. "I thought the limo would be a nice surprise for you today. Did Giorgio get you there on time?"

For a second I just frown. Why did he ignore my question?

"Hello? Madelaine? Are you in there somewhere?"

"Yeah."

"How was it? Arriving in style?"

How the hell am I supposed to respond to this? Admit I'd rather have taken the L, and I'd be ungrateful. Respond enthusiastically, and I'll be finding myself riding in hired cars for all of eternity. I know, I know. Poor baby. But I don't want to be that girl.

I shrug. "Giorgio's great."

"And the audition? Like I always say: walk in there like you've already got the role."

"And I did."

"Great. You amaze me, kid. And I think I might have a connection," Dad says. "A mutual friend of the director."

I don't want to get a role based on Dad's connections. I want to earn it.

"Before you start on your idealistic speech again, how do you think everyone else gets a foot in the door?" Dad asks. "It's who you know. I'm your manager, this is my job."

Up to a point it is. But I often wish that, instead of leaning on his friends to get me parts, he'd give me the tools I need to develop my talents and land jobs on my own merits.

"So tell me more about the audition, kiddo."

I don't want him to know how much I'm stressing over it. I search for a positive spin. "She said I was a strong tapper."

"You are." He'd say that even if I weren't because he doesn't know enough about tap dancing to know if I'm good or not.

He doesn't have an artistic bone in his body, but he manages to get me the right auditions with the right companies at the right time.

"My tap shoes are pretty worn."

"It's your mother's turn to buy a set, yes?"

A lump forms in my throat. I hate when they do this. "But maybe you could pick up the tab this time? For your favorite client?"

Dad takes a deep breath. "Maddy, I want to talk to you about something."

He's the only one who calls me Maddy, and usually I don't mind, but something about the way he says it raises my hackles tonight. Or maybe I'm pissed about the car, the dinner out when we were supposed to eat together at his house, the weekend visit that has somehow whittled down to only an hour or so at Morton's, and the fact that he's ready to haggle with my mother over a pair of tap shoes.

"Your mom's taking me back to court," Dad says.

"What? Why?" And now I'm pissed at Mom. I'm so over their fighting.

"She wants more money, but with the visitation schedule being fifty-fifty, I don't see any reason for it."

"Can you meet her halfway?" I ask. "Settle out of court?"

"I give her extra occasionally, when things come up and I can't see you when I'm supposed to. I don't know what more she thinks she needs."

Well, that sounds reasonable. Still—"She wouldn't take this step unless things were bad."

And even though Dad technically has me fifty percent of the time, he reneges almost weekly—case in point, this cop-out dinner at Morton's—so Mom's left robbing Peter to pay Paul.

Several weekends once last month, she skipped breakfast and lunch when I was home but was supposed to be with Dad. She said she wasn't hungry, but now I wonder if she hadn't planned on my being there and was trying to save food.

"Didn't your mom go on a trip just last month?" Dad asks.

I nod.

"Maybe she shouldn't be going on vacation if money is tight."

Three days in Minnesota isn't much of a vacation compared to his taking Miss Karissa, Jennica, and the boys to Italy this past spring break. But I don't correct him. I just don't want to talk about it.

"Maddy."

I don't want to look up at him, either, but I meet his gaze.

"I'm not the one who did this. I'm not the one serving the papers, you understand? I'm not the one fighting."

"Okay."

"Don't you see the position she's putting me in? I give her ample support. If she mismanages the funds, that doesn't automatically mean that I have to come to the rescue. It means she has to better manage her finances."

I'm not hungry anymore, but our dinner arrives. I pick at my plate.

"It's not my responsibility to find her a decent job," he goes on. "And if she hadn't moved in with Mr. Wonderful, she wouldn't have forfeited her alimony."

I bite my tongue. It's called *maintenance*, actually, and it's been two years since Mom lost it, but it's still a sore spot for all of us. Ted Haggerty was actually really nice to me. Picture an absent-minded professor—graying ponytail, corduroy trousers and plaid button-down included—and you've got Ted. He's a psychiatrist who fancies himself an artist. He used to go to the

Factory on open mic nights—it's where Mom met him—and he'd bite on an unlit cigar, sit in the spotlight, and rant about whatever happened to be on his mind. He never prepared, but his off-the-cuff commentary was always entertaining, always had the crowd cheering.

For the six months he lived with us, I knew sort of what it felt like to have a normal dad . . . the kind of dad who stops for cheese fries on the way home because he knows you've had a bad day. The kind of dad who talks about buying you a dog because you've never had one before.

Mom asked me to keep the cohabitation a secret from Dad—nothing like putting me in an impossible situation—but Dad found out anyway. And then he was pissed at me, and bam! Dad changed the security code at his house because he said he couldn't trust me even with that, my visits there ceased, and my parents were back in court again to nullify maintenance.

As for Ted? Mom's diagnosis came two days before we were supposed to pick up a dog from the shelter.

Ted left the day after she went to the doctor. Too much reality for him, according to Mom. I have my own theories, but it was obviously a mistake for Mom to have him move in.

He still checks in with me occasionally. And every so often, he posts pictures of the dog that was supposed to be mine on his Facebook page. He went with the name I'd suggested: Vinny. Every time I see the dog, my heart aches a little.

"Your mom will have to work it out on her own," Dad says. "I can't be responsible for her choices. I'm not going to bail her out of this. She could always ask Mr. Wonderful to pony up."

Dad has a point. Mom could have thought of me, or at least made sure Ted was in it for the long haul, before she pulled the trigger on cohabitation.

Still, Mom's had some bad luck, and my career aspirations aren't exactly inexpensive. It's been tough and even though we moved in with Nana Adie, Dad can obviously still help.

I wonder if he would be more willing if Miss Karissa and her kids weren't part of the equation.

"That's kind of apples and oranges, isn't it?" I say. "Ted's not the one who lives in a mansion on the lake." This is guaranteed to piss him off, but I can't help it.

"I'm entitled to spend my money where I see fit," he says, in a voice you'd use to explain a simple rule to a toddler. "You never go without, do you? But what kind of dad would I be if I made everything easy for everyone? What message would that send to you? That you wouldn't have to work hard for everything you get."

There's no point in turning this into an argument. "Okay."

"What your mother needs is a little tough love," Dad says. "She's going to have to figure things out. She's a smart girl."

"Woman."

Finally, a smile appears on his face.

"So. Let's talk about something else. Have you been thinking any more about college?" Dad asks.

"NYU," I say.

"Still NYU." Dad nods. "*Only* NYU?"

"I know it's competitive—and expensive—but—"

"Don't worry about that."

A shot of relief rushes through me.

Dad clears his throat. "You do what you have to do to get there. Study hard. Dance, sing, and act harder. And I can definitely pony up half the tuition for NYU."

Just like that, the feeling of panic returns to me. Half is not nearly enough.

"It's in our papers," Dad reminds me.

"Well, then, what about performing arts high school?" I say. "Couldn't you at least pay for me to go to the academy next year? It's where I truly belong. You know that."

"I agree."

"Well, Mom can't afford to pay half of the tuition for a special high school—even paying for Saint Mary's is a stretch—"

"We both contribute to your education, and that wasn't *my* decision. That was the order of the court, of the judge."

"But that was when she was getting maintenance." It hits me that this is probably why she's going back to court now; this is what she wants Dad's money for. My tuition at the high school of my dreams.

"And again: it's not my fault she isn't getting it anymore. Don't let her make me the bad guy. Let's give her time to figure this out."

"But I've already missed out on three years," I say. "This was the plan before the divorce, right? I was supposed to go to the academy."

"And your mother's the reason you're not there."

I feel sick. Why did Mom have to let Ted move in? And it only lasted six months, to boot. Six months, and now I'm paying the price for the rest of my life.

But there has to be another way.

I can't exactly get a job at a coffee shop to afford the things I need. I have little time to spare as it is, and if I'm cast, I'll have even less. It's not like I'm not working, though. I've been performing professionally since I was four. I have earnings. I gain control of them when I'm twenty-five.

"How much do I have in my account?" I ask. "Maybe I can cover some of the tuition for the academy, and then with the right exposure, I should be able to get a scholarship to NYU."

"The money in your account is not for tuition."

"Well, how much is there? If it's mine, I should be able to spend it where I need to."

"And you will. When you're twenty-five."

Tears fill my eyes. I stare down at my phone so Dad can't see. *Don't cry, don't cry.*

My heart refuses to beat at a normal pace. I text Hayley:

Me: Trouble brewing on the home front.
Hayley: What's going on?
Me: Mom's taking Dad back to court for more support.
Hayley: :/
Me: It's a last ditch effort for senior year at the
	academy. He can afford it but insists on a battle.
Me: I mean, this is my future we're talking about!!!
Hayley: Love you.
Hayley: But maybe Ella needs to get her shit together.

Instantly, I tense up. Hayley and my mom used to get along. Like, really well. And I don't want Hayley to be mad at me, but . . .

Me: Why are you hating on my mom so much lately?
Hayley: I'm not.
Hayley: But it's the truth.
Hayley: If not for her own sake, she should do it for you.
Me: Maybe if your mom did something for you, my
	mom wouldn't be in this position.

It's a low blow, but it's true. My mom has been more of a

mother to Hayley than her own. Still, it was snarky of me to mention it.

I start to apologize, but before I can hit the send button, my sister sends me her Bitmoji raising her middle finger.

I delete my apology.

> Me: Must be nice to know Dad will pay 100% of your bills.
> Me: He won't do that for me.
> Hayley: He's done more for you than he's ever done for me.
> Hayley: Gain some self-awareness, will you?

I suddenly feel totally alone.

For the rest of the meal I respond just enough to Dad's attempts at chitchat so that he can't accuse me of pouting. As he's taking care of the bill, my phone pings. It's a friend request on Lyrically. I open it.

The name: Dylan Thomas. Obviously a pseudonym—props for literary taste.

I click on the info tab.

Gender: Blank.

Pronouns: Blank.

Age: Seventeen.

Bio: *Observer, music lover, quiet lurker.*

The profile picture is an image of a quill and a reserve of ink atop a draft of words on parchment.

The message: *I saw the pic of the origami. I left that moon at the Factory. Let's talk?*

CHAPTER 4

The rain lets up by the time Giorgio pulls up to our place on West Evergreen.

Dad's chattering about some show getting ready to close on Broadway. I haven't done more than *half* listen to him since he offered to pay *half* my tuition at NYU—I've been pondering Dylan Thomas and the moon and whether I should accept a friend request from a stranger—until I hear the name of one of my Broadway idols. Suddenly, I'm all ears.

"Do you know how awesome it would be to meet him?" I say.

Dad smiles at my sudden interest. It's the most I've said since I picked at my dinner.

"Maybe we should go then," he says. "I can get you backstage for a meet and greet."

"For real?"

"It'll be a good experience for you. You can speak with the performers about life on Broadway."

"Incredible. I get to meet the cast? Really?"

"You want to go?"

"Of course I want to go!" Any opportunity to be on Broadway, even as a spectator, is a good one, but this . . . wow. It's more jackpot than opportunity.

"Great. All set."

All set? Did he mention a date? But I can't ask him now, or he'll know I was tuning him out earlier. "As long as it doesn't interfere with rehearsal," I say. "If I'm cast."

"You got it in the bag."

I roll my eyes. Spoken like a true dad-slash-manager.

"See you soon, kiddo," Dad says. "Shopping, maybe, next week? Before the trip?"

"For tap shoes?"

"Maddy." His sigh is exasperated "Didn't we talk about that? I'm only asking for your mom to pull her weight."

"Yeah, okay." I'm so over trying to convince him, and so tired of the back and forth between him and Mom that I have to remind myself that *we're going to Broadway*. Good things are on the horizon.

I gather my audition stuff and go to get out of the car.

"Hey."

"Yeah." I look back at him.

"You know I'll get the shoes for you if she won't. But try. Put a little pressure on her. It's what's right. I'll see you soon." He puts his hand up for a high five.

I half-heartedly slap it, exit the car, and climb the steps to our place.

We're on the top floor of a building we in Chicago call a three-flat. A young couple who just adopted a baby rents the basement unit, and a chick in her forties with a penchant for patchouli rents the main floor. It's not a bad place to live, but if I ever make it big, I'm buying my mom and Nana the kind of house where they can spread out—a dance studio for Mom, a little office where Nana can draw and paint to her heart's content. Especially because I took the room where she used to have her easel and art supplies.

As I climb the stairs to our unit, the familiar scents of tomato gravy and sausage and peppers filter down to meet me, and classic Madonna rings in my ears. Nana is singing along.

I close the door behind me and reset the alarm. Nana appears in the doorway. She's wearing a long turquoise-and-fuchsia tunic in a geometric pattern over pale pink jeans she cut off at the shins. Her pink-framed glasses are perched atop her dark curls like a headband. "My Madelaine."

"Hi, Nana."

"Thought you were with your dad tonight."

"Yeah, well . . . you know how that goes." I drop my dance bag on the bench by our door and shove off my shoes.

"Oh, Lainey. I hate that he's constantly canceling on you."

Even though I've been thinking along the same lines all night, my guard goes up instantly. "It's okay. I mean, it's not like I don't have a life of my own."

"I just want you to know you're worth more than that."

"Mom home?"

"She had an appointment in Minnesota late this afternoon. She'll be home soon."

"Minnesota again?" She was in Minnesota last month, too. There are a couple of great theaters there. Hope floats to the surface. Maybe she trekked out there for a callback. "What for? A job?"

"No."

And just that quickly, the hope crashes.

If it's not a callback, this appointment is probably more date than interview. I wish she'd just tell me if she's seeing someone, although I guess I can understand why she wouldn't.

She's not good at dating.

Her relationships are borderline disastrous, as evidenced by Ted Haggerty's abrupt exit. Before Ted, there were others. Rick comes to mind; he hummed while he ate and was addicted to painkillers. Then there was Rex, who stole one of her bracelets. My gut sort of hollows out in anticipation for the hurricane about to come.

"How was the audition?"

I blink away thoughts of Mom's worst mistakes and say, "Oh!"

Nana smiles. "Remember the audition?"

"I have to work on my vibrato, I'm just not good at belting, and I wasn't expecting to tap, and it was an improv piece, so I don't think I exactly nailed it, if you know what I mean, but—"

"Did you do your best?"

"Yes."

"You can't expect more of yourself than your best. What will be, will be."

If you're not determined to make a life in theater, maybe this is good advice. Maybe you expect to flub numbers occasionally if your life's ambition is to sit at a desk, but you can't flub anything and expect to succeed on stage. I know I have to do better than my best if I'm ever going to be on Broadway. And . . .

"I need new taps."

Nana sighs. "I suppose your father won't—"

"He says it's Mom's turn."

"Do me a favor. Don't mention it to your mom tonight. Or at all this month. You know what? I'll give you my card. Go get yourself a pair tomorrow."

"Nana." She's on a fixed income. She shouldn't have to do this.

"It's settled. I'll pop for tap shoes this time."

This whole thing is absolutely ridiculous. Dad and Miss Karissa and Jennica and the boys. Mom and her string of bad boyfriends. And my parents won't talk to each other, but they're communicating in their own little *fuck-you*s through me.

The tears I've been keeping at bay since dinner come like a torrential downpour.

"Oh, honey." Nana Adie gathers me into her arms.

I let her, even though I'm not usually one for physical contact, and breathe in the scents of tomatoes and peppers seemingly always embedded in her clothing.

"Do you ever feel like you just want out?" I pull back from her embrace. "Like nothing you do is good enough to make things work?"

"Are you kidding? I've got three ex-husbands and seven decades of mistakes behind me."

"So you're saying life just sucks, and I have to get used to it." "I'm saying life is *wonderful*." She takes me by the shoulders and studies me. "No one is born with all the answers, and no one can skate through this world without screwing up. It's all trial and error, honey. I'm still trying to figure things out at my age."

"Doesn't sound too wonderful to me."

"It's all about point of view. Think about possibility. The whole world is out there for us to explore. The whole world. Close your eyes and imagine it."

When I imagine the whole world, I imagine Times Square.

I absolutely love New York, and nowhere else will give me a leg up in my chosen industry like NYU.

"You know when you feel like you belong somewhere?"

Nana nods.

"I feel like it's just out of reach. Like I'll never get there."

"You will. If you want it bad enough, if you try hard enough—"

"What do you do if the only avenue to your chosen life is too expensive?"

"Honey." She sighs. "A girl like you . . . with your father's salary . . . the words *too expensive* don't apply to you."

"It's not Dad's salary I'm worried about. It's Mom's. How can I ask her—"

"Your mom is taking steps to fix all that."

"The court case." "I see he mentioned it," she mutters.

"I wish she'd just get a better-paying job."

"Do you think she's marketable? With a performing arts degree and a giant gap in her resume?" Nana crosses her arms. "She did a valiant thing, staying home to take care of a child who wasn't hers. She could have worked in productions, even if she wasn't performing, but she chose to take care of Hayley instead because your father was going to provide. That was their deal. And when you came along, she ran herself ragged. She did everything she was supposed to do, down to the letter, and your father split. She's trying to make lemonade out of spoiled, rotten lemons, young lady."

I don't want to look at her. I feel like a brat, like I'm demanding things I don't deserve. I know Dad screwed up when he left, but so did Mom. "But he has a point. If Mom hadn't let Ted move in, we wouldn't be in this situation, and I have to agree—"

"Stop right there."

I shut up when Nana raises her voice, which is an extremely rare occurrence.

"Your mother was broken after your father left her for that *Miss Karissa*. She was entitled to make a mistake or two."

"And to leave me paying for it?"

She chews on her words for a moment and then spits them out one by one. "Tell me: what kind of world do we live in where a woman can do the right thing, sacrifice her job for her children—and she didn't have to do that for *you*, let alone Hayley—and our court system allows a man to financially control her? She put in her time. She earned every dime of that maintenance and more, like so many women who stay home with children, and the courts allow the men to control her decision to live with someone or not. What would happen to the American family if no one stayed home with the children?"

"Oh, so it's my fault she quit working and stayed home? I didn't ask her to do that."

"The point I'm making: your mother made it all possible. Your dad wouldn't have gone very far in his career if he were chasing around town, getting you and your sister everywhere you had to be or staying up all night when one of you had the flu. That's why your father still has his money, but your mother's the one who should inspire you."

I want to tell her that Mom does inspire me. By being an awesome mom, by staying home with Hayley and me and by teaching me to dance and to love myself and to love the good in other people, and by always, always, supporting me.

What I can't tell Nana is that deep down, I'm worried none of that is enough—for Mom or for me.

And I'm still mad at Mom for letting Ted move in and ruining everything. Or maybe I'm pissed that she couldn't keep him. He may be a coward for taking off instead of staying to support Mom through the cancer, but he was nice to me.

"You shouldn't have to make your own way," Nana says. "But I want you to know you can. You have it in you to do marvelous things."

I wish I didn't have to ask either of my parents for another single thing. But that doesn't seem likely. "If I'm not called back for this audition—"

"If you're not, there'll be others. Or you'll write your own musical to star in. You'll blaze your own trail."

I roll my eyes. "Not all of us are Lin-Manuel Miranda."

"Not all of us are Madelaine Emmah Joseph. But you are. And you can. The only thing stopping you is right here." She taps me on the forehead. "Get out of your head and *do it*."

I shake my head.

She doesn't get it.

CHAPTER 5

Hayley: Another theory about the Vagabonds hiatus.
Hayley: Go check it out!

I guess Hayley's not mad at me anymore.

My fingers are instantly at work, rushing over my screen, tapping out directives to the Vagabonds website, then to blogs that discuss it.

Since the band abruptly went on hiatus, the fandom has uncovered all sorts of cryptic clues as to what they might be up to.

I scan through the latest evidence that a tour may be on the horizon. It's an interesting theory, although fans are often on wild-goose chases. Some people are interested in the mystery aspect of it all. Some people are simply jonesing for more music.

Me? All of the above.

But the real reason I'm addicted to rumors of a return: I relate to the need to fade away every now and then. Just like Vagabonds.

They've made it to where I want to be. Everyone knows their names, but that doesn't mean they want the world to scrutinize every move they make.

I'm the same way. I love music. I love the stage. I can't imagine a day when I won't love performing.

But I know it comes with an intense, heated spotlight. There's no way around it.

The stage equals invasion of privacy. Society doesn't generally respect that some of us don't want notoriety; we just want to perform.

I screenshot the new theory, file it in an album, and text Hayley.

> Me: I think you need a degree in astrophysics
> Me: To figure out all those clues!
> Me: But secretly, I totally want to do what they did.
> Me: Disappear on my own terms.
> Me: And if someone pays enough attention
> Me: They'll know where to find me.

Just as I hit send on my last message, another from Hayley shows up:

> Hayley: They'll know where to find you.
> Hayley: HA!
> Me: HA!
> Me: You still finish my sentences.

I wish I could find just one Hayley at Saint Mary's.

It's fair to say I don't exactly fit in at school. First, because at fifteen years, ten months, and three days old, I'm the youngest in the junior class. My parents started my education early because they say I was already reading—music and words—at age four. But really, I think they just wanted to be kid-free

41

a whole year faster so they could travel the world together, attending operas and ballets and musical productions—all of which, they assumed, I'd eventually be starring in.

When I first started performing, we celebrated every role together. We ate pastries at my favorite little café, and my parents held hands across the table. They cuddled and dreamed out loud together. Little did they know they'd end up hating each other's guts just a few years later.

They've been fighting over me ever since they separated when I was six. Sole custody versus joint. This percentage visitation against that. And now, I see Dad for mere hours at a time, and Mom's very often out late.

It's nearly ten by the time my mother walks in the door tonight. The murmur of her conversation with Nana echoes down the hall.

"Ella?" Nana asks. "How'd it go?"

"Oh, you know. Just about as expected." She sounds sad.

Like I said, she's not good at the dating game. She trusts too quickly and too broadly. She's a terrible judge of character. She sees the good in everyone, which means she sets herself up almost daily for heartbreak. She once told me that if she were in a room with twenty straight men, she'd be a magnet for the one who was the worst for her.

That's what's weird about Ted. He didn't seem bad. He didn't even seem bad *for her*. Until he just split.

I pop in my earbuds and let my own notes sift through my ears. I lounge on my bed, drifting between homework, the Vagabonds website, and Lyrically, where I'm making little progress on my score.

I meander to my recent friend request from Dylan Thomas. A name like Dylan could belong to anyone—guy, girl . . . And not that it matters, I guess, how they identify, but I don't want to this to turn into some kind of weird romantic entanglement. There's enough drama on the stage, is how I see it, not to mention all the theatrics involving my parents, and I need to remain focused on my aspirations, not whether someone else thinks I'm worthy of a relationship. This person's underlying motives for contacting me could get in the way of my focus. Besides . . .

What if I inherit my mother's bad judgment where men are concerned?

Dylan Thomas lives in Englewood, just a few trains away. I wonder what they were doing at the Factory. Surely, they can get a cup of coffee in their own neck of the woods. But this person, like the artist for whom they're obviously named, is a poet, and I'm in desperate need of words.

What the hell.

I accept the request and text Hayley, bringing her up to speed.

Me: I just accepted the origami moon poet's friend
    request on Lyrically. Someone going by the name
    Dylan Thomas.
Hayley: HOLD ON
Hayley: Some random guy is messaging my BFFLS?

That's short for Best Friend Forever Little Sister.

Me: Not sure it's a guy. And not totally random either.
Me: I'm thinking we could maybe collab on a song.
Hayley: Well, I'm all for that.
Hayley: You could use a little push from your
    comfort zone.

Hayley: For some of us it's dating, for you I guess
it's this.

Me: Ugh

Me: You know I don't like to get distracted with
dating.

Hayley: I don't know how you do it.

Hayley: Or DON'T do it

Hayley: As the case may be.

Me: I'm changing the subject!!!!

Me: Wanna go meet Andy Randy with me?

Hayley: The openly gay Broadway star you insist
you're going to marry one day?

Me: That's him!

Hayley: When's that happening?

Me: Dad just set it up.

Hayley: Seriously? You're meeting your idol?

Me: I don't joke about my openly gay future husband.

Hayley: Ha!

Hayley: Your life is so different than mine.

Me: Well?

Hayley: Not sure.

Hayley: When are you going?

Me: Not sure yet.

Hayley: In all honesty, I probably can't.

Hayley: Finals.

Me: :(

This is one thing that sucks about not having friends. Real friends, anyway, who want to hang out with me whether or not my dad's paying their way into some amazing experience. If my sister can't make it, who's going to come with me to New York?

"Lainey?" Mom's voice. "Can I come in?"

"Sure."

She doesn't say anything about the basket of laundry I still haven't folded. She doesn't ask why I'm here when I should be at Dad's. She doesn't ask about my audition or ride me about the homework I'm obviously not doing.

She wades through the clutter of my room and curls up at my side. She's so small and thin. And for a minute, I feel so sad for her. I want her to be happy and comfortable. I want to see her dancing in the kitchen again.

I want to tell her what she used to tell me when she'd tuck me in at night when I was little: *Love you to the end of the universe and back a million times.*

The scent of cinnamon rolls filters through my memory, and I flash back to our kitchen in our Kenilworth house. The *Thoroughly Modern Millie* soundtrack is playing in the background, and we're all dancing around the island—Mom, Hayley, and me—singing "Forget about the boy. Forget about the boy . . ."

It was an idyllic existence.

But it's been supplanted by memories of screaming fights echoing down the hall from my parents' room, an ugly five-year court battle, and insults disguised as compliments: *Oh, your father sent a car . . . .how nice that he wants you to arrive in style . . . how nice to provide stuff for your teenaged daughter. Stuff goes a long way . . . almost as long as love.*

I'm just plain sick of it. All of it.

I shrink away from her and pop in my earbuds to listen to the track I've been working on. Dylan Thomas's words—the few that I've committed to memory—seem to flow with my notes.

"Lainey?" She touches a curl at my temple.

I flinch. Don't want to be touched right now. But I pause my track and look at her.

"I love your hair," she says.

I look at her. "Court again? Really?"

She sits up straighter. "I've been compiling receipts and cataloging all I've done pro bono for your career since the divorce. Your father, as your manager, should have been paying me to scuttle you all over town the same way he pays Giorgio. What he owes me in back charges would more than cover your tuition at the academy next year. My lawyer says it's a slam dunk. We just have to put up with his contesting, with his continuances. And if a judge awards me for the back charges, you'll be at that school next term."

I sigh. "But Dad's contesting it."

"Let him. He can't intimidate me. Everything I do," she says, "I do for you."

We stare at each other in silence for a few seconds.

"What's in Minnesota?" I ask. "New guy?"

She shakes her head. Her hair—pin straight and golden— ruffles against the pillow. "You don't have to worry about it."

"I do, actually. In the five years since you and Dad have been divorced, and even in the five years it took you to get divorced, I've watched these guys absolutely crush you, and I don't like it."

"Oh, Lainey."

"It's true. You're awesome. They're all idiots."

"Yes." She laughs a little. "You're right about that. It's okay, though. I tried. I did my best. Just like an audition, baby girl. You do your best. Sometimes you win, sometimes you lose. How'd it go today?"

"Don't change the subject. You lose a lot these days."

"I've fallen for twenty idiots over the course of my life," she says. "The twenty-first time I fell in love was forever. It doesn't matter if I lose for the rest of my life."

"Who's the twenty-first? Dad?"

She sighs, and one corner of her mouth turns slightly upward. She shrugs a shoulder.

It was Dad.

I think about the day her diagnosis came in. The first thing she did was call Dad. Ted and I were in the next room, and we heard it all.

Jesse, I have cancer. After all we've been through, you need to know I love you.

"Is that what happened with Ted?" I ask. "Did he realize that you were never going to get over Dad? Is that why he left?"

"He left"—she rolls out of my bed—"because he couldn't handle the reality of the situation."

"But—"

"Cancer's no picnic. He couldn't deal."

"Sure, but I just think that maybe if he hadn't heard you tell Dad you loved him—"

"He had to go. When you're older, you'll understand."

"But—"

"All you have to do is focus on you. And that's all I have to do, too. Focus on you. You make everything worthwhile."

I wish that were true.

CHAPTER 6
Sunday, April 30

Waiting for this callback list is practically going to kill me. They said tomorrow. It's tomorrow. WTF?

Mom and Nana are heading off to some antique show in the burbs, where my grandmother sells her hand-painted furniture. While Mom's in the bathroom, Nana slips me her credit card so I can buy a pair of taps today.

"Your father should be ashamed of himself," she mutters. "Nickel-and-diming you while that Miss Karissa and her kids are sitting pretty in that shoreline house . . ."

"They don't live there."

"Oh no?"

"No, Miss Karissa has a place in Evanston."

"Having a place and living there are two different things. Do you think any woman of his is going home to a cramped two-bedroom bungalow night after night? Don't be naïve."

I honestly hadn't considered that. Could Dad be playing family with Miss Karissa and Jennica and the boys? Is he casting me out to bring in a new crew? I feel like I'm going to be sick.

***

My phone alerts. I pounce on it before the text tone gives away that it's only my sister.

> Hayley: Taking a break.
> Hayley: Thought I'd see how you're doing.
> Hayley: Did you get a callback?
> Me: Don't know yet.
> Hayley: Fingers crossed!
> Me: Can I ask you something?
> Me: You were little when my mom and Dad got together.
> Me: Did you ever feel like u weren't part of things?
> Hayley: Not really.
> Me: Because I do.
> Me: I haven't seen Miss Karissa since I met her in passing like three years ago
> Me: And it was an accident.
> Me: He didn't expect me to be there.
> Me: It's like Dad's hiding her from us.
> Hayley: He's entitled to have a life without us, u know.
> Hayley: I haven't even met her yet.
> Hayley: But I'm not complaining.
> Hayley: If they're going to go long term, I'm sure I'll meet her eventually.
> Me: It's been years now.
> Me: It IS long term.
> Hayley: Doesn't mean it's serious.
> Hayley: If it were, I'm sure I'd meet her.
> Me: But you're at school.
> Me: You're busy.
> Me: When was the last time you saw Dad?
> Hayley: He swings by occasionally.

Hayley: Takes me out for lunch etc.

Me: But he doesn't bring Miss K.

Hayley: Fine with me.

Me: She's a big part of his life.

Me: Her KIDS are a big part of his life.

Hayley: And???

Me: And we're not part of that life.

Hayley: That's not true.

Me: He's supposed to have me every other weekend.

Me: He cancels all the time.

Hayley: He's a busy guy.

Me: He's not too busy for Miss Karissa.

Me: Or "Jennica and the boys."

Me: Nana's sure they're living there.

Hayley: Nana should stay out of it.

Me: But you have to admit he has us totally separated from these people.

Hayley: You're too old to be playing this card.

Me: What card?

Hayley: It's time for you to grow up.

Hayley: Let Dad have this.

Hayley: Not everything has to be about you.

Me: That's not the point.

Me: It doesn't have to be about ME

Me: But shouldn't we be part of the equation?

Hayley: Typical.

Hayley: Who says you aren't part of it?

Me: ???

Me: Have you been listening?

Me: Scroll up. Read.

Me: This is about US.

Hayley: Since you were born, everything has been
    about you.
Hayley: Did I complain?
Hayley: My whole childhood was about getting you to
    auditions.
Hayley: The world revolved around you
Hayley: And now, the second something doesn't go
    your way, you're losing it.
Hayley: Grow up.
Hayley: Stop complaining.
Me: I'm not throwing a fit because Dad's dating
    someone.
Hayley: Really? Sure sounds like it.
Me: Easy for you to say.
Hayley: I love you
Hayley: But you're being a brat.

My fingertips go numb, and suddenly it feels as if I'm closing out the rest of the world. All I hear is static in my ears. It's
hard to draw a deep breath.

It's okay, I tell myself. It'll pass.

I call this a Mini Panic Episode, or MPE. There was a time
these feelings might have exploded into some serious struggles,
but during the six months Ted lived with us, he taught me to
acknowledge the panic and let it go, like a fleeting thought.
Some attempts are more successful than others.

And this one is needling me. My sister, who's always supposed to take my side, called me a brat, and I'm worried she
might be right (because she usually is). If someone who knows
me as well as she does can label me that way, how might the
outside world see me?

I imagine gossip columns of a future I may never know filled with testimonials about some bratty thing Madelaine Joseph said or did. Worse than not performing: being famous . . . for negative reasons.

I scan my text exchange with Hayley carefully. I really don't think I was being a brat. She's just not understanding what I'm saying.

I'm not angry, or sad, or disturbed that Dad's dating. That's what happens when parents get divorced, isn't it? I'm upset that he has something important in his life and doesn't think enough of me to involve me in it.

I screenshot the conversation and think to send it to someone for feedback. But who? Nana would be my first choice, but I don't like that Hayley basically thinks Nana's out of line.

Ted, maybe. I used to be able to talk to Ted about all of this. But inviting Ted into this situation could only set me up to miss the way things used to be.

I'm alone in this.

Me: I can't believe you'd say that to me.
Hayley: Oh wow.
Hayley: I mean I get that it's an adjustment.
Hayley: But after the things you've said to me today
Hayley: Major eyerolls.
Hayley: Stop obsessing about things you can't control.
Hayley: I'm here for you.
Me: Right.
Hayley: I am!
Hayley: But I'm not going to pretend you're not
    being egocentric.
Me: You just aren't listening.

Hayley: For fun, here's a compilation of all my pics
    of Vagabonds.
Hayley: Click here for my montage.

A link comes through. It's a series of photographs and clips that ends with the lead singer strumming his guitar in slow motion. I send an array of hearts to Hayley.

Haley: I MISS THEM!
Me: #intouchwiththatemotion

I click over to the website to see if there are any new clues as to when they'll be back in business. But there's nothing. No new tweets on either of their accounts, nothing on Instagram.

No amount of wishing will make them come back into the limelight until they're ready. *If* they're ever ready, that is.

And what about me? Am I ready for what I have to do next? No one else is going to make life easy for me. I'm not happy with the way things are going—I don't like Saint Mary's on the Mount. I belong somewhere else, living a life that's more me. If I want things to change, I have to make them happen for myself.

On Lyrically, I message Dylan Thomas: *Yes. Let's talk.*

I send them my work in progress. If they realize that the notes flow with the words they wrote on the origami moon, I'll believe it's not just my imagination. And maybe we really can collab and make all these single elements into something magical.

As soon as I hit the send button, I panic. God, what if my song sucks? What if Dylan Thomas listens to it and decides I'm a talentless idiot? Or what if they think I'm being presumptuous, like they'd *really* want to hear my creation?

Breathe. Just recall the message.

My finger hovers over the recall button.

I hesitate. I have to put myself out there if I ever expect to go places.

And so what if Dylan Thomas thinks I'm an idiot? I don't even know this person, and they live in Englewood. It's not like I'm likely to bump into them.

Still . . . maybe I should at least have a conversation with him before I decide to bare my soul to him. Because that's what sharing creative forces is—especially when there's no character standing between you and your work.

I go to recall the message, but a split second before my finger hits the screen, Lyrically alerts me that he's opened it.

Too late.

Nausea spins in my gut.

There's nothing I can do. Dylan's already holding my proverbial heart in their hands. If they're a jerk, they'll squeeze the life out of me, belittle me, make fun of me for thinking I can actually be someone someday. If they're not, they'll politely say they like what I've done, and I won't know whether or not they're telling the truth.

Lose/lose.

Maybe I'd feel more confident in my abilities if I were studying under people who can give constructive feedback. That's the problem with this world. Everyone's a critic, but no one knows the true art of criticism. The internet, for all its wonderful attributes, makes bashing and name-calling an art form. Everyone's got an opinion and everyone wants to share it, but no one's as much of an expert as they think they are.

I curl into a ball and imagine a barrage of insults popping up in tiny conversation bubbles on screens of all sizes.

You suck.

Talentless hack.

Don't quit your day job.

I can't.

I just can't.

Why did I share that song?

I hear my mother's voice in my head: *Shut the world out. Just perform. This isn't about anyone out there. It's about you . . . you and that stage. You love it. Share your time with it, your heart with it, your soul with it, and it will love you, too.*

I will.

It's a vow I speak practically every time I sing, even if I'm just singing in the shower.

I pull myself up. Picture myself on the stage. Maybe I'm playing my guitar. Maybe I'm singing along. Maybe I'm dancing.

"For*get* ab*out* the boy, for*get* ab*out* the boy, for*get* about the *boy!*"

I obey the song and shake off the feelings of inadequacy. I replace them with focus.

I will be what I strive to be.

Make it happen, I tell myself. One way or another, make it happen.

Step one: I pull up the site for Chicago's premier performing arts academy, and I begin to draft a note to the dean of admissions: *My name is Madelaine Emmah Joseph. I auditioned and was accepted into the academy three years ago. However, due to financial circumstances beyond my control, I have been unable to enroll . . .*

Maybe she'll be willing to help me figure out tuition since my parents can't put their differences aside to make it happen for me.

Next, I start compiling an online portfolio, including the programs of all the shows I've been in, tracks of bits of music I've written, snippets I've played on the ukulele, guitar, piano— and even a little bit of flute. If the dean gets back to me, I can share this with her as proof of my commitment.

An alert from Lyrically distracts me.

It's a message from Dylan Thomas.

CHAPTER 7

Dylan: So you're a composer.

Me: Sometimes.

Dylan: Dancer.

Dylan: Actor.

Dylan: Mezzo soprano.

Dylan: Anything you don't do?

Me: I'm not a poet.

Me: But you are.

Dylan: Eh.

Dylan: Every once in a while I come up with
    something vaguely poetic

Me: The origami moon . . . your words are
    beautiful.

Dylan: Like I said.

Dylan: Every once in a while.

Dylan: But I'm not like you.

Dylan: Your song is amazing.

Me: Thanks.

My profile page has my profession listed simply as "performer."
My location: Stting on a cornflake.

Goals: To be as vibrant and varied as the Ultimate Crayola Collection.

Me: How did you know all that about me?
Dylan: Research.
Me: You researched me?
Me: Stalker. :P
Dylan: Not quite.
Dylan: I just looked you up online.
Me: I've never been googled before.
Dylan: Yes you have.
Dylan: You have a career.
Dylan: (congrats on that btw)
Dylan: But because of that career,
Dylan: Of course you've been googled.
Me: How would you like it if I googled you?
Dylan: Go ahead.
Dylan: All you'll find are stories about a guy who
     drank himself into an early grave.
Dylan: "Do not go gentle into that good night."
Dylan: And all that stuff.
Dylan: It's interesting.
Dylan: But it's not about me.
Dylan: Just a window into a life that'll never be mine.
Me: You talk like a poet.
Dylan: Every once in a while.
Me: Can you give me a hint about yourself, at least?
Me: Which pronouns do you use?
Dylan: Does it matter?
Me: Not really.
Me: I'm not looking for a romantic connection. :P

Dylan: But if you're not looking, and I'm not looking, it's irrelevant information for our purposes here.

Me: I was just curious.

Dylan: I guess that's how you can describe me, too.

Dylan: Curious.

Me: Just don't want to misgender you.

Dylan: Like, if you talk about me to someone else?

Dylan: Am I a hot topic of conversation?

Me: Dude, forget it.

Me: There, I just potentially misgendered you.

Dylan: Ha. Fair point. I use he/him pronouns though. So no worries.

Me: Got it. Thanks.

Me: Why were u at the Factory?

Dylan: Wanted some coffee

Me: No coffee shops in Englewood?

Dylan: Met a friend there.

Dylan: It's halfway.

Me: Are you in the habit of leaving folded parchment at coffee shops?

Dylan: I didn't know I left the moon there.

Dylan: I didn't mean for anyone to find it

Me: Actually . . .

Me: Did you notice your words fit with my tempo?

Dylan: No.

Me: Can I use them as lyrics?

Me: I'll give you credit

Me: And maybe you can give me pointers on how you did it.

Dylan: Like I said

Dylan: I'm not really a poet.

Me: And I'm not used to working with people

Me: but would you consider a collaboration?

Dylan: Presumably, my part is already done.

Dylan: Right?

Me: :)

Me: I still need your permission to use your words, though.

Me: And maybe you'd be up for working on something else together?

Me: I mean, if this song does what it should do

Me: it could go places.

Me: If the right person sees it, we could be famous.

Dylan: Do you want to be famous??

Dylan: You don't even post pics of your face.

Me: Only because it's the internet.

Me: People are assholes when they're hiding behind a screen.

Me: I haven't posted a pic of my face since I was in eighth grade

Me: And someone rated me a six.

Dylan: That's terrible.

Me: Everyone's a critic.

Dylan: And yet, you're willing to share your work online.

Dylan: You open yourself to criticism

Dylan: From the whole world.

Me: Not usually, actually.

Me: Being onstage in a role is one thing.

Me: I can be someone else onstage.

Me: But singing a song I wrote . . . well, that's something else.

Me: That's being ME out there.

Me: There's a difference between Me-for-real, and Me-on-stage.

Me: I struggle with that.

Me: I'm shy.

Me: But I have my eye on the goal, here.

Me: I'm putting myself out there.

Dylan: What's the goal?

Me: I want to make it big.

Me: I want to be on stage.

Me: Like my mother.

Me: She was a dancer.

Me: She was an understudy on BROADWAY.

Me: But I want to be more than that.

Me: My dream:

Me: To write a musical score

Me: To star on stage.

Me: To sing

Me: To dance

Me: To be IT.

Me: But I can't seem to get the part that you refuse to admit is poetry.

Me: And you're talented!

Me: Why wouldn't you want to use that talent?

Dylan: I just don't think I'd be a good fit for what you have in mind.

Dylan: And if you want to do it all

Dylan: you don't need my help.

Dylan: Have u read your posts? They're all poetic.

Dylan: Downpour of peonies and all that.

Me: You DID stalk me.

Dylan: Just checked out your Instagram.

Dylan: You're an interesting person.

Me: Just say you'll think about it.

Dylan: I will if you will.

Me: You're frustrating.

Dylan: So are you.

Me: Ugh. Forget it then.

Dylan: ok

Me: Fine.

I slam my laptop shut.

A few minutes pass.

What just happened?

I was having a perfectly normal conversation one second, and then I was arguing with a guy I don't know . . . all because he doesn't want his work out in public?

Maybe Hayley's right. Maybe I do expect the world to revolve around me.

I open the laptop. Dylan Thomas is still online.

Me: Hi.

Dylan: Hi.

Me: I'm sorry.

Me: Of course I respect what you want to do with
    your talent.

Dylan: I'm not talented.

Dylan: Not the way you assume.

Me: I'm sorry I got mad.

Me: It's just that I'm sort of stressed out.

Dylan: You live in a stressful world

Dylan: The profession you've chosen is brutal

Dylan: It's bound to get to u from time to time

Dylan: I think that's why so many famous people

Dylan: Go off the grid.

Me: Speaking of . . .

Me: Do you listen to Vagabonds?

Dylan: Who doesn't?

Dylan: What's your theory on why they went silent?

Me: They're working on something.

Me: They don't want the influence of the outside
world

Me: Like I said, the internet can make people mean.

Me: Judgmental.

Me: Hypercritical.

Dylan: What other music influences you?

Me: Anything sincere and raw.

Me: I have everything from Sinatra to Sublime on my
playlists.

Me: My sister says that means I don't know what
I like.

Me: But really, I think it means that I know EXACTLY
what I like.

Dylan: Siblings.

Me: Yeah.

Dylan: Any other brothers and sisters?

Dylan: Or just the one?

Me: For now, just an older half-sister.

Me: But my dad's dating someone with little kids.

Me: The oldest is eight, I think.

Me: The boys are twins. They're five.

Me: So maybe I'll be a big sister someday.

Dylan: You sound ok with it.

Me: Trying to be.

Dylan: It's hard sometimes.

Me: Been through it?

Dylan: Twice.

Me: And you survived.

Dylan: It's not Everest.

Me: Sux though.

Dylan: Sometimes.

Me: Did you ever feel like your parents never stopped fighting?

Me: And like you were constantly refereeing?

Dylan: Girl. Please.

Me: We just might have something in common.

CHAPTER 8

My chat with Dylan Thomas lasts most of the morning. Shortly after I've signed off and started my Sunday chores, "Raspberry Beret" signals an incoming message. I practically jump on my phone. The Weekes twins might have news about the callback list!

Brendon: Did you see the email?

Me: No.

Brendon: They want an extra day to post the list.

Me: No!!!!!

McKenna: I can't even.

Me: Did they say why?

Brendon: Of course not.

Brendon: It's like being on an airplane

Brendon: And the plane isn't moving

Brendon: And you're stuck on the runway

Brendon: And you know something's wrong

Brendon: But the crew won't tell you what it is.

Brendon: Or why the fuck you're not going to be on time.

McKenna: I HATE THIS.

Me: Maybe they have some tough decisions to make.

McKenna: I'm sure they do.

Brendon: And the whole time you're wondering

Me: Maybe it's a good thing they're taking
   their time???

Brendon: Mechanical failure?

Brendon: Is the president making a surprise visit?

Brendon: Or better, is someone actually important
   coming to Chicago?

McKenna: Don't say you'll have the list posted

McKenna: If you have no intention of posting the list.

Brendon: Like maybe Panic! At the Disco is coming
   to town.

Brendon: I'd gladly wait on the tarmac for my
   namesake to show up.

Me: We did our job too well.

Me: They can't decide.

McKenna: Or maybe the opposite . . .

McKenna: Like, if I'd nailed it, they wouldn't be
   indecisive.

Wow. McKenna gets insecure about her auditions too.
Who knew?

Me: Same! So it's good and bad for both of us.

Me: I wish we weren't up against each other
   for Pepper.

Brendon: I saw him once

Brendon: at United Center

McKenna: Who?

Brendon: Brendon Urie!

Me: OMG I saw him once too.

I start typing that it was right after I saw him in *Kinky Boots* on Broadway. He shook my hand. He signed my program and asked the Sophias and me if we liked the show.

But I delete.

Brendon and McKenna might like this story, but I don't want to sound as if I'm bragging, so I don't elaborate.

McKenna: Beautiful guy
Me: Yeah. And mega talented.
Brendon: Duh.
Brendon: Why do you think I named myself after him?
Me: ???
McKenna: Brendon's his stage name.
Brendon: Because I'm as fabulous as he is.
Me: What's your real name?
Brendon: Screw it. I'm going out for cheese fries.
Brendon: Wanna come?

Obviously he's talking to McKenna. Why would they invite me out for fries? They live closer to the Loop. Surely they don't expect to go farther than the nearest corner.

But the conversation stills.

McKenna: Did you just call Panic! At the Disco more
     important than the president?
Brendon: Obv.
Me: HAHA
Brendon: Panic! might actually change the world.
Me: Warped but true.
McKenna: So wanna meet us?
Brendon: We can meet halfway.

McKenna: If we're going to wallow in post-audition
    blur
McKenna: we might as well binge on junk food.
McKenna: We won't be able to eat like that
    during rehearsal.

My first instinct is to shove the essentials in my backpack and go.

But then, once we're out together, what if it's awkward? What if I start talking about having an actual conversation with Brendon Urie? What if I start talking about going backstage at the Vagabonds show and playing Timothy's ukulele? What if they think I'm a brat who's on every stage I've ever been on because my dad is a manager with connections?

Brendon: Quick! Check her pulse!
Me: Hahaha
Me: Have to finish my homework.
Me: And laundry.
Me: Ugh.
McKenna: Groan.

Actually . . . since I'll be going out anyway to buy my tap shoes, maybe I *should* try to meet McKenna and Brendon. It might be fun to meet in the middle.

My heart starts shimmying at the thought of waiting in some strange place for people who might decide at the last minute not to show up. Or maybe I'll screw it up and be waiting at the wrong location. Or maybe everything will go as planned, but I'll get there too early, and I'll have to sit and wait while strangers try to take the seats I'm saving.

Sticking to texting is better. Safer.

I like my neighborhood. I like the café at the Factory. I like counting on just me.

But I have to put myself out there.

Me: But I'll do it all later.
Brendon: Why do it now when you can do it later?
Me: Where are we meeting?
McKenna: Counter Offer?
Brendon: An hour or so?
Brendon: Gotta do my hair.

It's good to venture out. Take myself out of the comfort zone.

Good practice for the day Dylan Thomas might be meeting his friend at the Factory again, when maybe I'll catch a glimpse of him in person. Maybe he'll be as beautiful as the words he writes, and I can enjoy looking at him from a distance.

Not in a creepy way. Or in a romantic way. Because I don't get mixed up in romantic hassles.

But if I wanted to . . . maybe Dylan would be the kind of guy I'd fall for.

I meander over to Lyrically and read his bio again: *Observer. Music lover. Quiet lurker.*

I learned that much during our hours-long exchange. I've never felt as comfortable so quickly talking to someone I've never met before, and I think that's because I know he doesn't want to meet for coffee and take things to the next level.

Even if we happen to bump into each other, there will be no pressure to sit down and make small talk over lattes. Dylan values his privacy just like I value mine. This means, of course, that we probably *would* talk, but we wouldn't have to. He'd understand if I waved hello and went back to my work. He wouldn't think I'm being a snob if I just wasn't into people at that moment.

He doesn't have much posted on his page. Not even the origami moon poem, which has me wondering: if he didn't mean to leave it, why was it so prettily printed and folded? And yet, if he wanted to share it with the outside world, it would be posted on his page. Did I infringe on his privacy by posting it on mine?

I scroll through his page. There are two pictures. One is of Nirvana's *Nevermind* album cover. The other is of a dog.

He likes dogs. Bonus.

I click over to Ted Haggerty's page just for a glimpse of my Vinny-dog. He's a mutt—a little lab, maybe some Jack Russell. I wish he could have been mine for longer than the hour I spent playing with him at the shelter.

Why did Ted have to bail?

My phone buzzes again.

McKenna: BTW
McKenna: how did it go with your dad?
Me: ?
McKenna: You were going to talk to him
McKenna: about coming to our school.

I don't want to get into the whole thing, so I keep it simple.

Me: Yeah, he's still undecided.
McKenna: You should at least visit again.
McKenna: Shadow me for a day.
Me: I'm going to do AT LEAST that.

McKenna: You will LOVE it!

McKenna: I can tell you EVERYTHING about
auditioning.

Me: I actually already auditioned.

Me: Was accepted years ago.

McKenna: So why aren't you here already?

I start typing about the whole ordeal with my parents. About the maintenance and Ted and my dad's stubbornness. But by the time I'm even halfway through it, I've already written paragraphs and . . . who cares? Like McKenna Weekes really needs to know all that.

Delete.

Instead I change the subject.

Me: Long story. How's your new guy?

Brendon: Me, or McK?

Me: You.

Brendon: Puhlease! He's so last week.

Brendon: I'm sort of into this chick now.

McKenna: You have relationship ADD.

Brendon: A guy could have worse things.

A text from Dad pops up.

Dad: When are callbacks?

Dad: When does rehearsal start?

Dad: Would like to finalize plans for the trip
to NYC.

Dad: Thursday is ideal.

Dad: Could have you home by Sunday evening.

I swipe away the conversation bubbles. I don't even know if I'm called back yet, and I don't want to jinx things by planning around a production schedule my name may or may not be on.

A series of tinkling notes fills the air, and I practically jump. I never closed out of Lyrically, and now I have a message.

Dylan: Been thinking about your song.
Dylan: It's soooo good.
Dylan: You should post it.
Me: I can't.
Me: Besides, it's not ready.
Dylan: We'll help you make it ready.
Dylan: Just do it.
Dylan: Don't think about it anymore.
Dylan: Just open the track, and click post.
Dylan: I'll count down for you.
Dylan: 5

I find myself opening the track. Can I do this?

Dylan: It's soooo good!
Dylan: 4

I tag Dylan.

Dylan: 3
Dylan: 2
Dylan: 1

I close my eyes. *Click.*
And now it's out there. For the whole world to hear.

My hands tremble. It wasn't ready for public consumption. It was too rough. Why did I send it to him? Why did I let him convince me to post it?

Ping!

Ping!

Ping!

And people are already commenting on it.

I don't want to look. Or do I?

I dare to scroll.

HayleyJo21P: Awesome!

MusicLover4871: Who's Madelaine Joseph?

Dylan: You'll know her name one day.

RadioHeadAddict: She blows.

I feel a little sick.

Here we go. The online world is about to crush my soul.

I brace myself. Close my eyes. Talk to me, Mom: *Shut out the world . . .*

Ping! Ping! The alert of postings silences the Mom-in-my-head.

My eyes slowly open, and although it's dangerous, I peek at the screen.

HalfwayTo500Miles: Nice flow.

HalfwayTo500Miles: Would love to hear it when
    it's done.

BurningUrine: Try it in E minor.

BurningUrine: Somberer.

RadioHeadAddict: SHE BLOWS

BurningUrine: STFU

RadioHeadAddict: Blow me.

HayleyJo21P: ur a creep RadioHead.

I have to laugh at Hayley's reference to "Creep," the song that arguably put Radiohead on the map.

HayleyJo21P: My sister is so talented! <3

Just for that, I forgive her for her harsh words earlier.

I reach for my guitar. BurningUrine might be on to something. I plug in, start an audio recording, and play.

It sounds incredible. It flows now, like a ballad. Sad, lonely notes drifting off into oblivion.

I post the recording to my page and rush out to meet the Weekes twins.

CHAPTER 9

I wait for McKenna and Brendon outside Counter Offer, which is incredibly crowded. But it's not bad outside, weather-wise, so if we can't get a table, we can eat at the park across the street.

> Brendon: Almost there.
> McKenna: We see you!
> Brendon: Girl, you are ROCKING that hat.

It's an actual raspberry-colored beret. I thought they'd get a kick out of it. It's a shade or two deeper than my pink hair, and I paired it with my John Lennon glasses.

> Me: Thanks. Going for a starving artist vibe.

McKenna is wearing pink-and-yellow striped leggings under an oversized men's dress shirt, and Brendon . . . very Elvis Costello today. He hugs me as if we're lifelong friends, and we pose for a selfie together, which McKenna posts to her Snapchat.

It's not until later in the afternoon, when I take a screenshot of her story, that I see a figure lurking in the background.

I put aside my homework, which I'm finishing at the kitchen table, and zoom in. I'm pretty sure this is the guy who was looking at me through the window at the Factory.

"Nana?"

"Hmm?"

I look up from my phone, then back to the picture of the guy half-hidden by a hardcover novel.

He's sort of looking at us, but sort of not.

Then again, we do look like figurines from a revival cast of the 1980s *Strawberry Shortcake*. It wouldn't be surprising if we drew a few stares.

Ever since I was little, I've had all kinds of irrational fears pinging around in my head, threatening to paralyze me. I have enough real problems—I don't need to draw people's attention to the imaginary ones.

"What's up, hun?"

"Never mind."

CHAPTER 10
Monday, May 1

My phone won't stop buzzing.

I pull myself out of dreamland—more like nightmare island, considering the terrifying images I've been seeing in my sleep—and silence my phone, which is whirring like a blender with nothing in it.

I glance at the time. 6:30. Shit.

Mom's texted four times, and my alarm is going off. It's been buzzing for over five minutes.

Monday. Ugh. At least getting dressed is easy when you go to Catholic school. I have one leg into my khakis—which are wrinkled, but whatever—before I'm even on my feet.

Teeth brushed. Pink hair in a ball on top of my head. Apple in hand, and homework—finished thanks to a 2 a.m. sprint—in backpack.

When I walk out the door in a record eight minutes, Nana's still asleep; she's up later than me most days. I leave her credit card and a big note on the kitchen countertop: *Thanks for the Capezios. You're the best.*

I text Mom on my walk to the L. Before I was old enough to get myself around the city, Mom took me everywhere. I suspect she'd still do it, if she wasn't juggling two jobs. She likes to know

I've gotten where I'm supposed to be on time . . . and safely.

Me: On my way!
Mom: Have a good day.
Mom: Text me when you get there.

I pull out a tiny mirror and begin to apply the limited amount of makeup we're allowed to wear at Saint Mary's, when suddenly, a wave of dejection hits me. Still no callback list. And still no reply to the email I sent the academy, which means there is no definite future ahead of me.

Everything is at a standstill.

My phone buzzes. It's on vibrate because I'm on the train and I try to be courteous to those around me, unlike the guy talking at volume level three thousand a few seats over.

Dad: All set for NYC.
Dad: Show tickets purchased.
Dad: Front row, center.
Dad: Backstage meet and greet.
Dad: Bought extras.
Dad: Bring friends!

Excitement-slash-awe-slash-mortification rises in my chest.

Sure, I'm excited to go to New York. I flipping LOVE New York. And I'm excited about finally having time with Dad. And the meet and greet . . . it's like a million cherries on top of an already decadent sundae.

Me: Thank you!!!
Dad: We leave Thursday at four out of O'Hare.

Dad: Text me names of three or four people you'd like
    to bring.
Dad: I'll purchase airline tickets this afternoon.
Dad: Any other shows you want to see while we're
    there?
Me: Not sure.
Me: But probably.
Me: :)

Instantly I post: *NYC bound in 5, 4 . . .*

Wait. Leaving Thursday means I'll be gone over one of Mom's weekends, and I'll bet Dad hasn't cleared it with her. It's probably okay, considering he's dumped me on my mother more often than not lately, but if she had something planned for the two of us . . .

Great.

I can imagine how this conversation is going to go, but since I've already posted about it, I should probably break the news to her before she sees it online. Texting is the easiest way.

Me: Dad wants to take me next weekend.
Mom: I'll believe it when I see it.
Me: To NYC.
Mom: . . .

The ellipses disappear, which tells me she's contemplating how to respond. Or maybe she typed something snarky, then decided she didn't want me to see it, and deleted it.

I stare out the window, at the city rushing by, with my song, now strummed in E minor, piping through my earbuds.

In my head, I put Dylan Thomas's words to the song.

It really could be beautiful.

When we pass the neighborhood where McKenna and Brendon's school stands, I press my palm to the glass. It seems that's as close as I'll get to setting foot on campus.

Mom: Sounds like fun.
Mom: Just you and your dad?

Oh. That went better than I thought.

Me: He said I could bring a few friends.
Mom: Who are you going to bring?
Me: Not sure yet.
Me: Hayley can't come.
Me: Maybe some people I met during Peter Pan.
Mom: What show are you going to see?

I bring her up to speed on our plans and speculate about which other shows Dad might buy tickets for. The more I type, the more excited I get.

Mom: Your dad should be talking to me about this
Mom: instead of making plans around me.
Mom: It's my weekend.

And there it is. The bottom dropping out.

Me: I know. I'm sorry.
Me: Did we have plans?
Mom: We don't now.
Me: What were we going to do?

Me: Can we do it some other time?

Me: It's just that if I'm cast as Pepper

Me: this will be the last weekend

Mom: Exactly.

Me: So either I go with him this weekend

Me: or I don't go at all.

Me: I don't want to pass it up.

Mom: I'm glad you get to experience all of
these things.

Mom: I just wish I could experience some of them
with you.

Mom: But I can't afford to take you

Mom: not to mention an entourage

Mom: first class, all expenses paid, Broadway

Mom: and I don't have connections anymore
for backstage.

Me: I know. It's ok.

Mom: It's not ok.

Mom: When you're looking for college tuition, it won't
be ok.

Mom: What he's going to drop on theater tickets,
meals, airfare, lodging . . .

Mom: Staying in Times Square again?

Me: I don't know.

Mom: What he'll spend in four days is more than
I earn all year.

Mom: What he'll spend would pay for my portion
of a year's school for you.

Me: That's not my fault.

Me: I wish I could go with you.

Me: But you could at least be happy for me.

Mom: I'm sorry.

Me: Me too.

Mom: I'm sorry that you're mesmerized

Mom: By all these sparkly things your dad dangles in front of you

Mom: And that I'm just a boring has-been who works all day.

Me: That's not how I think of you.

Mom: In a perfect world, I wouldn't have to remind you of these things.

Mom: I can't get through to your father.

Mom: You have to.

Mom: You have to be the messenger.

Mom: ASK HIM TO PUT THIS MONEY TOWARD SCHOOL

Mom: Because he refuses to talk to me.

Mom: It's not your fault.

Mom: But it's not mine, either.

Me: It's a little your fault.

Mom: How so?

Me: Ted Haggerty.

Mom doesn't reply.

A sense of satisfaction filters through me for having gotten the last word.

I get her point. I do. But I can't just *not* go to New York. I can't just not meet my idols.

Especially if I can't go to performing arts high school, especially if I might not be able to go to NYU, I deserve to have these experiences. And Mom obviously agrees with me because she isn't even trying to retort.

After a few minutes, however, the satisfaction wanes. And guilt settles in.

I try to imagine what it must be like to be my mother. Alone. Broken, in some ways. A shadow of what she used to be.

All because Dad was never home. Because she stayed home to raise us, she lost her connections, lost her friends, lost her last opportunities to perform.

She loves us all more than she loved the stage. I know that means she loves us *a lot*.

And because Dad wasn't home, he fell out of love with Mom, and he left.

And Mom fell in love with Ted, and he left, too.

And now my mom is struggling and has no money and can't possibly compete with what my dad can give me.

But she's surviving. No thanks to me.

Maybe Hayley's right. Lately, I'm not my best self. I stare at a holographic reflection of myself in the train window, and I touch my pink hair.

I text Mom an apology. While I wait for a response, I snap a quick pic and post it on Instagram: *Feeling all sorts of Blizzard and Cerulean. Could use some Purple Mountains' Majesty.*

CHAPTER 11

I'm heading to the dean's office because . . . lunch. I've texted Mom about a hundred times, but she still hasn't replied. I scroll through our earlier messages. On the train, I read her messages as sort of snotty, like she was annoyed.

But now that I'm reading them again, I feel like she was annoyed, but she was also upset. Sad.

One of the Sophias knocks a shoulder against mine in passing.

I stop. She stops. Our glances meet for a second.

She purses her lips and raises a brow. "Want to hit the Factory after school?"

I look over my shoulder, certain she's talking to someone else, but there's no one there.

Sophia 2 nudges her way next to me, and suddenly we're a clump in the hallway, with other students rushing past us, like a river flowing around an island.

"Grab some coffee?" Sophia 2 asks. "And I'm dying for one of those vanilla scones."

"Um . . . I really can't. I have—"

"Come on," Sophia 1 says. "We haven't hung out in, like, forever."

"Did you hear what they're saying?" Sophia 2 asks. "If you click on some link on the top of the Vagabonds website, it takes you to a page with a code. Some people think it's part of some big puzzle, and if you decode it, you'll find a link to free songs."

"Timothy's gotta be behind it," Sophia 1 chimes in.

"Of course he is," Sophia 2 says.

Sophia 1: "And Wade is like, I'll do whatever."

Sophia 2: "It's just the kind of thing he does!"

She wouldn't know what kinds of things the band does if it weren't for me. I was there the first time she heard any song too obscure to be played on the radio. Specifically, she was in a suite at the Drake, which Dad rented for us for my last birthday. When she walked into that hotel, she didn't know the band was anything more than "Tense." She walked out with a whole new obsession.

The sad thing is there's a small part of me that really wants things to go back to the way they were. Talking about Vagabonds . . . counting down the days until the next concert . . .

Until I remember it was all a big joke to them. They never really liked hanging out with me. They thought I was weird.

But if they're asking now . . . maybe they're sorry. Maybe they didn't mean everything they said, or they see me differently now, or . . .

"So." Sophia 2 props a hand on her hip and looks down at me. "Saw you're going to New York again. When's that happening?"

Ah. They want to come. "End of the week," I say.

"We had such a blast with you in New York," Sophia 2 says. "And Brendon Urie! Swoon!"

"Seriously," Sophia 1 says. "Let's meet at the Factory after school."

"Sorry." I take a step toward the dean's office. "I have plans."

"Some other time?"

I take a deep breath and keep walking.

Fool me once.

My phone erupts with "Raspberry Beret," and I practically fumble it.

Brendon: We're all called back!

I go to my email and see the official invitation to callbacks. My heart takes a running leap.

Me: Unbelievable!

Me: To celebrate, how do you feel about

"Miss Joseph."

I stop typing. I was going to take a chance and invite them with me to Broadway. I figure, it's a nice way to seal the budding friendship, even if one of us isn't cast. But I look up from my phone to see Sister Mary Angela treating me to a hard-nosed stare. She puts out her hand, palm up, and wiggles her fingers. "Phone."

"I'm on my lunch hour," I say because phones are allowed during lunch. This doesn't mean I don't constantly check it throughout the day, but at any other time of day, I would have been more discreet.

"You're in the dean's office," Sister Mary Angela says. "Did you miss the sign on the door?"

"I'm sorry," I say. "I've been waiting forever for this callback list—"

She presses a finger to her lips, and I shut up. "You can pick it up at the end of the day."

A day without a phone is sort of like a day living under a rock even under normal circumstances. But I have this amazing news to share. Sure, it's not an actual, official role, but I made it past another hurdle!

I can't wait to tell my family, and I want to celebrate with the Weekes twins. Not to mention, I should inform the academy that I've made it over another roadblock and will likely be working in a big production. And if I were attending a special school, all my academics would be in the morning before rehearsals begin, but juggling school and Saint Mary's is going to be hell—at least until summer vacation gets underway.

I'm getting ahead of myself anyway. I'm just called back. Not cast. Maybe it's too early to celebrate.

I shrink into the corner, where the good sister put me the day I showed up looking like an Easter parade landed on my head, and I eat.

CHAPTER 12

I've missed sixty-two text messages, and the Lyrically icon on my phone may as well have a flashing neon arrow blinking at it.

That always happens when people post something. Everyone chimes in to comment.

The Lyrically community can either be really supportive, or really evil. And I can't deal with the latter right now. I have too much to be excited about. I'm not keen to be brought down by haters.

I'm going to New York to meet one of my idols. I was called back for another show today. I'm gonna ride out this glory and not ruin it with a lot of negativity.

I open the "Raspberry Beret" thread, where the Weekes twins are wondering why I went radio silent.

Brendon: Madelaine, where'd you go?
McKenna: Maybe she fainted.
Brendon: Get over the shock.
Brendon: You're fabulous, ok? We all know it.
McKenna: Maybe we should call an ambulance.
Brendon: Or . . .

Brendon: if you're celebrating with someone other
    than us
Brendon: I can't even.

I'm smiling. They're funny. And even though McKenna and I are in direct competition for the part of Pepper, we're still friends. I love that. I finally weigh in:

Me: Haha, sorry, Sister Evil took my phone!
Me: To celebrate, how do you feel about hitting NYC
Me: and taking in a Broadway show?
Me: We'd leave the day after callback auditions.
Brendon: Gurrrrrrrrrrl
McKenna: Are you serious?
McKenna: (About NYC, not Sister Evil)
Me: Ha! Yes.
McKenna: Hellz yeah!
Brendon: How are we gonna make that happen?
Me: My dad offered.
Me: He'll take care of everything.
McKenna: I effing love your dad.
McKenna: I don't know him.
McKenna: But I love him.

I'm about to respond with all the details when, out of the corner of my eye, I catch sight of another origami moon balancing on the handrail of the school's front steps.

One of my fellow students brushes it with her elbow and it falls to the steps. No one's on the lookout for something like this when we're about to gain a modicum of freedom for the rest of the afternoon. Leaving this place at the end of the day, especially this time of year, is sort of like getting a stay of execution.

Everyone else is in deep conversation, doing a pretty good job of pretending I don't exist. I'm in my own little world, separate from those around me, and that's just fine with me. If I were heading to the Factory with the Sophias right now, maybe I would have been engrossed in a discussion with them, and maybe I wouldn't have seen the moon.

I wait at the top of the stairs, keeping an eye on the moon as my peers shuffle their way out of the building. When enough of the masses have gone, I go to where it's abandoned on the sidewalk, now marred with the treads of shoes and—a bicyclist zips past—the track of a tire.

Once it's in my hand, I test the weight of it. It's made with the same thick paper as the first, but this one is a pearly white that shimmers when it catches the sunlight.

I sit on the steps of Saint Mary's and carefully unfold the moon.

As expected, there are words on the back of this one, too. I read the poem, which is only four lines:

Weaving through the mysteries
Of life before I've lived it
Waffling through present time
For gifts before they're given.

I snap a picture and send it to Hayley.

Me: Dylan Thomas strikes again.
Hayley: Whoa.
Hayley: Are you sure it's the same person?
Me: I mean, obviously, this isn't a coincidence.

Hayley: No. Can't be.

Hayley: But they're not following you or anything?

Me: I don't see anyone here.

Hayley: They just left you a note.

Me: When you say it that way, it sounds creepy.

Hayley: I mean, isn't it?

Me: Maybe, maybe not.

Me: If he really wanted to be creepy, he'd wait for me
     and give it to me in person.

Hayley: Uhhhh

Hayley: Is there any chance this Dylan Thomas goes
     to your school?

Me: Maybe.

Me: How else would he know I'd be here?

Hayley: If you notice someone starting to follow you

Hayley: you should call the police.

Hayley: Can't be too careful.

Me: Actually . . .

I pause. I'm tempted to tell my sister about the guy outside
of the Factory, and the guy lingering in the back of my selfie
with McKenna and Brendon outside Counter Offer. But I'm
not even sure it's the same guy. And I don't want to overreact,
let my fears get the better of me.

Hayley: Actually what?

Me: Nothing. I'm not worried about Dylan though.

Hayley: Even though you don't know anything
     about them?

Me: Him. See, I know a little now.

Me: And I sort of like the mystery about him.

Hayley: Wait.

Hayley: Does that mean you're into him?

Me: What?! I don't even know him.

Me: How could I be into him?!

Hayley: Just be careful, if you decide to be
into him.

Me: It's a choice to fall for someone or not?

Me: Maybe someone should let my mom in on
that secret.

Hayley: Ha!

Hayley: You're different than your mom.

Hayley: It IS a choice with you.

Hayley: You're the only person I know

Hayley: who leads with her head and not her heart.

Me: Haha

Me: This is definitely a business relationship.

Hayley: Well, let me know if he does something like
this again.

Hayley: It's weirding me out.

Me: Noted.

This is a new dynamic for us. Usually I'm the one freaking out about something, and Hayley's the one talking me down, reminding me to chill, poking holes in my ballooning fears.

Hayley: Any word on the audition?

I love that my sister knows I don't post the results online, and she knows I don't brag about getting cast ever. I wait for people to ask, and then I tell them. And this particular news, I've been *dying* to share!

Me: I'm called back.
Hayley: Woohoo! Awesome!
Me: Thx!

I scroll through my remaining text messages. A few from Nana Adie, who's wondering if eggplant sounds good for dinner—and asking for an update on the callback list.

Mom hasn't texted all day. She's probably still mad at me.

My heart seizes with the thought of it. It's not like Mom to give me the silent treatment.

I text her now, just in case she doesn't believe my apology was sincere.

Me: Sorry about this morning.
Me: I just hate being in the middle all the time.
Me: You're an amazing mom.
Me: I don't need you to spend money on me
Me: I love you to the end of the universe and back.
Me: A million times.

"Vinny!"

When I hear the name, and the jingle of dog tags, I look up from my screen.

I scan the stream of people walking down the sidewalk, hoping to see a little black lab-slash-terrier-slash-whatever-he-is with white paws bounding up the steps of Saint Mary's.

Instead, I see a pair of friends do the guy-hug where a high-five turns into a grasp of hands, they pull in closer, and then they wallop each other on the back. "Good to see you, Vin."

At the same time, a woman walking a dog that looks like a tiny dust mop prances past, tags a-jingling.

My heart sinks. I miss the dog that was supposed to be mine.

I tap on the Facebook icon on my screen to look at Ted's pictures. No new ones of Vinny.

But Ted's online.

Should I . . . ?

What the hell. I message him a "Hi" and start walking toward the L stop. Half a block later, my phone pings.

Ted: Lainey!

Ted: Nice surprise.

Ted: Good to hear from you.

Ted: How's school?

Me: Ugh.

Ted: How's the stage?

Me: Good.

Me: Just saw a dog I thought was Vinny.

Me: How is he?

Me: Pic?

Ted: We're heading out for a walk.

Ted: Why don't you meet us?

Ted: I could take him to Wicker Park.

Me: Just leaving school.

Me: Have to catch the L.

Ted: We're just heading out now.

Ted: If you want to come, we'll wait.

Should I?

I want to see the dog. Would Mom mind if I happened to see Ted at the same time?

I'll decide on the way.

I high-tail it to the L stop, where the Sophias are waiting

for the next train. I pretend I don't see them—or the guy in the black coat behind them who keeps looking this way . . . *creepy*—and try to keep my gaze pinned to my phone.

But he's familiar. He could be the same guy I saw outside Counter Offer . . . maybe even the same guy outside of the Factory.

Or . . . it could be a coincidence. It's a big city, but we usually stick to our neighborhoods, and neighborhoods can feel a little small.

I snap a pic of the moon in my hand and post it to my Instagram with a caption: *Sometimes the world gives you snow-capped hills on the midnight horizon.*

And, just to be safe, I sneak a pic of the guy who keeps looking this way. I'll compare the pictures later.

"Sure you don't want to hit the Factory with us?" Sophia 1 asks.

I look up. "Oh. Hi."

"My treat," Sophia 2 offers.

But I see right through them. They want to go to New York. They don't want to go with me, but if that's the way they'll get their free tickets, they'll endure the boredom of being near me.

"I'm meeting my stepdad," I say. "Sorry."

The moment the word stepdad fumbles out of my mouth, I want to suck it back in. He was with my mom for ten months, lived with us for six, and then ditched us. Calling him any kind of dad is giving him too much credit.

"Oh. Well, if you change your mind . . ."

"Hey, by the way," Sophia 1 says. "Any new productions coming up?"

I don't want to ruin the good news about the callback by letting them pretend to be happy for me. As if they don't remember saying that they think I'm a talentless spoiled brat. "Nope."

"Well, we'd love to come see your next show, so be sure to let us know . . ."

Her words are drowned by the rattle of the oncoming train.

But I nod and keep my mouth shut. Even though all I really want to do is tell them to stop being so fucking fake. I want to remind them that I'm the same weird girl they used in order to meet Brendon Urie during his Broadway run. The same weird girl they pretended to like in order to get backstage at the Vagabonds concert last year.

I board the car behind theirs.

I study pictures of creepy guy number one and creepy guy number two.

Similar coat. Similar build. But the second guy is balding. I can't really tell if the first guy is—his hood is up.

I send the pictures to my sister and ask for her input.

Hayley: Hard to tell.
Hayley: But probably not the same guy.

I ride. Images of my Vinny-dog flip through my mind like one of those digital photo albums reviewing the highlights of your year's postings. But seeing Ted could be harder than I think—could bring back all the heartache we felt when he left Mom.

That's one thing that sucks about parents looking for their next forever. It's up to them and their significant others when to end the relationship. As little say as I had as to whether they got together, I had even less of a vote when it came to their breaking up. If Ted had told me he was going, I would have begged him to stay. I would have pled on my hands and knees.

He made Mom so happy.

Until he didn't.

I should play it safe. I should just go home and forget that I ever almost had a dog.

But when I exit at Damon, the Sophias exit, too.

If they're really going to the Factory, they got off one stop too early.

I take this to mean that they plan to walk with me, to try to convince me to be friends again. Instantly, I decide to follow through with the park plan. The last thing I need is them hanging around on my doorstep, lingering until I invite them in and staying until I invite them on a first-class flight to LaGuardia.

I catch the glance Sophia 2 throws at me over her shoulder. It's the same bright smile she offers teachers when she needs an extension on an essay. "Coming?"

The guy in the black coat brushes between us. "Excuse me." But then he lingers near a lamppost, dialing and putting his phone to his ear.

"My treat," Sophia 2 says again.

The guy in the black coat keeps glancing at us. I'm halfway tempted to go with the Sophias because the guy seriously creeps me out. But . . .

"Can't. Bye." I already told her I was meeting Ted. I quicken my pace past them to the point that I'm almost running.

"Well . . ." Sophia 1 sighs behind me. "Might as well wait for the next train. I'm so not walking all the way to the Factory from here."

I keep up my ridiculously brisk pace even after it's clear the guy in the black coat isn't heading in the same direction as me.

But it smells and feels like rain this afternoon, and I don't know how long Ted will keep Vinny in the park, so I figure I should hurry even if I'm only being followed in my overactive imagination.

My cheeks are moist with the beginnings of a late afternoon storm by the time I arrive. I glance over the expanse of Wicker Park, looking frantically until I see him.

He's running, the leash dragging behind him, retrieving a Frisbee Ted just spun across the lawn.

"Vinny!"

The dog that was supposed to be mine skids to a stop and cocks his head to one side with the Frisbee firmly in his mouth.

I pat my legs. "Come here, Vinny! Good boy, good boy."

He beelines right toward me and jumps up. His muddy paws mark my khakis, but I don't care. Maybe he remembers me from the shelter, or maybe he simply recognizes that I love dogs. Either way, he looks so happy to see me. His little nub of a tail is twitching back and forth.

"Vinny! Down!" Ted's on his way now, an apologetic expression written on his face.

I grab the leash to hold him and let him lick my cheeks.

Pause.

You know Ted Haggerty. His profile picture is a portrait of Ivan Pavlov. His cover photo is a serene beach with an inspirational quote written in the sky with a jet stream. His laugh is as identifying as his too-long hair or nerdy wardrobe.

Anyway . . .

"Look what you did to Lainey," Ted says to the dog.

"I don't care," I say. "I'm just so happy to see him."

"We're happy to see you too. You don't message often. Except on my birthday. That was nice. Thank you."

I nod, not sure what to say. I'm still mad at him for leaving, but I don't want to start this conversation on a sour note.

"We, uh . . ." Ted sighs and tucks a grey wisp of hair—no ponytail today—behind his ear. "We live just west of here. You can drop in any time."

"Oh." He must have gotten a new place. "Really? You wouldn't mind?"

"Well, I think . . . maybe enough time's gone by."

He shuts up and, out of breath, plants his hands on his waist, one thumb hooking into a belt loop. He's wearing salmon-colored corduroys and a black t-shirt that reads TUCK FRUMP. On his feet are honest-to-goodness penny loafers (who wears those anymore?), but with nickels slid into the slits instead of pennies because he likes to aim high. He hasn't changed a bit.

"Why is it okay now?" I ask. "Isn't two years kind of an arbitrary statute of limitations?"

"Lainey, to be honest, I would've loved seeing you all the time, but I'm not sure how your mom would feel about your dropping by, so . . . It's really up to her. And you, of course. But you should talk to her about it before you just do it."

"Yeah, I will."

"How's she doing?"

"She's mad at me right now."

Vinny jumps up on my khakis again—Ted doesn't scold him this time—and I pet his perfect, black ears.

"Mad?" Ted squints at me. "What's going on?"

"Oh, nothing. Just that my dad wants to take me to a couple of shows on her weekend, and she thinks he's showing off or something, but I think he just wants me to have these amazing experiences, so . . ." I shrug. "I'm just over trying to have to worry about hurting Mom's feelings if I want to take my dad up on these things, and—"

Shut up, Madelaine. None of this is Ted's business anymore. After a moment or two of silence, Ted clears his throat. "I know you blame me for what's going on with your mom. The finances—"

"How do you know about that?" It seems like an infringement on my family's privacy. He's not part of my family; he shouldn't be talking about it.

"She told me. I took her to Minnesota a couple of days ago."

"You did?"

"We talked all the way up and back. About lots of things."

"Why would you take her—"

"I shouldn't have mentioned it."

"Wait. Why would you ask how she's doing if you just saw her? What's going on?"

"It's something she would've told you if she wanted you to know. I shouldn't have said anything—"

"I thought she was there for a date." Wheels turn in my head. "Was the date with *you?*"

"No. Not a date."

"Then why?"

"You should ask her. Really."

"But if wasn't a date, and it wasn't an audition—"

"Thanks for wrangling this little guy." He takes the leash from my hand. "And you"—he's talking to the dog now—"you shouldn't be so naughty. Those muddy paws all over Lainey's uniform!"

I'm not going to let him distract me from this. "If you must know, I don't blame you for what's going on," I say.

"I would understand if you did."

"I don't. I blame Mom. She should've given it more time, been more sure that you would stick around before you moved in. But you should know you ruined things when you left—important things, like my education. And I want to see Vinny. I do. But I don't know how I feel about seeing you because you broke my mother's heart."

"Is that what she said?"

"She didn't have to say it. I saw it. And you let me down. I thought we got along. I thought I mattered to you. You treated me like your daughter. You said you wouldn't have kids of your own, but it was fine because you had me. But you . . . you just left. Like I didn't even matter."

"That's valid." He slides a hand into a pocket and bobs his head.

I give him a second to expand on that. He doesn't.

"I know it's valid," I say. "I *know* that. What I want to know is . . . why aren't you sorry?"

"I am."

"You left her when she got cancer. You said you loved her, but the second things got tough, you split. And now you're taking her to Minnesota, and you're walking your dog in my park."

"It's the city's park."

"It's the park closest to Nana's and you know it. Aren't there other parks in West Town?"

He nods. "Yeah, but I like Wicker Park."

"Are you and my mom back together?"

He thinks for a minute. "No."

"Do you want to be?"

"Think she'd have me?" He grins.

I shake my head. This whole thing is so ridiculous. "I should go. Thanks for letting me see Vinny, but maybe I shouldn't have come."

"You probably need to get to rehearsal."

"No."

"No work on the horizon?"

"I was just called back for a revival of pretty big production, so . . ."

"*Thoroughly Modern Millie?*"

He knows it's my favorite. He remembered. I soften a bit. "God, I wish."

"Someday."

"Hopefully."

"It'll happen."

I shrug.

"Dating anyone?"

"No."

"Still sticking to that no-dating policy?"

"Considering my parents, I have enough drama without it."

He rocks back on his heels. "That's true."

"You know about the court case, so . . ."

He nods, and for a couple of uncomfortable seconds, things are silent.

"You know, though," he says, "if you ever need someone to come over and intimidate some guy before he takes you out . . . I'm there for you."

"Yeah. Like that'll ever happen."

"Hey. I can be intimidating when I want to be." He flexes muscles he doesn't really have.

He's not the kind of guy who would show off the guns if he had any, but because he doesn't, I can't help smiling at his joke. And it feels good to banter with him again. "I meant some guy taking me out."

"That's *your* decision. It doesn't mean some guy wouldn't be lucky to have you."

"Doubtful."

"You know why you feel that way?" Ted takes a step down the path.

I fall in line next to him.

"You feel that way because your dad was never there for you. It's textbook."

"He's there for me."

"On his terms."

I shake my head. "Spare me the psychobabble."

"Okay," he sighs. "I wanna come to your show, though."

"It's not my show. Not yet. I was just called back."

"Well, when you get it, then. I'd like to go see it. Would that be all right?"

"Sure. Buy a ticket."

"You'll let me know when it opens?"

"Or you can look at the banners on State Street."

"I prefer a text. Or hell, maybe even a phone call."

"How about a carrier pigeon?"

"Hey, I'm hip with the technology," he says, even though those very words belie the sentiment. "Speaking of which. Who's Dylan Thomas?"

"Huh? How do you know—"

"I see some guy tagged in something near and dear to you, like a song you wrote, and I gotta wonder. Who is this guy?"

Ah. I wonder if Ted still gets an alert every time I post or every time I'm tagged in a post from someone else.

"Just someone I met on Lyrically. Strictly business."

"You finally posted one of your songs."

"Don't make a big deal out of it."

"Was that you playing guitar on that track?"

"Mmhmm."

"You're getting pretty good. Taking lessons?"

"Teaching myself. Thank God for YouTube."

"You're so talented, Lainey."

"Well, I have to work ultra hard." I start babbling again, reiterating my hopes and dreams to the guy who's the very reason I might not get to the right school to accomplish them. And we're walking through the park, a dog leash in my hand, just like it's any other day, like Vinny's still my dog. Like there's still a chance Ted might be a dad to me someday.

I wonder, and not for the first time, if he would have been the kind of dad to pick me up from school if I were feeling sick. If he would have taught me how to swing a bat, how to clean and steam fish after we catch them, whatever else dads teach kids.

If Ted were my dad, would he have taught me to ride a bike? Mom tried, but ultimately, it was Hayley who taught me because I never allowed Mom to let go of the bike.

My dad didn't do those things. He never had time. He was never in the same place long enough, never stayed home for more than a day or so before he was heading out for this actor's debut, or that show's opening night.

It was business. He was working. I understood. And maybe I wouldn't be where I am—career-wise—if he were, say, a human resources manager. I wonder if I would have wanted to be onstage so badly if I hadn't grown up in the realm. If having a semi-absent dad is what it takes to get where I'm going, maybe it's worth the sacrifice.

"Hot dog?" Ted asks when we near a vendor.

I probably shouldn't take him up on it, probably shouldn't succumb to the normalcy of it all, but the truth is that I'm *starving*, and because I opted to meet him and Vinny, it'll be that much longer before I'm home to grab a snack.

"No mustard," I say.

"I know. I remember. It hasn't been *that* long."

He buys me a hot dog, complete with tomatoes and pickles and celery salt.

We sit on a bench and eat. Vinny curls up at our feet. I watch people pass us by, and I wonder if they're thinking that we're father and daughter. I used to muse that even though we don't look alike, we share a similar style, prone to upcycling vintage finds at thrift stores. Most people aren't observant enough to look past the surface.

But I'm not most people. I observe strangers all the time.

The expressions of the Wicker Park patrons are combinations of burnt orange, buttercup, blaze, and blue skies. It takes all kinds of moods to usher in the storm about to break over this city.

"All these people," Ted says, as if reading my mind. "They have one thing in common: they're walking as if on a mission, as if they know where they're going."

I know Ted well enough to recognize a philosophical speech coming on, but when he doesn't elaborate, I figure I should comment.

"I want to be like them," I say. "I wish someone would just give me a map, and show me the shortcut, because I want to get there yesterday."

"Where's there?"

"You know. New York. Broadway."

"Life's not like a city, kid. There's no map detailing the L routes and bus schedules. You gotta find your own way. And I know you will. I know you'll be a big star one day."

"Do you really think I'm good enough?"

"It seems the only person who doesn't know you're better than good enough is sitting right next to me."

I roll my eyes.

"I just worry that I'll end up like Mom. You've seen her. You know she's not happy doing what she's doing, and the only thing that will fix it is a freaking time machine."

"The world hasn't seen the last of Ella Norini," Ted says. "I promise you."

I chew in silence for a minute. "Ted?"

"Yeah."

"Why were you with my mom in Minnesota?"

He dribbles mustard onto his corduroys and treats me to a stare that's full of both hope and sorrow. But he says nothing.

"She came home sad. I want to know what happened."

"Did you ask her?"

Did I? I'm not sure there was an opening. He should know my mom well enough to know she wouldn't tell me something bad even if I did ask to hear it.

"Did you emotionally skewer her again?" I press. "Because if you did—"

"Lainey."

"What?"

"Finish your hot dog."

It's only about half gone, but I'm so done with everything right now. I toss it at a trash can a few feet away—miraculously, it goes in—and hand over Vinny's leash.

"Lainey—"

"If you don't want to tell me, it must be bad news. You're the cause of enough bad news in my life, so . . ." Once my arm is through the strap of my backpack, I stand and start to walk away.

Vinny squeals at my back. My heart aches. Love you, too, pup.

But it wasn't meant to be.

"Good or bad," Ted calls after me. "It's not my news to tell."

I'm halfway down the path. I still hear Vinny whining. I didn't even say goodbye to him.

This is the only reason I look over my shoulder.

My would-be stepfather is holding a half-eaten hot dog, watching me. There's a blotch of goldenrod on his salmon corduroys.

But the skies are about to split open and wash all this away.

CHAPTER 13

Nana Adie is singing "Like a Prayer" in the kitchen while she slices eggplant. I'm doing homework at the table.

My heart lifts when I see a message pop up on my phone.

Mom: I'll be home soon.

It's the first I've heard from her since our argument this morning. Maybe she's finally forgiven me for being such a horrible daughter.

Me: <3 <3 <3

I haven't even put my phone down yet when it buzzes again with a text from my BFFBS.

Hayley: Been thinking about this Dylan Thomas thing.
Hayley: It's strange that another origami moon
    showed up.
Hayley: Is this guy stalking you?
Me: I haven't seen anyone but those guys that
    I sent pics of

Hayley: And like, he's in high school, right?

Hayley: So how would he even be able to leave the moon at Saint Mary's?

Hayley: He should have still been in school.

Me: Unless he's on a different schedule.

Hayley: He can't get from Englewood to your school in ten minutes.

Me: I don't know.

Me: I don't even know if he's in high school.

Hayley: Lainey!

Me: Not sure it came up in conversation.

Me: We talked about music

Me: About art

Me: hopes, dreams, etc.

Me: I haven't even seen a pic of him.

Hayley: What if he's seen you?

Hayley: Don't tell me you haven't thought about it.

Hayley: Why else would you have sent me the pictures?

Me: So I'm a little paranoid.

Me: I don't feel threatened by him.

Me: On the contrary, I feel very much like myself with him.

Me: Like I feel with you.

Hayley: . . .

Me: Not that anyone could ever replace you.

Hayley: I was gonna say . . . LOL

Me: It's just that I like the anonymity of it.

Hayley: But how does he even know where you go to school?

This gives me pause, and my breath sort of catches in my

throat for a second. How *does* he know? Did I tell him about Saint Mary's? It seems like something I'd normally keep to myself online. Maybe that day when we messaged for hours . . . Could I have mentioned it?

Hayley: Just be careful.
Hayley: Don't trust the way your mom would.

I log in to Lyrically and click on my messenger. While it loads, I continue to text Hayley.

Me: I'll be careful.
Hayley: Maybe you should stop talking to him.
Me: But he writes the most beautiful words.
Hayley: You don't even know if he really wrote it.
Hayley: You posted a pic
Hayley: and he claimed it was his work.
Hayley: How do you even know the truth?
Hayley: How do you even know who he is?

Hayley has a point. I don't really know.

I read through the conversation we shared the night after I found the first origami moon.

School never came up.

He did admit to Googling me, however.

So I Google me.

And I scan through the items that pop up. This production. That production. I give all my bios (I write new ones for every show) a quick once-over to see if I ever mention the name of my high school. I doubt it—it's not exactly brag-worthy to announce to theater-goers that I attend a stuffy, normal

Catholic high school where I'm remanded to the dean's office for tinting my hair—but I check just in case.

No mention of Saint Mary's. So how did he know where to leave the second moon?

I message him.

Me: Got your second moon.

I wait.

I drum my fingers on the keyboard of my laptop.

It's clear he's not going to respond.

And I still have a gazillion messages on my page that I've yet to look at. I know they're going to be responses to my revised song in E minor.

I know most of them are going to be mean responses. It's the internet. People are asshats on the internet.

But I have to deal with it sooner or later. And like Dylan Thomas said when we chatted: my chosen profession is brutal, and people are going to be overly critical at times. If I can't take it when it comes through a computer screen, how am I going to take it face-to-face?

My finger hovers over the mousepad, about to click over to my homepage to deal with whatever awaits me over there.

Just do it. I hear Mom's voice in my head: *Just you and the stage.*

With my eyes tightly closed, I click.

I open one eye, then the next.

My jaw drops. My song has been shared hundreds of times. It has twenty-five thousand views.

With numb hands I pick up my phone.

Me: 25K people have listened to my song.

Me: Do people like it?

Me: I can't look.

Hayley: Hold on, I'll check.

Me: Thanks.

Hayley: It's in the job description for BFFBS.

Me: I CAN'T stop talking to Dylan now.

Me: He's the reason my song is spreading online.

Hayley: Not the only reason!

Hayley: I shared it.

Hayley: Ted shared it.

Hayley: BurningUrine shared it.

Hayley: And you're the one who wrote it

Hayley: and changed it and reposted it in E minor.

Hayley: YOU did this.

Hayley: Dylan Thomas may have encouraged you

Hayley: But you're the reason it's awesome.

Me: Let's just hope other people like it.

Hayley: People LOVE it.

Hayley: OMG

Hayley: People LOVE it!

Finally, I brave the comments. The first few aren't all that great. RadioHeadAddict was sure to remind me that I "blow," for example, but loads of people have given it a thumbs-up. I skim over the *obviously an amateur* comments and focus on the good things people have to say. So many people have commented with specific things they like about the song, and some have even suggested ways to improve it. I don't agree with most of the advice, but at least most of the commenters seem to have good intentions.

Tears of joy fill my eyes. I burst into the kitchen and interrupt the choir singing backup for Madonna.

"Nana, listen!" I cue up my song, then turn down her music.

I grab her hands, which are slightly sticky with eggplant breading, but I don't care. "I wrote this song, okay? And I thought I'd take a chance, so I posted it online. And—"

"Take a deep breath."

"And people are liking it! You want to hear it? 'Cause I really want to play it for you. It's like the best thing I've ever written, and it sort of has lyrics, but it sort of doesn't. And I'm going to send it to the dean of admissions at the academy. I've been compiling a portfolio to see if I might qualify for any grants—"

"Good idea."

"—because I want this *so bad*. It's like you said. I can make my own way, and this song . . . it's the first step."

"Let's hear it," Nana says.

I push play, and my music filters through the speakers on my laptop.

Suddenly, life feels like it used to, when I was little, living in Kenilworth and dancing around the kitchen.

I've been hearing Dylan Thomas's words in my head whenever I work on this song, so I start to sing them as the notes play.

When the song is over, Nana hits repeat, and we listen to it again and again. By the fourth time, even Nana is singing a few of Dylan's lyrics she's caught onto, and she's holding my hand, and spinning me like we're ballroom dancing, and we're laughing.

God, what a great day!

Halfway through a spin, I see Mom as she emerges from the hallway.

She's drenched from the rain, and she looks positively exhausted, but she smiles.

I hit pause on the song. "Mom, it's a song I wrote, and I put it on Lyrically, and this has *never happened to me before*—"

"I heard it," she says. "I love it."

I jump into her arms, and she holds me so tight, as if our spat this morning didn't even happen. And that's the way it always is with Mom. She always wants me to feel loved. Always wants me to feel good enough.

Nana resumes the song, and we start singing it again, but really, we're more laughing than singing, and we manage only the last four words: "Abiding like the ti-i-ide!"

When I turn off the music, Mom takes a seat and Nana slides the eggplant into the oven.

"Oh, my Madelaine," Mom says. "You sing beautifully."

I sit across from her and start to tell her all about the first origami moon I found—I don't mention the one that showed up at school—and explain how I met Dylan Thomas online and hope to convince him to collab.

"The words inside are serendipitously perfect for this song," I explain. "I have to convince him. I just have to."

"Dylan Thomas, huh?" says Mom, raising her eyebrows. "Interesting."

I can tell she's not totally sold on the idea of me chatting with a stranger, so I change the subject. We talk—or rather, I do—about my callback and about my plan to stay in constant contact with the performing arts dean of admissions.

"That's a great idea," Mom says with another tired smile.

"Isn't it?" Nana looks at me and gives me a nod.

I lean toward my mother, and she gingerly brushes my hair from my forehead, like she used to when I was a little girl. "It's like I've always told you," Mom says. "Talent finds a way to the spotlight. If only you believe . . ."

She sounds like such a dreamer sometimes.

It's no wonder, now that I think about it, that I ended up with such aspirations, given she's been whispering things like this in my ears since before I was born.

"Now." Mom laughs a little. "What happened to your khakis?"

I take a deep breath. "Vinny happened."

"As in Ted's dog?"

"Yeah. I sort of . . . I met up with him today in Wicker Park. He bought me a hot dog."

"How did that happen?" There's an edge to Mom's voice. Or maybe she really is just tired.

Nana shakes her head and *tsk*s.

"It was *fine*," I say. "Actually, it seems like I'm not the only one who's seen Ted recently."

Mom nods.

"Are you getting back together?"

"As much as I think you'd like that, Madelaine—"

"I just want you to be happy."

"—I don't think so."

"So why did the two of you go to Minnesota together?'

My mother and grandmother share a glance.

I straighten. "What?"

"Maybe it's time to tell her," Nana says.

"Tell me what?"

My mother shakes her head.

"Ella, for God's sake," Nana says.

"It's nothing," Mom says. "I've been putting together a proposal for choreography, and Ted took me to present it last Saturday. It was just a favor. He agreed to take me, and that's the end of it."

"Choreography?" I'm brimming with excitement now. It's a job in the theater. So much more fitting for my mother than secretarial work, and I can imagine it would be that much more satisfying. "How'd it go?"

"I'm not sure," Mom says. "But here's to hoping."

Nana shakes her head again.

"I sort of let Ted have it," I say.

"You don't have to do that, baby girl," Mom says. "I know you liked him."

"He said I could visit my dog whenever I wanted."

"Okay."

"Would that bother you?"

"We'll talk about the possibility. Just not tonight, okay? I'm so tired."

"But it bothers you that I'm going to New York with Dad this weekend."

Nana drops a spatula—it clangs against the floor—and swears in Italian.

"It seems it doesn't matter whether it bothers me or not. Your father is going to do what your father wants to do." My mother pushes back from the table and covers a yawn. "I'd better try to lift the mud out of those khakis."

I'm about to thank her when Nana gives me a stern look. "You can take care of your own pants, can't you?"

I get up. "Mom, wait."

I follow her down the hallway.

It's not until I see the tears in her eyes that I know: She lied to me about Ted. Maybe she really did propose a choreography package, but there's more to it. And she isn't telling me what it is.

"You know, Mom . . ."

She looks at me over her shoulder and wipes the tears from her eyes. She looks so sad that I almost don't want to call her on it. But . . .

"I don't like being lied to."

"I can't imagine anyone does."

"I feel like Dad has a life that doesn't include me. I don't want you to have a life that doesn't include me, too."

She sighs. "Everything I do," she says for the millionth time, "I do for you."

"Then let me in on it. I don't deserve this sneaking around. I'm honest with you. Transparent, you know. And you're keeping something gargantuan from me."

"You know, I just . . . for once, I'd like to know: do you talk to your father this way?" Mom asks. "You say he has a life that doesn't include you. Does he know how you feel?"

"I don't have to tell him these things! Nothing I say will change what he does!"

"Then why do you demand it of me? Why does your father get a free pass every fucking time—"

I flinch when she swears in English, which almost never happens.

"—but I have to always do the right thing. Always say the right thing. You don't allow me the courtesy of being human, and I've had it!"

My heartbeat picks up. I didn't mean to start another fight. "I apologized for earlier," I remind her. "But if we're being honest, I do think you screwed up. I *do* think things are hard now because you're an absolute *idiot* when it comes to relationships!"

"Madelaine Emmah!" Nana says.

"Your father controls you. He manipulates you."

"Ella," Nana interjects. "Think about—"

I cut Nana off. I'm not letting her intrude on this argument. "That's what you think of me? You think I'm easily manipulated?"

"This isn't exclusive to you. He manipulates *everyone*," Mom says. "He sure manipulated the hell out of me, didn't he? He gets what he wants because he has money. You go to New York because he has money. You do what he wants, when he wants, because he's holding the purse strings, and you think if you're the perfect daughter, if you don't disagree with *anything* he says, you'll get what you want."

This is so unfair of her. She wasn't at Morton's the other night, when I defended her and pushed back at Dad. She has no right to accuse me of *letting* my father walk all over me.

"You think that ultimately, he'll pay for your last year of high school at that performing arts academy, when he could have opened his checkbook years ago and paid for all of it with a single stroke of a pen. You should've been there since day one. And he has you thinking *I'm* the reason you're not going." Her tears intensify, and she leaves a black streak of mascara over her cheek when she wipes them away.

"Ella, enough," Nana says.

Mom slams a palm into the wall and leans her head there. "I'm asking you. Just this once, baby girl. Stand up to him and demand what you deserve, and I'm not talking about a trip to New York. I'm talking about your future. Don't let him control you with the almighty dollar sign. Don't let him steal your opportunities from you the way he stole mine from me."

"Mom." I'm crying now, too, and I go over to hug her. "I'm sorry. I won't go on the trip. Is that what you want?"

"I want you to go." Her tear-moistened fingers meet my cheek. "Of course, I want you to experience all these wonderful things. But I wish he'd see that he's not hurting me when he demands fifty percent of your tuition. He's hurting you. Because I don't have it, and no matter how hard I work, even if I work these two jobs until the day I die, I won't have it."

"Ella," Nana tries again.

"I'm done fighting," Mom says. "I'm tired, and I'm done fighting."

Nana Adie is suddenly behind me, her hand under my elbow, helping me up. "Madelaine. Go wash your pants."

CHAPTER 14
Tuesday, May 2

It's after midnight, but I can't sleep, even though we all hugged and cuddled on the couch for a while and calmed down.

Nana's watching reruns of *Gilmore Girls*, so I hear her laugh every now and then. And I hear my mother's soft sobs drifting down the hallway.

No one wants to tell me what happened, but if Ted brought my mom to Minnesota last weekend, he probably accompanied her last month, too. Which means that whatever happened between them has been happening for a month.

And judging by her tears tonight, it's not going well.

I play around on the internet, try to crack the Vagabonds code. But I'm so tired, and it's like a mathematical mindfuck, so I give up and tweet: *Vagabonds, life without you is outer space with hints of slate. Come back into the unmellow yellow.*

I message Ted.

Me: Talked to Mom. Want to tell me
what's REALLY happening between
you two?

But he doesn't reply.

He's probably out with some other woman right now, promising her that even though he's never had kids, he'd love to be a dad. Maybe he'll actually mean it this time.

If so, he should know how she's feeling right now. I drive it home.

Me: She's been crying all night.

I plug in my guitar, and my headphones, so I don't wake the baby downstairs—no one's sleeping in our place, obviously, so I wouldn't wake anyone here—and I play. But even the notes can't take my mind from the words my mother spoke tonight.

The whole thing makes me so sad. She's the one who's been there for me. Come hell or high water, she's there.

She came to my shows in the midst of chemo, even when I was on stage for mere minutes. She's never missed a recital. She was there when nightmares woke me in the middle of the night. She was there when I was sick with the flu.

And when my father sent my mother and me packing, Mom's the reason I wasn't afraid.

I scroll through a photo album that contains pictures of Hayley and Mom and me throughout the course of my life. For so long, it was just the three of us. Three chicks making it happen together.

I didn't even know Hayley wasn't Mom's daughter until I was going into kindergarten, and when I found out, Mom simply said it didn't matter. That I was her firstborn, but Hayley was her first baby.

I've been so hard on Mom. I mean, I get that she made a gargantuan mistake by having Ted move in, given the way the papers were written. But that doesn't mean she should have to pay for it forever. Her life's hard enough without me making it worse.

But I don't know how to change it.

I think of all I'd sacrifice if I weren't on Dad's good side. He could start treating me the way he treats Mom. If I piss him off, the trips will go away. So will the concert tickets. And that's okay.

But what if he stops trying to get me auditions? It's unprofessional, since he's my manager, but it could happen. What if he, out of spite, decides I need some tough love, too?

Nothing is going to change with him. Ever. Who am I kidding?

Unless something *else* changes, unless the dean of admissions finally decides that I'm too good an asset to pass up and helps me find a way to pay tuition, I need my father too much to do the right thing.

I scroll through my phone and find my favorite picture of my mom, sister, and me. I post it to my Instagram: *All the good things in life. Cotton candy and pink lemonade.*

Lyrically alerts me that I have a message. I shoot over to the site.

Dylan: You there?
Me: Here now.
Dylan: So about that moon
Me: Yeah
Me: Word on the street is it's kind of sketchy to leave
    gifts for a stranger at her school
Dylan: Oh man
Dylan: Not trying to be sketchy
Me: I didn't think so

Me: but this is quite a cloak-and-dagger way
        of sharing your work with me
Dylan: I do have a flair for the dramatic
Dylan: and a playfully mischievous nature
Me: Does this mean you'll let me use your lyrics?
Dylan: It means I'm game to keep talking.
Dylan: Saw your tweet. You had a bad day?
Me: A little good, a little bad.
Dylan: Such are most days.
Dylan: Wanna talk about it?

And surprisingly, I do.

CHAPTER 15

I didn't hear Mom leave for work today. And I barely slept. But still, I trudge down the hallway to the bathroom.

The Sophias have texted.

> Sophia 1: Who's up for coffee during zero hour?
> Sophia 2: Hand in the air!
> Sophia 1: I'll bring it.
> Sophia 1: Text your order.
> Sophia 2: Americano with two pumps mocha.
> Sophia 2: Thx!
> Sophia 1: Madelaine?
> Sophia 1: You want to join?

I type *I see right through you.*

My finger hovers over the send button, but at the last second, I delete it all instead. And as an extra measure, I block them both.

Better to simply ignore what they think is a cunning attempt at getting back into my life than to call them on it. If I respond at all, they'll defend each other, try to make me feel like I'm being unreasonable, try to convince me I misconstrued what I know I completely understood.

"Madelaine?"

I stop and peek into Mom's room.

She's standing at her dresser, wearing a pair of jeans and a tunic sweater that's the same shade of pink as my hair. It's her favorite color, and I love seeing her in it, even if it sort of takes me aback. This isn't usually the kind of ensemble she wears to work, and I wonder why she's wearing it today.

In her hand is a mascara wand. She leans toward the mirror and brushes her naturally thick lashes with a coat of black.

"Running late?" I ask.

"Not exactly."

I check my phone for the time. Maybe I'm the one off-schedule today. But no. It's just past six.

Instantly, my mind goes to Ted, and I jump to the conclusion that she's prepping for a day out with him. Playing hooky, he used to call it. "Taking the day off?"

"No."

"Going in late?"

She looks at me. Smiles. "I quit my job last night."

"What? Which job?"

"Both of them. I was just so tired, see, and I think that's why I lost it on you. And I can't do that, Lainey. I need to be my best self for you. After all that happened yesterday, I started thinking about it. Really thinking about it. And I emailed my boss at Hembry after you went to bed and told him I'm done. Then, I called my boss at Walton and told her the same."

My brain scrambles to process this information. "No two weeks' notice?"

"Nope. I'm just done."

"Won't that make them mad? I mean, you always say the way you leave a job could affect the next job. Wouldn't you want to leave on good terms?"

"I think there are better things I can do with my time. I hated those jobs, Lainey." She rummages in a drawer for the next cosmetic. "Hated them. I decided life's too short to spend my time getting coffee for other people."

It feels as if someone just carved my heart out of my chest. How does she think we're going to make it? Money's already tight. Already we can't afford things. And, God, not to mention . . . . "The courts aren't going to like this."

"Don't worry about the courts."

I take a deep breath. Maybe, if not for the emotional evening we shared yesterday, I'd really let her have it. How does she expect me to react? What she's just done is again putting me in an impossible situation. My dreams of attending the academy may as well be chalk drawings on the sidewalk in the rain.

Everything's blurry, and I feel like I'm either going to cry or scream. I don't know what we're going to do.

Unless . . . "Did you hear from the Minnesota people? The choreographer position?"

"No. I'm not sure my heart's quite there, either."

"Mom."

Maybe Dad's right. Maybe Mom is in her financial situation exactly because she refuses to change it.

And yet I remember her discipline on the dance floor. I've never seen her perform live, but I've seen Nana Adie's old videos. My mother was the picture of grace. Until, that is, I came along.

"I want to tell you what I'm going to do today instead," Mom says.

"Okay." I lean against the doorframe.

She brings her hands to my cheeks. She's been doing this since I was little, holding my face in her hands.

But I don't like to have my face touched.

I pull away, but instantly regret it when I see the expression on her face. It's the same look she had when she told me Dad wanted out of their marriage, and when she told me Ted had moved out of our place. It's the result of rejection, and this time, I'm the reason for it.

She turns away. "We're going to see the dean of admissions at your dream school."

I feel my mouth fall open. "Yeah?" Please let this be more than Mom's deciding to storm the office and demand a meeting. I still haven't gotten a response to the email I sent.

"I asked for the meeting last week," she tells me. "They emailed last night to confirm. Private visit. Today. They still want you if we can work out the finances."

I throw my arms around her. At the moment, I don't care about anything but the chance to tell the dean about all I can offer the school. I'll worry about the mistake she's probably making with her job later.

"I'm going to find a way to make this happen for you," Mom murmurs in my ear.

"I'm going to make you proud," I say.

"You've already done that."

I shower and dress in a unitard—in case they offer me an impromptu second audition—a fun poncho, and ankle-high boots. I gather all my dance and music stuff, and Mom packs apples for the L.

I can't remember the last time we went anywhere like this together, as if we share a quest. Before the cancer, for sure.

She links her arm in mine—I let her in close this time—
and together, we descend the front steps. Nana Adie's voice
filters down from the open window upstairs. She's singing "Ray
of Light." Appropriate, I think.

Things definitely could be looking up.

And even if nothing comes of this visit, I'm not at Saint
Mary's today. That's a win in my book.

I see something on the bottom step. Is that another moon?
I pick it up before Mom sees it. The last thing I need is for Mom
to start worrying about how the mysterious Dylan Thomas
knows where I live.

Although . . . I wonder the same.

Did he cyber stalk me to learn our address?

I bury my uneasiness. He's harmless. We're fellow artists,
potential collaborators, nothing more. If he wanted something
more, wouldn't he be lurking somewhere nearby, hoping to
force contact with me?

I glance up and down the street, but don't see anyone.

I shove the red-and-white checkered moon into my pocket.

CHAPTER 16

The L is crowded, so we can't sit next to each other. Mom's a row up, and if I were still a little girl, I'd be sitting on her lap. She glances back at me; I assure her I'm fine with a wave. Once she turns back, I open the origami moon.

The poem inside is inspirational, almost as if Dylan Thomas knows what I'm doing today. One line in particular pinballs around in my head: *Keep your heart in the stars and your dreams in your arms.*

I can't stop thinking of it, of the images it evokes.

I snap a picture of the words and send it in a private message to Dylan on Lyrically.

> Me: If you still don't call yourself a poet . . .
> Me: shame on you.

This settles it. I'm going to finish the song and play it at open mic night at the Factory.

And maybe Dylan will come, and I'll invite the dean of admissions at the academy.

The lyrics will flesh out the musical notes I've arranged, and my performance will help prove there's range to what I can do. Everything will fall into place.

If, that is, Dylan Thomas agrees to let me use his words. But if he does, I could tap into the stars in my heart: I'd really love to write an entire original score for a musical. He could write the lyrics.

I refold the moon, stash it in my backpack, and open a track in progress as the L stops at the next platform.

The guy next to me gets up, so I call to Mom to alert her to the empty seat.

"Whatcha up to?" Mom says as she slides in next to me, gesturing at my earbuds.

"I think I'm going to sing at open mic. And I'm going to write a musical about making it in this business. It'll be about you. And me. And Hayley."

"I love that idea," she says.

"Sort of like *Gypsy*, without the neurotic mother and obnoxious costumes."

Mom laughs. Her laughter is like a music box. It's been so long since I've heard it. I love her laugh.

I lay my head on her shoulder. She leans her head against mine.

That's when I realize the man from the platform—the one who was looking at the Sophias and me—is in the next car. He's looking right at me.

When I look at him, he looks away.

"Mom?"

The train lurches to a stop at Webster.

"Yeah?"

I was going to ask her if she recognized the guy, but he's getting off the train. Maybe it really is a coincidence.

"Love you."

"I love you, too, baby girl."

CHAPTER 17

"They were impressed," Mom tells Nana Adie later as we all sit around the kitchen table. "Lainey really showed them what she could do!"

"Of course," Nana says. "My granddaughter is brilliant."

"And then there's the bad news," I say. "Grants are based on aptitude and need, and with Dad's salary, there's no way in hell I'll qualify."

Nana Adie frowns.

"But!" Mom raises a finger and turns to me. "I did the math again last night, and despite what his lawyers insist, my half of your tuition at the academy is almost exactly the same percentage of your earnings your father takes as your manager."

Insert record scratch. "Wait. He charges me?"

"Standard fifteen percent," Mom confirms.

"Why didn't I know this?"

"He charges all his clients for his services, Madelaine. That's what managers do. Why did you think he'd do anything different when it comes to you?"

"Well, because . . . I guess . . . 'cause he's my dad."

She raises a brow. "He's your manager."

"But *you* don't get paid for what you did for my career when

I was little. You did it because you wanted good things for my future. Why would Dad *charge* me?"

My dad's always made calls to put me in front of the right casting directors in the right venues and at the right time. But it was usually Mom's responsibility to take me to meet every casting director, to take me to all of my lessons—until she had to go back to work. Now I take the L, or Dad sends Giorgio in the limo. And he's paying for that limo out of his percentage of my earnings.

"Well, he gets your foot in the door," Mom says. "He definitely works for that percentage."

"But—if Dad earns x amount and tuition is almost exactly x amount, if he'd donate what he earns back to me—it's like I'd be paying for myself to go to school then."

"That's one way to look at it."

"So you're saying that we should ask him to put his fifteen percent toward my tuition?"

"No. I'm saying that if you didn't have a manager, you wouldn't have to ask for that fifteen percent back. We'd still be putting away the majority of your wages for your future, and you could put the extra toward school."

It takes a minute for me to catch up to what she's implying. "You want me to fire my father?"

"We don't say fired in this business. We say we went another way."

"What other way can we go? I mean, I still need someone to get me auditions. I still need someone to make calls, to follow up on the auditions."

"*I* can do it. I'm familiar with his system. I know how it works. I can get your foot in the door. I can follow up—"

"You don't have connections anymore." The numbness

returns to my fingertips, and a heavy feeling settles in my chest, as if an elephant just sat on me.

"Maybe not like I used to. But you do. Your resume will speak for itself now. Lainey, what you've managed to do in such a short about of time . . ."

"I don't know, though. Firing Dad?"

"Aren't you always saying that you don't want to get parts based on who your dad knows?"

"Yeah, but . . ."

"Let me try it. And if I can earn enough—if I can help you earn enough—you'll be able to go to performing arts school next year, even if your dad delays the court case for eons."

"You want me to replace my current manager, *my father*, with you."

"Yes, baby."

"On a whim."

"It's not a whim. It's a means to an end. You deserve to go to that school. This is the best way. I can fill out forms online to incorporate my new business, so once you tell your father—"

"I don't know how I'm going to do that," I manage to say. At least I think I say it. But my ears are clogged with the *shazam*s of panic.

"Lainey." My mom sounds like she's underwater.

"No. I can't. Mom, it's not like I don't trust you, but . . . fire my dad?"

Mom goes to brush hair from my forehead.

I flinch away. "I can't be constantly forced to choose between the two of you!"

"But you're not," Mom says. "You're choosing *you*. Don't you see?"

"Nice rationalization, but you're not the one who has to actually do it."

"He probably knows this is coming. I've already been trying to discuss it with him. But we'll explain it to him together, if you want," Mom says. "I'll go with you."

This only brings more panic. "You mean . . . the two of you? Together?"

"When will you go?" Nana asks.

"I don't see any reason not to go right now," Mom says. "As long as he's in town."

"Could we just . . ." My fingertips still feel numb. I'm tempted to take my pulse just to make sure my heart is still beating. "Can we wait until after New York, please? I don't want to ruin things."

For a long time, Mom doesn't reply.

The clamor in my ears gets louder. Of course, Mom doesn't care if New York is ruined. Dad ruined whatever she had planned, so maybe it's poetic justice.

It's getting harder to breathe.

Finally, Mom places her hand on mine. "Sure. That'll be easier for you, so that's what we'll do."

CHAPTER 18

Choosing between my parents.

There's no other way to describe what's about to happen.

No matter the rationalization, no matter the soundness of Mom's reasoning, I'm still going to have to sacrifice my relationship with my father if I want to get into performing arts school.

I snap a picture of my steps from the kitchen to my bedroom and post to Instagram: *Walking between boulder and bedrock.* My message thread with the Weekes twins is the only thing keeping me calm.

> McKenna: First, I can't believe your dad won't
>   make this happen for you.
> McKenna: Second, there has to be another way.
> McKenna: You can't possibly give your dad the ax.
> Brendon: BUT you can't possibly not come to our
>   school next year!
> Me: So what do you suggest, wise ones?
> McKenna: For now, we concentrate on callbacks.
> Brendon: And we have a blast in New York this
>   weekend!

I wish I could keep brainstorming with the twins—it's fun even if it's not particularly practical—but before long, they're off to voice lessons. For a while, I attempt to decipher the clues about Vagabonds. When I'm thoroughly confused, and half-convinced all the clues mean absolutely nothing, I log into Lyrically and play around with my piece, strictly for the distraction. But lately, the distraction seems to be whether or not the mysterious poet is online.

I find myself checking the Friends bar to see if Dylan's there.

On the fifteenth glance, I see his name pop up.

I wait. Maybe he'll approach me first.

Ten minutes later—and only because I'm afraid that if I don't make a move, he'll log off—I cave.

Me: I have now found three moons.
Me: All yours, I presume.
Dylan: . . .
Me: Are you ready to collab?
Dylan: You don't need me.
Me: That's for me to decide, isn't it?
Me: Have you listened to the song with the lyrics
    you wrote?
Me: It's all so perfect.
Dylan: What would you say if I told you
Dylan: that the moons aren't mine?
Dylan: That they're yours?
Me: You just don't want to work with me.
Me: Why not?
Dylan: I already told you.
Dylan: You don't need me.

Me: Wow, thanks.
Me: That's just great.
Me: Awesome end to this awesome day.
Dylan: You have more bad days than anyone I know.
Dylan: Do you even try to have a decent time?
Dylan: You're only here on this planet once, u know.
Me: I'm trying.
Me: It's just hard.
Dylan: Tell me all about it.

And, God knows why, but I find myself again relaying the details of my day. Actually, a lot of good happened . . . until Mom hit me with her plan.

And Dylan listens. He offers feedback and consoles me as if he knows me, as if he's known me forever, as if he completely understands how it feels to be wrung out and stretched between two families. He also pulls no punches.

Dylan: Maybe some of this would improve if you
    aimed for a more positive attitude.
Me: I know my attitude sucks from time to time.
Me: My sister tells me that.
Dylan: You're a pessimist.
Me: I am not.

But I wonder if Dylan has a point. If so many people are telling me the same thing, maybe I should think about it.

Dylan: You see the dark in things when you have lots
    of light.
Me: I'm a realist. There's a difference.

Dylan: Then I'm sure the realist in you knows that this
     situation could be a lot worse.
Dylan: These are some classic first-world problems,
     after all.

I can't argue with that. Yes, it's awful that Mom and Dad are on opposite ends of the earth when it comes to everything that matters. But I have two parents who do a lot for me. That's more than plenty of people have.

Dylan and I talk until it's nearly one in the morning. And even with his brutal honesty throwing me off balance, I don't want to get off line.

Dylan: Good talking to you
Dylan: But I have to go.
Dylan: I have to get up early.
Me: This was nice.
Me: Thanks for talking things through with me.
Dylan: :)
Me: It's been a long time since I've talked like this to
     anyone.
Dylan: . . .
Me: I appreciate it.
Dylan: . . .

When no words follow, I feel like maybe I've been too touchy-feely. Maybe some of this (most of this?) could have been left unsaid. Maybe I should've just vented a little and then refocused on what this site is all about: music.

I scroll up. God. The whole conversation is about me and my family dramas. Same as last night.

This guy is never going to want to talk to me again.

I begin to type an apology when . . .

Dylan: Want to meet?

Relief, and maybe a little excitement, rushes through me . . . followed by the familiar twinge of panic.

Me: Just for a coffee or something?
Dylan: Why not?
Me: The Factory?
Dylan: Sure.
Me: Then again . . .
Me: There's something comforting in this.
Me: The screen between us.
Me: Something that keeps us anonymous.
Dylan: If u want, we won't even talk face to face.
Dylan: We'll message thru Lyrically.
Me: And we'll happen to both be at the coffee shop at the same time.
Dylan: If we're comfortable, we'll meet face to face.
Dylan: If we're not, we won't.
Dylan: Tomorrow after school?
Me: I have a callback.
Me: But I usually get a coffee before.
Dylan: So . . . ?
Me: Sounds good.

It occurs to me as we're finalizing plans and saying goodnight that maybe this is not such a wise idea. He's already managed to leave moons at my school and my home. He obviously knows more about me than I know about him. He knows what I look like. I won't know if he's at the next table, or across the room, or even sitting in his bedroom in Englewood.

And if he wants to meet, it's probably because he's interested in discussing more than music. *I don't do the dating thing*, I think to say. But I can't type the words because suddenly, I don't know if they're 100 percent true.

Because despite my better judgment, despite all my worries, I'm finding myself looking forward to this. And if we hit it off in person the way we have online . . . maybe . . .

Eesh. I need to chill out. It's just coffee. Just half an hour. It's not a date.

Unless we want it to be.

CHAPTER 19
Wednesday, May 3

"Order for Madelynn."

I roll my eyes, get my coffee, and look for a place to sit.

The place is crowded—it always is—but I manage to snag a stool next to my favorite spot. I scan the space for anyone who looks like what I imagine Dylan Thomas might look like: maybe tall, lanky, Buddy Holly glasses. And I don't know why, but I keep picturing him wearing some sort of hat. Not a cap, a *hat*.

No one in the place fits the description in my head.

Not many of us are here alone, and while Dylan didn't say he'd be alone, I assumed if he's going to hold a conversation with me on Lyrically while he's here, he wouldn't come with someone else.

There's a guy in a Bears jersey on the other side of the room. He's on his phone. Maybe that guy is Dylan.

I pop in my earbuds and scroll through my Vagabonds playlist. I tap on the *One-Hundred-Foot Cliff* album and hit shuffle. "Traveling" fills my ears.

Me: Are you here?

I stare at the screen for a bit and sip my mocha roast.

When nothing pops up, I go to Instagram and post a picture of my coffee cup: *Sifting through shades of caramel and cocoa. Breathe. #Todayisagoodday.*

I check Lyrically again, but Dylan still hasn't replied to me.

I start to type another message, but then delete it all.

If he changed his mind and didn't have the courtesy to tell me so I didn't have to come all the way out here, he doesn't deserve to hear from me.

When I look up from the screen, it's directly into the deadpan stare of a man a couple of tables away.

I scroll through my pictures. Quickly. It's *him*. The one who was waiting outside of Counter Offer.

He's alone.

His laptop is open.

He's staring right at me.

And he doesn't look away fast enough.

I shift my gaze away, discreetly aim my phone in his direction, and snap a pic. I hope it wasn't obvious. But I don't like the way he's looking at me.

I send the picture to Hayley.

Me: This guy's making me uncomfortable.

I pack up my things and, coffee in hand, head out the door.

I keep looking over my shoulder on my way to the L stop. But he doesn't follow.

Luckily, a train is already hurtling toward the stop. I board under the hypnotic tones of Vagabonds.

Hayley: Answer your phone!
Me: Sorry. It's on silent.

Hayley: Are you ok?

Me: Yeah.

Hayley: Who's the guy?

Me: I don't know.

Me: Just some guy looking at me.

Hayley: Maybe he saw you in a production and
     was trying to place you???

Me: Oh. Maybe.

Me: But is it the same guy I texted you before?

Me: The last time wasn't even in this neighborhood.

Hayley: Do you feel safe?

Me: I do now.

Hayley: Text me when you get to the studio.

Hayley: I'll try to meet you there after your callback.

Me: It's ok.

Me: You don't have to.

Me: I know you're in the middle of stuff.

Hayley: Text Ella.

Hayley: Someone should be there.

Me: Mom has enough to worry about.

Me: I'll be fine.

But as the train rolls away, I see him on the platform, waiting for the next train.

CHAPTER 20

The Weekes twins and I emerge from the dance studio on Webster after a grueling callback audition and step out into another downpour. No sign of the coffee shop lurker. I allow myself to exhale.

"No matter what happens," McKenna says as we huddle under an awning, "friends."

"Friends," I say.

Brendon puts an arm around me, and the other around his sister. McKenna completes the circle by looping her arm through mine, and for a second, we're standing there in a group huddle. "And no matter what happens," he says, "we're gonna rock New York."

I love this. They get me. I get them. And I'm not sure—because I've never really had real friends—but I think this is what friendship is supposed to be like.

A horn beeps—it's their mom—and Brendon turns to me. "You okay, Madelaine?"

"Yeah, I'm fine."

"Girl," Brendon calls over his shoulder. "You're fabulous!"

"So are you!" I tent myself under my backpack, but before I can head toward the L, I see my mom coming up the sidewalk toward me. "Hayley texted me," she calls out, waving from under her red umbrella. "She said you seemed like you could use some company for the trip home."

I'm torn between being annoyed that Hayley went behind my back and being grateful that Mom is here.

Mom's umbrella is obviously a more effective shelter than my backpack, so I duck under it with her. The moment she puts her arm around me, I feel a rush of nostalgia. This is what life was like before the divorce, before the hired car, before Mom started filling out applications and sitting behind a desk for minimum wage: just Mom waiting on the curb, and the two of us—or three of us, if Hayley was tagging along—strolling home.

I didn't know until right now how much I've missed Mom's part in all this.

"Cookies?" she asks.

I try to exercise willpower and say no, but warm cookies with Mom on a rainy day like today . . . *heaven*. I grin.

We're about to head toward the Mrs. Fields on Devon when suddenly, I hear "Maddy."

I turn toward my father's voice. He's looking at me through the lowered window of Giorgio's car.

I glance at Mom, then back at Dad.

"Hop in," he says. "There's no reason for you to walk in the rain."

"I didn't know you were coming today," I stammer.

"I *always* send a car in this weather, and I have a little time this evening so I thought—"

A nest of butterflies stirs in my gut, and my head gets light and fuzzy.

I have to choose between my parents right now, if only temporarily.

"Go ahead," Mom says.

Relieved to be let off the hook, I take a step off the curb, but much to my surprise, Mom's tagging along, in stride with me.

"Your father and I are adults," she says when she catches the question in my expression. "There's no reason we shouldn't be able to be in the same place at the same time."

To my knowledge, they haven't been within fifty yards of each other since my eleventh birthday party, and that was disastrous. My heart starts galloping.

Mom tucks an arm around me, and together, we approach the car.

"Hi, Jesse," Mom says.

Dad's jaw sets. *Tat tat tatatatat.* The rain patters in fat drops against the umbrella.

Mom tries again: "Can you believe this rain?"

He looks at me instead of her, and smiles. "How about some shopping? For New York?"

"We didn't say today, did we? Mom came to get me."

"Well, she's not usually here this time of day, is she?" Dad asks.

"She is right here," Mom says. "Jesse—"

Dad keeps talking, but to me: "Our agreement says I'm able to exercise visitation any day of the week before five. It's ten till." He's still smiling. "Get in."

"For crying out loud, Jesse," Mom says.

"Dad, could we—"

"If we don't go today, we don't go," Dad says. "I have a full week."

"Could we maybe do it after dinner? Mom and I were going to—"

"Can't," Dad says. "I have a dinner meeting at seven, and

I'm heading out of town tomorrow."

Horns blare as cars cut around the limousine.

"So if we're going to go," Dad says, "we've gotta shake a tail feather, Maddy."

It's technically before five; it's his right . . . I look to Mom, who's already shaking her head in defeat. "Can we get cookies later?" I ask. "After dinner?"

She gives me a hug and kisses my cheek—I let her this time—and turns to go the moment Giorgio steps out of the car to open the door for me.

She keeps the umbrella firmly positioned over my head, although she's already stepped away.

Maybe it's just the rain on her face, but I think she's about to spout some waterworks of her own.

"Mom?"

"Just go," she says.

I keep an eye on her as I back into the car. Even as I'm sitting down, I know I should run to her, if only to thank her for coming to get me, to remind her that I love her, but Giorgio's out in the rain holding the door open for me, and Dad has barely two hours, and I *did* tell him I wanted to go shopping.

A sense of ickiness rushes through me, and I feel for a moment as if I'm going to be sick. Mom came all this way. And now she's alone. But what was I supposed to do?

"So, where to first?" Dad asks.

I shrug and open my text thread with Hayley.

Me: Ugh. Parent drama.
Hayley: What now?
Hayley: Did Ella meet you?
Me: Yeah.

Me: You didn't tell her everything, did you?

Hayley: No, but I think she should know.

Me: Ended up with a more immediate problem.

Me: Dad showed up too.

Me: And he flat-out ignored Mom.

Me: Pretended she wasn't even there.

Hayley: He did that? Why?

Me: I've been trying to tell you.

Me: Since you went to college, things have gotten ten times worse.

Me: and Dad and I didn't exactly have plans

Me: and Mom and I didn't exactly have plans

Me: but they both showed up

Me: and I had to choose.

Hayley: They really need to grow up.

Me: #thingsthatwillnevercometopass

Hayley: Sigh

Hayley: Did you tell them about the guy?

Me: Didn't want to worry them.

Hayley: But this dude you keep seeing is seriously creepy.

Me: I know!

Me: But what am I supposed to do about it?

Hayley: What if he's Dylan?

Me: No.

Hayley: You have to stop talking to this Dylan guy.

Me: You don't really think it was him, do you?

Hayley: It would make sense.

I think about it. He's been at or near two places I've found moons—the Factory and Saint Mary's.

"Maddy."

"Huh?" I look up from my phone.

"Are you going to pout all night? If so, I'll just take you home."

"I'm not pouting. It's just that . . ." I consider telling Dad about my suspicion that I'm being followed. But that reminds me about how Mom came to meet me, and about how now she's walking back to the L stop in the rain all alone while I'm riding in a hired car. I don't like the way that makes me feel, and now that I think about it, I'm sort of worried about my mother.

But I know Dad won't get it. He'll just give me some bullshit rationalization about how Mom gets what she deserves, and how she shouldn't have come anyway because he has parental rights until five.

"I don't know why she continues to put you in this position," Dad says.

I could try to explain things from Mom's point of view, but I know it won't do any good. So I just shrug again.

"You need clothes for New York, am I right?" Dad asks.

I nod half-heartedly. I don't really need anything.

"Well, I don't see your mother ponying up to buy them." He shakes his head, as if he's utterly disgusted with my mom.

Defensiveness rises in my chest. "She works hard."

"If that's the case, why isn't she at work right now?"

"I didn't ask." It's not a lie. I didn't.

His phone rings. He raises a finger to tell me we're going to be finishing the conversation in a minute. The second he shifts in his seat and angles away from me, I know it's Miss Karissa calling.

"Hello? Yeah. Yeah, I told you I would." His eyes meet mine for a split second before he turns away again. "I have Maddy with me now. Okay, but it's going to have to wait until I get home. Well . . . if that's what Jennica wants to do, we'll make it happen."

The words stab at my heart. For the past three years, I've been begging him to pay for performing arts high school to no avail. But sure . . . if that's what *Jennica* wants, he'll *make it happen*. I roll my eyes and pop in my earbuds.

Dad stays on the phone the entire ride, which is just fine with me. At this point, the evening could go either way: he could hold a grudge against me because I dared to defend my mother, or he could let it all go.

The car rolls to a stop in front of the mall. I pause the video on my phone.

"Don't worry about that."

I catch Dad's glance in the periphery. He thinks I'm still listening to music and can't hear him. Not that I was raised to eavesdrop, but I've learned that doing so is the only way I'll learn anything about my father's life.

He continues: "My lawyer says that by the time he's done filing continuances . . . Kari, wait. Listen."

I don't know about Miss Karissa, but I'm listening *hard*.

"It'll be moot by then. I promise you. She'll run out of money before that happens."

I put the pieces together. Dad's going to frustrate the legal process. He's going to spend enough money to drain Mom's resources.

Dad'll be fine.

Mom'll be broke.

And nothing will have changed.

And maybe for the first time, I fully realize the power of money in the courtroom. I've always known my father held sway in the audition circuit. But I guess I never thought about how much his wealth could help in a legal battle.

My breath catches. *It's for me*, I want to scream. *I know you won't do it for Mom, but can't you be decent for me?*

He says goodbye to Miss Karissa. Complete with the "Yeah, me too. I do."

Not spoken: *love you.*

Does he think I'm eight? Does he think I haven't realized he's in love with someone else?

Does he honestly think that just because I have earbuds in my ears I can't hear him talking legal strategy?

Dad touches my elbow. "Let's go," he says.

I pull out an earbud and bite back tears. I don't want to go anywhere with him right now. But I don't want to stay in the car, I know that much.

Giorgio opens the door. We get out in the rain and run to the entrance.

"Well, that was refreshing," Dad says with a smile. "Let's have some fun." So it's option B tonight for him.

As for me, I don't know if I can get over this so quickly.

✳✳✳

At the end of the night, just as the car pulls onto West Evergreen, Dad says, "I need the names of the girls you're bringing to New York."

"The Weekes twins."

"Have I met them?"

"I don't know. Maybe. We met during Peter Pan."

"First names?" He digs swipes at his phone, bringing up a notepad app.

"McKenna." I spell it. "And Brendon."

"*Brendon*? Is that a girl's name?"

"No."

"You want to bring a boy to New York?"

"Yeah. Is that a problem?"

Dad's brow knits.

"We're not . . . He was just dating a guy, so . . . It's not like what you're thinking."

"I can trust you in a suite together?"

"Obviously, Dad. He's just a friend. Besides, his sister will be there."

"Just the two of them?"

"Yeah, that's it."

"I bought eight tickets. I assumed Hayley would come, but she declined. And I thought the two of you would bring more friends."

I cringe. Logically, I know this isn't my fault, but I feel like I've let him down. "Sorry."

"Think about it. See if there's anyone else. I don't want the tickets to go to waste."

"Couldn't you just sell the extra tickets?"

"Think about it."

"I will, but—"

"Well, our first stop in the Big Apple is a salon. I thought I'd treat you and your friends to makeovers. Maybe do something about that pink hair of yours. Maybe this Brendon can wait in the lobby."

"Why can't a guy get a makeover?"

He bulldozes right past that. "And I got you a great penthouse suite. Three bedrooms and two pull-out couches. Plenty of room for more friends."

Perhaps he hasn't yet realized that I don't have more friends. I check my phone. It's seven fifteen.

"You're going to be late," I say. "Your dinner meeting."

"Don't worry about it."

I wonder if he even had a meeting at all.

Maybe he just had to rush home to Miss Karissa, Jennica, and the boys. Or maybe he needed an excuse to tank Mom's plans again.

"Giorgio's going to help you with your bags, and I'll see you Thursday night." And now, he's practically shoving me out the door.

Dad bought me a lot of stuff. Even stuff I only sort of liked. So, even if I wanted to refuse Giorgio's help, I wouldn't be able to do it. I can't carry all the bags, plus all my school stuff and rehearsal stuff, up to our apartment in one trip, and it's raining.

Sheepishly, I follow my dad's driver, laden with today's haul. God, I feel like a Sophia.

Nana Adie meets me at the door. "Well, well. I could've guessed you'd arrive with a load." And under her breath: "What that man does is shameless."

From here, I see Mom's lounging in the living room. She looks so tired.

Once Giorgio manages to place all my bags inside our tiny foyer, filling almost the whole space, I send him off with a thank-you and go to Mom.

I press a little kiss to her cool cheek. "I'm sorry about the cookies," I say.

Mom smiles. "There will be other times."

"Will there?" Nana Adie crosses her arms over her chest.

Her tone catches me off guard. "Nana—"

"Nice loophole, don't you think? As long as he gets you before five, he can keep you till all hours? It's manipulation. Any decent man would see that before five should imply keeping you only *until* five, but no. Not your father. He writes between the lines, but only when it'll suit him fine. He wants his freedom, doesn't he? He wants things the way he wants them, doesn't he? And if he doesn't want you on a day he's supposed to have you, then by God we'd better figure out how to make things work . . ."

She doesn't usually get so worked up, even when Dad pisses her off. What's the matter with her lately? "I don't know why you're mad at *me*, Nana."

"Will you once, Madelaine, make a priority out of your mother?"

It's like a bomb explodes in my head. Shouldn't it be the other way around? Shouldn't *they* be making a priority of *me*? I don't know what else I have to do to prove that I love them both. That I'm loyal to Dad, but that doesn't mean I'm any less on Mom's side.

"I can't do anything right," I say. "Do you know how hard it is to make everyone happy all the time? It's impossible. But I guess no one cares about that. No one cares about what it's like to be in the middle."

"I told her to go with Jesse," Mom interjects.

"There are other things you should tell her, too," Nana says.

I whip my head around to look at my mom. "Like what?"

"Don't worry about it, Lainey. We'll discuss it after New York." She peels herself up from the sofa and kisses the top of my head. "Night, baby."

"Night?" I follow her with my eyes as she walks down the hallway. "It's just after seven!"

"Yeah. Well, walking in the rain can tire a girl out."

"Mom—"

"Love you, Lainey."

"I love you, too."

What is she not telling me?

CHAPTER 21

I'm putting my new clothes away. My small closet is already jam-packed with stuff I rarely wear because . . . well, Saint Mary's mandates a uniform, and until recently, I haven't had much occasion to meet up with friends outside of school, auditions, and rehearsals. So I don't know where I'm going to put it all.

If only Dad were as generous with tuition for the performance academy as he is with clothes.

Wait.

I pull every new item out of my closet and fish the receipts out of the trash. When I add it all up, I'm numb. Slowly, I lower myself to my bed.

Three grand and change. Dad spent three grand on clothes I didn't really need. That's one month's tuition.

I feel awful, and not just because I chose Dad over Mom tonight, as Nana not-so-subtly indicated. But because all of this is very extravagant and unnecessary.

Yes, it was fun, and Dad needed to offer up some fun after the things he said about my mother.

But I'd rather have the education, thank you very much.

I fold all the clothes and pack them back into the shopping

bags. I haul the bags out to the living room, where Nana is watching TV.

"What's all this?"

"I want you to be proud of me," I say. "And not just for what I do onstage. I want you think I'm a good person."

Nana pauses her Netflix. "I do, Madelaine."

"The only reason I did this tonight was because I didn't know how not to do it."

Nana nods. "I understand."

"And I'd cancel New York if I hadn't already invited two new friends. But all of this . . ." I point to the clothes. "I don't ask for this. I don't expect it. My dad—"

"It's the only way he can show you he loves you," Nana infers.

"I guess so. I mean, I don't want to think that's true, but . . . maybe it is. I mean, I think about all the nights you and Mom and I hang out and watch shows. I think about all the times we cook together, and even do chores together. And we *laugh*. Even Ted . . . maybe he was a disaster, but he shared in it too, while Dad . . ." I swallow hard. "It's like he's never real. Like he's always performing. Showing me only what he wants me to see."

"Well, that's the profession."

"But Dad's a manager. Mom is a performer," I say. "She's real. Why can't he be?"

"I like the way you said that," Nana says. "Your mom *is* a performer."

"She is." I sit down next to my grandmother and settle against her. "I've never seen her live on stage, but I know I will someday."

"I hope so."

Things are quiet between us for a minute or two. I breathe

in the scent of her: tonight it's chocolate and raspberries.

Nana breaks the silence. "So what's with packing up all your new things?"

"I want Mom to return them while I'm in New York. Dad paid cash for a lot of it and gave me receipts in case something didn't end up fitting right or whatever. She should be able to get cash back. I want her to put the money toward tuition for next year."

Nana smiles. "That's sweet, Lainey. But you don't have to do that. The courts are going to take care of it. You'll see."

"I don't think that's going to happen," I say. "My dad isn't going to give another dime to my mother, no matter the reason why." I relay what I overheard when Dad thought I wasn't paying attention.

Nana's jaw sets. "He's going to starve her out. The same way he got her to agree to everything the first time around."

Which means I really am going to have to do what Mom suggests.

I'm going to have to fire my father to make a priority out of my future.

✳✳✳

Back in my room, I take a deep breath. This Mini Panic Episode could easily morph to a Major Panic Episode.

But I don't have a choice. I have to ride through it.

I have a message from Dylan. I don't feel like dealing with him right now, but I also don't feel like being alone with my thoughts.

Dylan: Hey, everything ok?

Me: Not remotely. Thanks for blowing me off
    this afternoon.
Dylan: I was there.
Dylan: Had some connection issues.
Dylan: I saw you though.
Dylan: You took off shortly after you got your coffee.
Me: Oh.
Dylan: Thought you changed your mind.
Me: I thought you did.
Dylan: Just working up the nerve to talk to you.

This isn't what I expected. It's such a . . . vulnerable thing
to say.

Dylan: Didn't want to approach you if I couldn't
    message first.
Dylan: Guess I hesitated too long.
Dylan: Why'd you leave so soon though?
Me: There's this guy
Me: I see him all over town lately.
Me: And he was there.
Me: Just sort of creeped me out.
Dylan: Ick. Totally valid.
Dylan: Sorry we didn't get to talk.
Me: It's not the worst thing that's happened
    to me today.
Dylan: :/ Would it help to talk about it?

I hesitate. I'm still annoyed, but . . .

Me: Maybe.

CHAPTER 22
Thursday, May 4

I can't sleep. Again. I text Hayley.

> Me: You up?
> Hayley: BFFLS!
> Me: Do you know what's going on with Dad
> and my mom?
> Hayley: You told me.
> Me: I mean about what Dad plans to do about the
> court case?
> Hayley: No.
> Hayley: But I really think we just shouldn't talk about it
> anymore.
> Hayley: Because I don't want to fight with u.
> Hayley: I don't agree with some of Ella's decisions
> Hayley: and she's your mom, so you defend her
> to the death.

I tell her what I heard Dad say anyway.

> Hayley: Can I play devil's advocate?
> Me: Of course.
> Me: Help me understand.
> Me: PLEASE.

Hayley: You let him spend extravagantly.

Hayley: These trips, the shopping

Hayley: I don't do that sort of thing.

Hayley: If you keep taking, you're perpetuating the cycle.

Hayley: Have you ever thought about simply asking him NOT to spend?

Hayley: Asking him to simply help Ella pay for your school?

Me: Yes, actually!

Me: He says he can't bail her out of this.

Me: It's like he doesn't see the connection.

Me: Like he wants me to blame her

Me: But I see how hard she's trying.

Me: I feel like nothing she does gets her remotely close to adequate.

Hayley: But like it or not, Dad has the legal right to file continuances.

Hayley: Technically, he's not wrong.

Me: It's not fair, though.

Hayley: Who said life was fair?

I fall asleep with my phone in my hand.

When I awaken, everything is fuzzy, like I'm on the other side of a static-y television. I blink a few times, and details start to come into focus.

It's nearly nine.

I bolt upright. I'm late for school.

And I've missed about thirty messages from "Raspberry Beret," all describing the nerves of waiting for the final cast list to post.

Music is playing in the kitchen. But it's not Nana's usual Madonna throwback. It's classical. Tchaikovsky's "Waltz of the Flowers."

I peek out into the hallway.

I see my mother's feet under the kitchen table. She's wearing her worn, pale pink pointe shoes, and while her feet may not be moving across the floor, she's dancing. I see them flexing and pointing in an entrechat.

The furniture in the living room beyond has been pushed to the edges of the room. Unless I slept through a tornado, Mom and Nana have moved the furniture to create a dance floor. I meander closer. "Mom?'

"Good morning, Lainey." She and Nana Adie are drinking coffee. Nana is already pouring me a cup of my own.

"My alarm didn't go off," I say.

"It did," Mom says. "You slept through it."

"Why didn't you wake me?" I ask. "Sister Mary Angela's going to ream me."

"Not if you don't go," Mom says.

"Don't I have to go?"

"And make it that much easier for your father to decide to pick you up directly from school, and take you straight to the airport?" Mom shakes her head. "We thought we'd try this instead."

"That's why I'm staying home?"

"I thought it would be nice to spend the day together," Mom says.

"All right, what's going on?"

"I already told you," Mom says. "Two can play at his game."

"Ohhhhkay."

"Raspberry Beret" chimes again. I check the messages.

Brendon: We're in!
Brendon: We're all on the cast list!
Brendon: NYC, here comes the cast of ANNIE!
Me: Hold on.
Me: Have to see this for myself!
Brendon: . . .

I tap my email icon and see the message from the casting director. I can't move for a good ten seconds.

I muster the courage and open the email. I scroll through the cordialities and finally find the cast list.

Pepper, Pepper, Pepper. . . . Please let me be Pepper!

Pepper: McKenna Weekes.

As happy as I am for McKenna, my heart sinks. My cheeks are hot, and the world starts to blacken at the edges until I feel like I'm looking at the cast list through a pair of binoculars.

It's not like Pepper's a big part. It wasn't a goal too high to aim for. And I didn't reach it.

"Lainey?" Mom asks.

"Wait." I scroll to the end until I see the list of ensemble cast. Instantly, I pick out Brendon's name, but I don't see mine.

I shove away jealous thoughts—Brendon and McKenna have been on the audition circuit half as long as me, and they're in and I'm not—and I'm going to have to spend the weekend with them in New York. I'm going to have to pull myself together and be happy for them.

But Brendon said I was in.

I check the ensemble cast list again. There's a Madeline Jameson, which is sort of close to Madelaine Joseph. Maybe Brendon just misread the name.

It's okay if I didn't make it. There will be other auditions, other opportunities.

But I wanted this opportunity.

With everything going on in my family life, I need a character to slip into. I need the escape. And now . . .

There's no escape on the horizon.

I get it. I'm a little too tall to be a Pepper. Not quite old enough to play one of the leads. I'm in that strange in-between age. But to not make even ensemble?

This must be how Mom felt on those few auditions when she attempted a comeback: not quite right for any particular role. I look at the ballet shoes on her feet. Someday, I'll be dancing only in my apartment, too.

I swallow my disappointment and go back to "Raspberry Beret."

Me: Congrats, guys.
Me: But I wasn't cast.
Brendon: Ummm, yes you were!
McKenna: . . .

I look again, reading more slowly this time. Then I see it.
July: Madelaine Joseph.

I let out a little yelp. I'm in. My name will be on a program. Not where I wanted it, but it'll be there. I'll have another production to put on my résumé. One step closer to NYU. One step closer to my dream.

I swipe back to "Raspberry Beret" to see that McKenna sent a screenshot of my name circled. I type a quick OMG YES! and look up at Mom and Nana. "I'm in! I have lines! I have a *singing solo*!"

Nana kills the music. "Oh, Lainey!"

"Now there are *two* reasons to stay home from school!" Mom says. "Let's celebrate!"

"Wait. You already knew!"

Mom's eyes are sparkling. "You went shopping with your dad. I had a drink with the casting director. She said she'd call if she had any news." Mom grins and gets to her feet. "She called half an hour ago."

I catapult into her arms.

"Let's go to that little pastry shop you used to like." She leads me in a spin with all the grace and control I've seen on the old footage of her performances.

I watch her step across the floor.

I hear the notes of my song, pairing with every footfall.

CHAPTER 23

Dad: What do you mean you're not at school?

Me: I stayed home today.

Dad: Why?

Me: I needed the sleep.

Me: Couldn't sleep last night

Me: I was so nervous about the callback.

Dad: I guess I can understand that.

Dad: And congrats again on the role. I knew you'd nailed it.

Dad: But I'm not paying private school tuition so you can ditch.

Dad: That's twice this week.

Me: Wait. How do you know I wasn't at school the other day?

Dad: Same way I know your mother's no longer working.

Dad: I pay attention.

Dad: I knew she wasn't supposed to be off work last night.

Dad: I made some calls.

Dad: Found out she quit.

A sickening feeling spins in my gut. I'm either going to have to defend my mother to my father, or I'm going to have to try to ignore his little jabs.

Dad: Do you see what I mean, Maddy?
Dad: If your mother would commit to a job,
    maybe you'd be going to the academy.

I feel the panic starting to squeeze at my heart. But I know nothing I can say will make any difference.

Dad: I was going to pick you up from school on
    the way to O'Hare.
Dad: Now I have to make other arrangements.
Me: I wouldn't have had my bags with me anyway.
Dad: I would have sent Giorgio to pick them up.
Me: Here's an idea:
Me: Brendon, McKenna, and I will meet you at
    the airport.
Me: Done.
Me: No more arrangements to be made.
Dad: I don't want my daughter lugging suitcases
    on the L.
Dad: I'll send Giorgio.
Me: Sure
Me: whatever you want

I know he won't register my sarcasm, but it still feels good to put it out there.

Two hours later, Brendon, McKenna, and I are in the back of Dad's limousine, singing show tunes.

"Angelica!" McKenna belts.

"Eliza!" I sing.

"And Peggy," Brendon croons.

I can only imagine what Giorgio must think of us. But he unloads our baggage at the curb, and we go inside to check it and get our boarding passes.

One foot past security, I stop in my tracks.

The Sophias are there, waving enthusiastically at me.

"What the hell is this?" Brendon murmurs. "It's like the cast of Toddlers in Tiaras grew up."

"Can you believe it?" Sophia 1 says, running up to me.

"Your dad called us," Sophia 2 says, right behind her.

No, Dad. You didn't.

"We've been trying to message you, especially when you didn't show up at school today," Sophia 1 says.

"Yeah, why weren't you there?" asks Sophia 2.

"I needed a break." Unspoken: *from people like you.* "Why are you here?"

"Your dad invited us," Sophia 2 says. "He said he talked to you."

"Come on, we're good friends, right?" adds Sophia 1. "It's time to put all that other bullshit behind us."

Brendon clears his throat. "Bullshit?"

"It's nothing," I say. "Forget it."

"Oh no you don't," Brendon says. "Do tell."

I look from the Weekes twins to the Sophias. I could smooth it over. I could grit my teeth and pretend everything's okay, so that we can have a nice weekend, free of awkwardness.

But that would be a lie. I'm so sick of secrets and lies and things that aren't what they seem to be. I take a deep breath. "I caught them talking about me on a group text."

McKenna gasps—nice and dramatic—and loops an arm through mine.

"They don't think I'm talented," I continue, looking from one shocked Sophia to the other. "They think I'm bratty, and they think my dad's gotten me every role I've ever landed."

"Outrageous," Brendon says.

"Her dad didn't set foot in the casting hall for *Annie*," McKenna says. "And she freaking landed it!"

"*Annie?*" Sophia 1 says. "Like, the lead?"

"Here's the thing," McKenna says. "There's nothing more prestigious about a lead than a supporting role. The prestige is in the art form itself. You're impressed only if she lands the mothership, but we love her even if she's in the orchestra pit."

"Look, if we're going to have a good time this weekend?" Sophia 1 says, "we should start off on the right foot? So maybe we should start over?"

My heart is hammering, and I'm half-thrilled and half-horrified that I've been so blunt. "I don't know why my dad invited you," I say. "I didn't ask him to do that. And I'm not going to pretend we're friends. But since you're here, I agree: we should make the best of it."

"Great!" Sophia 2 says brightly. "We're going to have so much fun."

"Or we'll go our way," Brendon says, "and you go yours."

"Perfect," I say.

"So rude," Sophia 1 mutters as the two of them saunter off toward the gate. "We come all this way, and he has the nerve—"

"Oh my God," Brendon says. "Is that what you deal with every day at school?"

"Yes. Every day."

"You so need to get out of that place."

I get a text from my dad.

Dad: Karissa and I are already in the
    first-class lounge.
Dad: Come on up.

My jaw drops. "He brought Miss Karissa."

"Who's Miss Karissa?"

"His girlfriend. The one he's been with for years. And for some reason, he usually keeps us far away from each other. So this is a big deal. I have to tell my sister." I'm already texting Hayley.

"Interesting," McKenna says. "Let's go meet her."

A sense of calm washes over me. None of it matters—not the Sophias, not Miss Karissa. I'm heading to New York with my two new best friends—my colleagues.

And someday soon, we're going to take a bite of that apple ourselves.

CHAPTER 24

You know Miss Karissa.

Younger than my mom, and since Mom's too young for Dad, Miss Karissa is *definitely* too young.

Very thin. Long dark hair with a part down the middle. Cheekbones so sculpted you're looking for the plastic surgeon behind the curtain.

If I were looking at her profile picture, I might read something like this on her bio.

Occupation: *gold digger.*

Location: *nearest Tiffany's.*

Philosophy: *smiling gives you wrinkles.*

"She's gorgeous," Brendon whispers as we enter the VIP lounge.

I shrug. "She is."

"Do you think she's sucking on a Lemonhead?" McKenna asks. "Or do you think her lips are just naturally puckered?"

Dad and Miss Karissa are in the depths of a conversation that looks rather pinched. Maybe that's why she looks like she just ate something sour.

When we approach them, Dad jumps up. "There you are, honey. And the infamous Weekes twins!"

"Dad, this is Brendon and McKenna. We were all cast in *Annie* together."

"Ah, excellent," Dad says. "Congratulations all around. And July!" He puts up a hand for a high five. "You'll kill it, kid."

I slap his hand—can't leave him hanging—although it feels childish.

"July's a little lost," Dad says. "Sad. But she knows there's a better tomorrow out there. It's the perfect role for you. You can play melodrama to the hilt, you know."

"She's fabulous," Brendon agrees.

"Got that right." Now Dad offers the high five to Brendon.

"Dad," I mutter. I know my dad thinks I'm awesome. He's supposed to think so. And I know he can talk roles to death, but this is hardly the place. My cheeks grow hot with embarrassment.

But Brendon slaps him five anyway and says, "Thanks for having us."

"Of course, glad you're here. Where are Sophia and Sophia?" Dad asks.

"I don't know," I say stiffly. "I'm sure they'll be here soon."

Miss Karissa stands up next to Dad. "Good to see you all," she says. She has a surprisingly deep, serious voice, like she's about to negotiate a merger with us or something. I don't know what she does for a living, but I assume it's not that.

She shakes hands with the Weekes twins and introduces herself, but just as she's turning to me Dad says, "Karissa and I are in the middle of something." He pulls his wallet from his pocket and hands me a few hundred-dollar bills. "Go grab some dinner, and we'll meet you at boarding."

Brendon's jaw drops. Once Dad is out of earshot he says, "Girl. That was cold."

"Sorry," I say to my friends. "This is just the sort of thing he does."

"There are worse things," McKenna says. "Might as well work it, right?"

"Yeah, I just wish he were more . . . genuine. I wish he actually wanted to spend time with me." I almost can't believe I'm speaking the words aloud. Admitting that he's been placating me with gifts, while withholding everything that matters ever since he and Mom split, seems rather pathetic.

"Well, our old man doesn't want to spend time with us or give us money," Brendon says. "You can't control what they do. Just make the best of it."

I nod. "Not a bad life philosophy."

"And speaking of life philosophies . . . cheese fries, anyone?"

CHAPTER 25

We get to Manhattan really late, and by the time we've settled into the suite at the Marriott, we're all exhausted.

I've barely spoken to the Sophias, and I think that's just fine with them. They accomplished their goal. They're here, and my father paid their way.

The suite is large enough that the Sophias can hang in one room, and Brendon, McKenna, and I can occupy the rest, so that's what's going to happen. Brendon's chosen a bedroom, the Sophias have chosen another, and McKenna and I will share the third.

My father sends up dinner for us to share, but even for that we don't attempt to mesh. The Sophias make plates for themselves and eat in their room, while we eat in the living room in front of the floor-to-ceiling windows overlooking Times Square.

Despite the fact that this weekend is turning out much differently than I expected, it's absolutely perfect.

The uninvited girls from Saint Mary's lean out of their lair. "We're heading out in pursuit of alcohol. Want any?"

"No."

"No."

"No thanks," I say.

"Suit yourself," Sophia 1 says.

"Be careful," McKenna says. But she rolls her eyes when she says it, and once the door is closed she punctuates with, "Or don't."

"I can't believe your dad did this to you," Brendon says. "I mean, it's great that he's trying to give you these experiences, but after the way those girls treated you . . ."

"Well, in his defense," I say, "he doesn't know about it."

"How could you not tell him?" McKenna demands.

I shrug. "We just don't talk about that stuff."

"Why not?"

"You don't talk to your dad," I say. "You already told me he's not super involved in your life."

"Right," McKenna says. "But your dad is involved in your life. He's your manager. You should be able to be honest with him."

"We just don't have that kind of relationship. I mean, we do talk. We have fun. But none of it's all that deep, you know? I think if Dad's really careful," I say, "we can go this entire weekend without seeing him."

The Sophias return to the suite with a snagged bottle.

"Ah," Brendon says. "Fruitful mission."

"Got it off a room service tray in the hallway," Sophia 1 says. "It's warm, but we're gonna get ice. Last chance. Want any?"

"We're good," I say.

"Okay, then," Sophia 2 says. "More for us." They disappear into their bedroom.

"We have an early day," McKenna says. "I'm gonna hit the hay."

"We won't be up too much later, either," Brendon says.

But once McKenna's gone, I stare out at Times Square at the Jumbotron flashing pictures and ads, and it feels so amazing to be here again. "I don't want this night to end."

"It's a pretty unbelievable place," Brendon says.

I imagine my picture flashing up on that large screen. *Madelaine Joseph IS . . . Thoroughly Modern Millie!*

"Do you think it'll happen for us one day?" I ask. "Do you think someday, some group of wannabes is going to be sitting here, in this room, looking out at the square and saying: I can't believe I'm going to meet Brendon Weekes tomorrow!"

"I can't believe Madelaine Joseph just shook my hand!"

We laugh.

"I just don't see any other way to do life," I say. "I love performing. I love being onstage, and—" I think of my mom. "I don't know what I'd do if I couldn't be onstage anymore."

"Then we have to make sure you're always there."

He's sitting beside me now, and together we gaze out at the glowing lights. "I love this city," I continue. "And it's not that I don't like Chicago, because I do. But this place . . . it feels like home."

He puts an arm around me.

I tense at first, but after a moment I relax against him. He's done this before, but always when McKenna was with us and in on the group hug, so it felt less . . . intimate.

"I think you truly belong here," he says.

"I just hope this city eventually learns to love me as much as I love her."

"She will. McKenna adores you, you know, but when she saw she was reading for the same parts you read for . . . she about lost her cool. Girl, you're legendary."

"Shut up."

"We saw you in *Mary Poppins* when we were kids, and McKenna was all . . . I want to be that girl."

I laugh.

"I'm serious. You're the reason we're here now. The reason we audition, the reason we go to the academy."

I look up at him. He looks down at me.

"You know what?" I say. "I want to play you a song."

He smiles. "What a coincidence. I want to listen to a song."

I tap on the Lyrically icon and find my song. My notes fill the room, and if I block out the rest of the world, it seems even the lights on the square below are flashing in time with the riff of my guitar.

Just you and the stage. Mom's voice is in my head. As always. And I sing, staring out at the city I love.

By the time I finish the song, Brendon has a hand over his heart. "You. Are. Talented." With his other hand, he touches my knee briefly, in a kind of pat-slash-squeeze, and while it surprises me, it doesn't bother me. "This is a whole other side of you."

"I know. It's the me side of me. It's still a performance, but it's different from, say, pretending I'm July. It's more like performing the truest, deepest version of myself."

Brendon nods. "That takes a lot of work. And guts. And—"

"Oh, sorry to interrupt." The Sophias rush through the room with the ice bucket. They snicker as they bolt out of the room.

I realize how close Brendon and I are sitting and lean back a bit. "I think they just got the wrong idea," I say.

"Wouldn't be the first time that happened to me."

We laugh, and suddenly I think of Mom, of how she'd love to be here. If she were here, she'd be in this suite with us, enjoying the view, watching movies, talking, telling stories about her days on stage until we couldn't keep our eyes open any more.

I miss her.

"None of this is happening the way it was supposed to happen," I tell Brendon. "My sister, Hayley, stopped coming along on these trips, and it's never the same without her. And since then, I've come with people I don't really fit in with because I don't really fit in with *anyone* at my school."

"Thus, you should come to our school."

"Trying! But I feel like we're really friends—you, me, and McKenna."

"We are."

"And when I saw the Sophias at O'Hare, I felt like they were ruining it all. But right now, I feel like nothing could ruin this view, this night, this whole experience."

My phone chimes with a text from Dad.

Dad: Meeting. Hallway.
Dad: Now.
Me: What? Why?
Dad: Get out here.
Dad: NOW.

"What's up?" Brendon asks.

The Sophias enter the room, giggling. "Sorry, *Maddy*. Daddy wants to talk to you."

CHAPTER 26

I meet Dad in the hallway. He's pacing. Running his hands through his hair. "You told me he was gay."

"What?"

"I paid for this guy to come along this trip, and now, I find out he's *not* gay, but kissing my daughter in a suite I paid for?"

"Dad, no."

"Go get your things. I'm putting you in your own room."

"No!"

"Sophia just told me. She saw the two of you—"

"You're going to believe the Sophias? Over me? You're not even going to ask me what happened?"

"I used to be a teenager, all right? You can't pull that over on me. I know what's going to happen."

"*Listen to me.*"

"You said he was gay."

"I said he was dating a guy. Which he was."

"So why is he kissing you?"

"He's not! He *won't.*" MPE coming on. Deep breath. "Dad, I don't even date."

He shakes his head. "I'm not stupid."

"I don't. I don't want the hassle of it. I want to stay focused on my career. Not to mention, there's enough drama in my life without it, thanks to the fact that you and my mother can't seem to be decent to each other even for my sake!"

"We'll talk about your mother some other time. Go get your things."

"*No.*"

"What's with this attitude lately?"

"Excuse me?"

"With your hair, and your—"

"What about my hair?"

"Do you know what I had to pony up to get you back in the good graces of the dear Sister Mary Angela?"

"Actually, I do. Hayley told me."

"And still, here you are. Pink hair. You're changing it tomorrow."

"No."

"Yes."

"No!"

"Why do you think I made appointments at the spa?"

"I thought you made appointments for *us*. For my friends and me. To have fun."

"You need to change the hair."

This is unbelievable. Anger, pure anger without any nerves attached, is bubbling up inside me. "Do you know what last month was, Dad? Why I dyed my hair pink in the first place? It was the anniversary of my mother's survival. And I know you don't care about that, but it means something to me."

"As your manager, I'm telling you, the pink—"

"The pink doesn't affect my work. I wear a wig to auditions. And I just landed a pretty decent part, so—"

"You're changing it tomorrow. For now, get your things.

You're getting your own room."

"There's no reason for me to get my own room. I haven't done anything wrong." My heartbeat is banging in my ears, and tears burn my eyes. I force an inhale. "Sophia made assumptions. There's nothing going on between Brendon and me, I swear."

And even if there was—the thought takes me by surprise, a mental image of Brendon and me together—should Dad really be losing his shit over a *kiss*?

There've got to be better ways for a parent to handle this. Mom's talked to me about protection, about consent, even though I've rolled my eyes and insisted I'm not interested in anything related to dating. She would never in a million years react this way if she thought I was getting close to someone.

Dad sucks in his breath. "One more word about that guy in there"—he points at the closed door—"and the room situation changes. Got it?"

"Yes!"

I watch my father storm down the hallway to the elevator.

I sink to the floor and pull my phone out of my pocket. I text my sister.

> Me: Dad just reamed me for something I didn't even do.
> Me: I so wish you were here right now.
> Me: You have to see how he's acting.
> Me: It's like he's not even the same guy.

I hear a whistle behind me. I turn to see Brendon standing in the doorway.

I wipe a tear from my cheek. "How much did you hear?"

"Enough."

"God, I'm so embarrassed."

"I changed my mind." Brendon points in the direction Dad just went. "You can fire that guy. No brainer."

CHAPTER 27
Sunday, May 7

Our plane is delayed at least half an hour. I'm sitting with Brendon and McKenna in the first-class lounge, fiddling absentmindedly with my hair. It's a pretty auburn now.

A little girl wearing a tiara sits across from us, staring at me like I'm about to be her first victim in a horror movie.

I try to smile at her—anything to get her to stop looking at me—but she only sticks her tongue out.

"Nice," Brendon says. "Real classy."

"Shh." McKenna elbows him. "She's a little kid."

"A bratty one," he says.

McKenna rolls her eyes. "Why are you letting her get to you?"

"I'm *telling* that you called me a brat." The girl sticks her lower lip out.

"Tell you what, honey." Brendon leans into the aisle between us. "Like it or not, this world is full of labels. If you act like a brat, people are gonna call you a brat. You know . . . see those two girls over there?"

He points in the direction of where the Sophias are sitting.

"They're more your people. Go bug them."

I'm biting back a laugh when my phone buzzes. It's Nana

Adie calling. "I gotta take this," I say.

"You're gonna leave us alone with this diva?" Brendon asks.

"I'm *telling*!" The child crosses her arms over her chest and stomps on a mission toward the opposite end of the lounge.

"Bravo, bravo," Brendon says. "Excellent exit!"

I step away. "Hi, Nana."

"How's your trip?"

"The shows were great, and the meet and greet . . . ahhhhmazing."

"You had a good time with your dad?"

I spy him and Miss Karissa on the other side of the lounge. He's doing a fabulous job pretending my friends and I don't exist, and that's just fine with me. "Not exactly."

"No?"

"I'll explain when I'm home," I promise. "And honestly, I cannot *wait* to get home. I love New York, but—"

"Honey, can I talk to your dad for a minute?"

I look at him across the lounge. For a split second, he meets my stare, and I see the same look of disgust I've seen all weekend whenever he's looked at me.

I don't get it. He was way out of line this weekend. Beyond strict: controlling. Like he wrote a script, I didn't follow it, and even though the audience loved the ad-lib, he considers the show a failure. I should be looking at him the way he's looking at me.

"Why do you need to talk to Dad?"

"I just . . . I need to."

I'm already making my way toward him, despite his obvious attempt at keeping Miss Karissa far away from me. "Is everything okay?"

"Just a few hiccups. I'll explain when you're home."

I hand my phone to Dad. "It's Nana."

Dad takes the phone. "Adie, hello."

I watch as Dad frowns, turns his back on me, and edges a few feet away from the table.

"I'm not sure that's a good idea, Adie. I . . . well, yes. But small doses to start would be better, and to be honest, she didn't mesh all that well with . . . oh. That *is* a dilemma. I just think if there's any other way . . . what's that? Uh-huh, uh-huh. Great. Yes, we'll do that." Dad hangs up and hands over my phone. "All settled."

In a flash, realization hits me: Nana called to ask my dad to keep me overnight at his place. And he refused. "You don't want me at your house?"

"I have an early meeting tomorrow, and you have school."

But he didn't say any of that to Nana. He just doesn't want me in his house!

"I can take a train, and you know it. You don't want me there. Why not?"

"Maddy. Don't make a scene."

"I'm not making a scene. I'm just talking." I changed my hair. I tolerated the Sophias. What more can I do to placate him?

"Now's not the place."

"I just want to know. Is it Karissa?" I cross my arms over my chest. "Does she not like me much?"

"Cut the sarcasm. And to be honest, I don't think you've been at your best this weekend, and Karissa has young children to think about."

"Doesn't she have her own place then? If she's worried about my rottenness rubbing off on *Jennica and the boys*, maybe they could stay at their own place tonight."

"Maddy, it's settled."

"Why does Nana want you to keep me anyway?"

"You're reading a lot into half a conversation."

"I know what I heard."

"We'll discuss this some other time. I suggest you get back to your friends and let me get back to Karissa."

✳✳✳

Mrs. Weekes meets us at baggage claim. The Weekes twins say goodbye to me, my father, and even the Sophias, who ride with us and Miss Karissa in Dad's car.

When we drop them both at Sophia 1's place, I do what I'm supposed to do. I hug them goodbye and thank them for coming.

"Coffee's on me tomorrow during zero hour," Sophia 2 says, as if they didn't orchestrate an enormous explosion this weekend by lying about what happened between Brendon and me. "Mocha roast with peppermint?"

"Two pumps," I say with a forced smile.

She probably won't bring the coffee. But if she does, I won't take it.

After they exit the car, Dad says, "Maddy, we should talk."

God, he's going to do this in front of Miss Karissa, who's suddenly putting her novel aside.

"I was hoping this weekend would have gone better," he says.

Me, too. But I don't say a word.

"I was hoping," he continues, "that you and Karissa could have some time together, which now, I see, was impossible with your friends. Maybe my inviting Sophia and Sophia without checking with you first was a mistake."

"Yes."

"I thought you were close."

"Not anymore. They use me, Dad," I say. "They're not my friends. They use me to go to concerts and to meet famous people."

"Okay, I see that," Dad says. "Karissa helped me see that."

I glance at my father's girlfriend, surprised. "Thank you."

She nods, then looks expectantly at Dad. "Jesse, you had something else to say to her."

Dad sighs. "I've realized you're growing up without my knowing much about what's happening in your life. Sure, I know about what roles you're auditioning for, what parts you hope to land someday, and your instructors tell me when you land a switch jump, or when you manage to hit a note you can't usually hit in your range, but—"

"Really? They tell you that stuff?"

"Of course they do. But they can't tell me what's going on in your head, in your heart. And when Sophia told me that you and this boy were kissing . . . I lost it. I wasn't on my best behavior, was I? It just blindsided me, to think you'd be at that stage in your life, and I wouldn't know anything about it—"

"There's nothing to tell. We're *friends*. And—"

"Okay, you're friends with *this* guy. But what about the next guy? You're growing up so fast, and there's so much I don't know about what's going on with you."

I clench my fists in my lap to keep them from shaking. "I told you I don't date, and you chose not to believe me. You believed a random girl you met a couple of times—over me."

"That was a mistake. I recognize that now. But you see where I'm coming from, don't you? I wouldn't have even invited those girls if I'd known you weren't friends anymore. But you never mentioned it . . ."

I look out the window so I don't have to meet his eyes. This is as close to an apology as I'm going to get, and I can sense how much it's costing him. I can feel the discomfort in his voice. My instinct is to tell him I forgive him and release the tension.

But I fight that instinct. I don't want to keep overlooking things he's done and the way he's treated me just because he might pay for something. That's how he always gets things his way, and I'm sick of it.

I fiddle with my newly auburn hair. "So I'm supposed to tell you everything that's happening in my life, even though you don't tell me anything about yours?"

Dad takes Karissa's hand. "Karissa actually made the same point when I was talking to her about this. And I—I want to be more open with you, I want our communication to be a two-way street. So—we have something to tell you."

I look over at them. "What?"

"Well . . ." Dad brings their joined hands to his lips and kisses her knuckles. They share a look.

"You're getting married," I guess.

"We got married already. It was just the two of us. A small ceremony."

". . . Oh." Maybe I shouldn't be surprised, given the covert nature of their relationship, but I can't help it. I can't believe Dad wouldn't involve us in something as official as a wedding.

But I look at my new stepmother and say, "Congratulations."

So that makes three words I've said to her this entire trip, and not because I haven't wanted to talk to her, but because Dad has kept us so isolated from each other.

She sort of smiles and says, "Thanks."

"Now that we're family," I say, "maybe we can get to know each other."

"I'd like that," she says.

"I'd appreciate it if you didn't say anything to your sister just yet," Dad says. "I'd like to tell her in person."

I nod, but I don't know if I can keep a secret of this magnitude from my BFFBS.

Dad puts up a palm for a high five, so I slap his hand. "Dinner next weekend."

"At your place?"

"You'll have rehearsal."

"I can come after."

"And commute to the city for Saturday's call? I don't want to put you through that. Besides, you'll need to get some good sleep."

I eye him. "Are you sure that's the reason? I haven't been to your house in years. You and Karissa are married now. I assume she's living there—has been for a while, am I right?—so there are no more secrets. Why can't I be at your house?"

Karissa folds her arms over her chest and looks away.

At first, I think she's pissed at me for asking, but I catch something in her expression—a sadness, maybe, crossed with irritation—that tells me she's just as frustrated with my father's compartmentalizing his family as I am.

"Later, Maddy," Dad says. "We'll talk about it later."

"It's always later with you." I get out of the car. For once, it's not raining. Giorgio has my bags, and he follows me to the building.

On the steps leading up to our three-flat, I see another origami moon.

This one is folded out of paper in an aqua-and-peach chevron pattern, and it's propped up as if waiting for me to come discover it.

So Dylan couldn't manage to show his face at the Factory, but he's still leaving me gifts. I don't know how I feel about that, and I don't have time to decide right now. I pocket it before Giorgio has the chance to kick it aside.

My father waves from the window. I give him a nod.

At the door, I grab the handle of my suitcase.

"Oh, I can take it all the way up for you, Miss Maddy."

"Madelaine," I correct him. "And I've got it. Thanks."

I unlock the vestibule door and lug my suitcase up two flights of stairs. "I'm home!" I call as I unlock the door to our apartment. But no vintage Madonna greets me. "Nana? Mom?"

"Hey there, Lainey."

"Ted." I drop my suitcase with a thud when I see him sitting on the couch, reading an issue of *Rolling Stone*. "Where's my mom? Where's Nana?"

He squints at me through the light. "Did you have a good trip?"

"It was . . . it was fine." I grip the origami moon in my pocket. "How long have you been here?" I wonder if he saw anyone leave the moon. "Where's Mom?"

"What's with all these new clothes? And receipts?"

I look over my shoulder at all the things I packed up for Mom to return. "She didn't take them back yet?"

"Lainey . . . why don't you sit down?"

"What are you doing here? Where's . . . did they go to another antique show or something? Was that why Nana wanted my dad to keep me overnight?"

"You hungry, kid?"

"I'm fine." But why isn't he answering me? My throat feels as if it's starting to close, and my ears go cloudy for a second. Something's wrong. "Where's my mother?"

This is too much for one day. My dad's married. My ex-nearly-stepfather is in Nana's apartment, and no one seems to want to tell me the whole truth about anything.

An MPE comes on fast and hard.

I wheeze with my next inhale. I'm going to faint. Or throw up. Or both. The world starts to spin.

"Whoa. You okay?" Ted asks. "Sit down a second. Let me get you some water."

But I don't want to sit down. I grip the back of the sofa for stability. "Where's Mom?" Tears burn my already tired eyes. "Is she . . . did something happen to her?"

I think of the man on the L. The black raincoat.

I think of my beautiful mother.

I link the two images—the predator and the prey—and wheeze again.

"Lainey, I'll take you to see her."

"See her? Where?"

"I'm not sure if you've noticed, but she hasn't feeling well. Your nana took her to the hospital."

"The *hospital*?" I'm pacing now. "Just tell me what's going on, Ted. Was there an accident? Or—"

"Remember when . . . Lainey, sit down."

I'm numb. He guides me to the sofa.

"Last month, your mom went to Minnesota for a few days."

"Yeah." I wipe tears away with the back of my hand. "Some potential choreography gig?"

"That's . . . no. No, Lainey." He looks me in the eye. "She went for a second opinion. For additional rounds of tests."

Realization dawns on me, and my heart kicks into high gear. "No."

"The team of doctors here suggested she seek a second

opinion, and I thought . . . Mayo Clinic. It's the best."

"No, no, no." Tears are pouring from my eyes. "This can't be happening. Not again."

"And when I took her back last week—"

"No!" I shove his arm away when he tries to comfort me. "It's not *fair*. She wasn't supposed to get it once, let alone twice. No!"

The cancer is back.

That's why she quit her jobs, I realize.

That's why she's been trying to squeeze in time with me . . . because what if we don't have that much left together?

God, what if it's too late already? What if no treatment can save her this time?

My head is spinning. "How bad?"

"A little farther along than last time. The surgeon had an opening in his schedule, so your mother took it."

"So while I was in New York, my mother was getting cancer cut out of her?" I backhand my cheek, rubbing at the tears. "It's not fair. This is bullshit."

"Your mother doesn't deserve this," Ted says. "That's absolutely true. *You* don't deserve it. But it's happening, so we have to deal with it."

"We?"

"Lainey, I know I wasn't around the last time your mom went through this."

Numbly, I say, "Mom said you couldn't deal with the reality of the situation."

"I guess she was right from a certain point of view. But it wasn't that I couldn't handle the cancer. *That* wasn't the situation I was avoiding. I walked away because . . . I didn't want to leave, but things were complicated. I loved her, but—"

"But she was still in love with Dad." I catch my breath and look to the hallway, where a week ago, my mother and I screamed at each other. I think of her words: *I'm done fighting.*

"The bottom line is, this time it's different. I'm here for you. I'm going to take you to see your mother."

I shake my head. "I'll call my dad. I'm sure, once he hears what's going on—"

"Your nana already told him."

"What?"

"When she called when you were at the airport in New York. I was right there, and Adie told him then."

"He knows the cancer is back?"

Ted nods. "We called when we found out she could have the surgery on Friday. He thought it best not to worry you during your trip. And we called again today when the doctor said he wanted to keep her another day."

"And he just . . . left me on the doorstep?"

"He knew I'd be here," Ted says. "Your nana told him I'd be here for you."

"And he had to be there for someone else."

Ted shrugs. "I guess so."

CHAPTER 28

Mom is asleep.

Hayley and I each sit on either side of her bed, and we both hold her hands. It's not until my sister smudges a shoulder against her cheek that I realize she's crying.

I still haven't stopped much, myself.

"So," I say. My voice comes out flat. "Dad got married."

Hayley sits up straight. "What?"

"Months ago. He told me earlier today."

My sister stares at me. "Today? *After* Adie called him to let him know about Ella?"

"Yup. Great timing, huh?"

Hayley lets out a long breath and shakes her head. "I don't understand how he could do such a thing. And then . . . just to leave you there with a guy who played your daddy for six months. This is our *mother*. She raised us. Maybe she wasn't getting a paycheck in the early years, but she *worked*. Probably harder than he did. She made my lunches, and taught me to tie my shoes, and stayed up with me when I was sick or scared and he was gone."

I nod. "Maybe you could get through to him, Hay. Whenever I try it doesn't seem to register with him. It's like he doesn't even care—about all she used to do, about everything she does now, and about everything she's going through—and I can't imagine how that must make her feel."

I don't speak my thoughts aloud, but come to think of it, this whole thing is unfair. Everything has worked out for him. He's married. He gets to keep his money. Mom, on the other hand, is out of luck just because she dared to give Ted a shot. They earned that money together. It's not fair that Dad has all the control, that he could do this to her.

It's appalling. I owe her so much, and my dad makes her out to be a lazy sponge.

"*And* he makes money off me," I say as if Hayley hasn't just made an excellent point. "Can you believe that?"

"He's your manager, right?"

"Okay, so everyone's focused on that right now. But I tell you: if Mom made money off me, and we needed that money to pay my tuition, she'd work for free."

"Yeah, I suppose, but—"

"I feel like he deliberately misled me," I tell my sister. "Like he *lied* to me about what she deserves. I was mad at her for not pulling her weight, for the court case . . . all of it. When all this time, he hasn't accused her of doing anything he hasn't done himself."

"Well, he does have the law on his side."

"It doesn't make it right! And for my sake . . . for our sake, he should do what's right, not what he can get away with."

"Look," Hayley says. "I'm mad at him, too. But we should talk to him. We should figure out why he's acting this way. If we did something he didn't like . . . like the whole misunderstanding about you and that guy in New York. How did it feel knowing he didn't want to hear your side?"

On the surface this feels like an excellent point, but I'm not buying it this time. "I have listened to his side. And all I ever hear is legalese. The paperwork says this, the judge declared that. What kind of justification is that? For using me. For pitting me against my mom. For dictating everything from my hair color to who I get to spend time with, for making me feel guilty when I ask for something he doesn't feel like giving me. For never, ever apologizing for anything. We're his kids. He shouldn't treat us that way."

Hayley looks about as uncomfortable as I've ever seen her. "Of course. I get that. Here's the thing, though: He's still our dad. Don't we have to give him the benefit of the doubt?"

I shake my head. "Not when he's wrong."

CHAPTER 29
Monday, May 8

It's eight in the morning. I'm supposed to be in physics class right now, but instead, I'm curled up in the same uncomfortable leather chair in the same frigid hospital room I've been in since Ted brought me here last night.

Mom's been sleeping since I got here, and for the past two hours I've been drifting off to sleep, too, only to waken with a start. When Mom wakes up, I want to talk to her. There's so much I have to say.

"Madelaine?"

"Mom?"

"Hi, baby girl."

"Mom."

"Where's Hayley?"

"She was here. But she had to go to class."

I think of the night Mom met me after my callback audition—the night I chose shopping with my dad for clothes I didn't really need over spending time with her. I think of this past weekend—the trip to New York, when Dad didn't even notice if I wore the new clothes or not. I should have been with my mother.

It's weird. You look at your parents, and you assume they'll always be there—at least for the foreseeable future—ready to tell you what to do, annoy you, restrict you, make you do the dishes. But when I consider that something worse could have happened . . . that she could have *died* while I was in New York . . . After all, if the cancer was aggressive enough that they thought they had to squeeze her in for surgery this quickly, anything could have happened.

"Mom." I hiccup over a sob. "I'm so sorry."

"Shh. You didn't know."

"I shouldn't have gone to New York. I shouldn't have gone shopping that night, I should have—"

"And I should have told you."

"Yes, but—"

"I didn't want to distract you from the audition. And you were focused. Obviously." She smiles. "Madelaine Joseph is July."

I decide right now: I'm going to dedicate my performance to her.

I bite my lip and try to stay strong. The last thing she needs right now is to watch me fall apart, but I'm raw and exhausted, and I don't know if I can hold it together. "What's going to happen now?"

"I'm going to fight." A soft smile touches her lips. "Fight like the devil. And you're going to that school next year."

"Mom, don't worry about that. I can just finish at Saint Mary's. It's okay. Everything will be okay if you just get better."

Taking over as my manager is going to be difficult, if not impossible, now that she has a long battle ahead of her. Unless Dad budges and opens his wallet, there's no way her plan will work now.

"It's all figured out. We're going to be able to pay half your tuition next year—and at NYU."

"Mom . . . how? The medical bills are going to be through the roof, and with your awful insurance—"

"The insurance is adequate."

"Sorry, Mom, but it's not." Even when she was working, corporations would only hire her part-time so they didn't have to give her benefits, and the insurance she can afford sucks.

"At least I have it. It's going to take care of what I need."

"Still. We can't afford performing arts school . . ."

"You got a grant." Mom smiles.

"I did?" I start to smile until I remember that Mom's on some pretty heavy painkillers after her surgery. Maybe she's mistaken. "How? Those are based on need."

"A grant from the Ted Haggerty Foundation."

"No. Mom, no."

"Yes."

"But then he'll expect to be involved."

"Would that be so bad?"

"He still loves you, okay? He's going to expect you to get back together. And you're still in love with Dad."

She laughs. Honest-to-goodness *laughs*. "Is that what your father thinks?"

"I heard you *tell him so*. That's why you and Ted broke up."

"Oh, that phone call. Listen, honey, I needed time to fall out of love with your father, and the past several years, with everything that's come to pass . . ." She laughs again. "Let's just say, mission accomplished."

"But you don't have to get back with Ted just because he offered to pay." "Of course not. This isn't the Dark Ages. He's offered to pay your tuition whether or not we're back together. On the other hand . . . how would you feel if Ted and I did try again?"

Tears prick my eyes, and I hold her hand and shake my head. "You're not good at this dating thing, Mom. I love you, but you're not. And watching you fumble all these relationships all these years . . . it's why *I* don't date."

She frowns at me. "Do you think you're going to have the same kind of track record I have in regard to romance?"

"Well . . . basically."

"That's ridiculous, Lainey. You don't have to date if you don't want to, but you shouldn't hold yourself back out of fear. This point in your life is the perfect time to start dating. You have to figure out how to be in a relationship before you're in one for the long haul. Sometimes things are messy. But sometimes they're not."

I've never seen what the *not* option looks like. I doubt Mom has either. "But with Ted . . . What if things go bad again? Then what?"

"Caring about people is always a risk." My mother smiles. "But it's also incredibly rewarding, even when it doesn't work out. If you never let yourself care, you'll never *know* anyone else. And worse, no one will know you. And *you* are wonderful."

I laugh a little and climb into bed with my mother.

"How's your song coming?" Mom asks.

"It's good. Still needs some fine-tuning, but it's getting a lot of shares online." I reach into my pocket and feel the outlines of the origami moon I found on the steps yesterday. "Dylan Thomas shared some more lyrics with me." I leave out the details about how he shared them, in case it freaks Mom out. "Listen to this."

I unfold the moon and read the poem inside, which weaves themes of aspiration with contentment: *"I reach for you, teach you / Everything you aspire to be . . ."*

When I'm finished, Mom is staring at me wide-eyed. "Someone *sent* that to you? Someone you met online?"

"Yeah," I say, not sure why she looks so unnerved. "I mean, it's like these words were written specifically for a music staff. When you're all better, I want you to choreograph a dance to it."

She smiles but still seems concerned. "Lainey, this Dylan Thomas—"

"Don't worry about it. He'll come around to letting me use his words. And then, one day," I continue, "we'll put it into production. I'll write and sing the songs, and you'll choreograph. Like Nana says: we can write our own musical. You want to collaborate, Mom? You want to work on something together?"

A pensive expression settles over her face. "It's a nice thought, isn't it?"

I kiss her cheek. "I'd love that, Mom. And someday we'll be onstage together."

CHAPTER 30

I've finally taken a break from my post at Mom's hospital bed. Now that I've finally showered and changed out of the clothes I was wearing when I got off the plane, I start to unpack my suitcase and sort my laundry. I set aside the goofy souvenir shirts I bought for Mom and Nana, plus the mini Statue of Liberty for Hayley because the first time she went to New York, when I was too little to go, she picked one out for me. And I pull the moon out of my hoodie pocket and I place it in my desk with all the others I've gathered over the past couple of weeks.

The place seems somehow quiet without Mom here, even though she's not usually awake past ten, and it's now after midnight. Nana's laughter filters down the hall every now and again (she's watching her shows), and nothing sounds different.

It just is.

And while Mom's probably going to be back home in a day or so, it's still hard to sleep without her here.

It's like tonight is a preview of what it might be like . . . when she's gone.

The thought is like ten stones of grief plummeting into my gut. I don't want to imagine it. It's too soon. She has to beat this evil entity again. She has to. There's so much we have to do together, so much we haven't gotten around to.

For the fortieth time since Ted told me about the cancer coming back, I bury my face in my pillow and cry hard for a few minutes. But like always, I have to pull myself back together.

I reread the poem in the last moon and begin jotting down notes, adding phrases of my own.

I plug into my amp, pop on my headphones, and start messing around with chords. Pretty soon I have the seeds of another song at my fingertips.

After recording a few versions, I pick my favorite one and post it on Lyrically with the caption: *For my hero, my mom.*

And because I promised Mom we'd be onstage together, I go out on a limb, certainly out of my comfort zone. I post a picture of the two of us and share the song on the public forum.

Instantly, my phone chimes with "Raspberry Beret."

Brendon: Girl, you are the shiznit.
McKenna: Totally addicted to your page already.
McKenna: You're going places!
McKenna: Remember us little peeps when you're famous!
Me: Awww, thanks.
Me: If I sign up for open mic at the Factory, would u come?
Brendon: You're like twenty one pilots meets Stone Temple Pilots meets Amelia Earhart.
McKenna: OF COURSE WE'LL COME.
Brendon: (was sort of going with the aviator theme there.)
Me: Got it.
Brendon: Amelia because she's legendary.

Brendon: Not because she disappeared.

Brendon: Because OMG, if you disappeared, like Vagabonds, I'd cry.

McKenna: How's your mom?

Me: We'll see.

Me: Supposed to be pretty routine treatment, so fingers crossed.

Me: But something good came out of it.

Me: Guess where I'm going to school next year?

McKenna: NO WAY! The academy?

Me: Mom made it happen.

McKenna: Let's chat tomorrow.

McKenna: There's no way I'm waking up early tomorrow if I stay up.

Brendon: Continuing with the aviation theme: I'm still jetlagged.

Me: Goodnight, cast of ANNIE.

And because I want to commit, I pull up the Factory's site and sign up for open mic in July. I would sign up for an earlier slot, but . . . baby steps.

It's not a big stage, but it's a start.

A message pops up on Lyrically.

Dylan: Hi.

Dylan: I love your new song.

Dylan: Where ya been?

Me: New York.

Me: And then, the hospital.

Me: My mom's sick.

Me: Cancer.

Dylan: Shit, that sucks. :(
Dylan: Anything I can do?
Me: No.
Dylan: I can listen.

And so I talk.

CHAPTER 31
Thursday, May 25

Rehearsal just let out, and McKenna, Brendon, and I are heading up the street for coffee. The weather has shifted and suddenly, in late May, we're edging on eighty. That's the way it is in Chicago. Sometimes you can get all four seasons in a week.

I'm still thinking about Dylan Thomas. And I remember Mom's advice: reaching for someone is always a risk. Maybe things will work out, or maybe they won't. It's a fifty-fifty shot at happiness. But not reaching out at all gives me a one-hundred percent chance at being alone.

I pull out my phone and tap on the Lyrically icon. I'm going to take a chance. I'm going to invite Dylan to meet us at Counter Offer.

"Maddy!"

I look up from my phone see my father's car parked outside the rehearsal hall: "Oh look," Brendon says. "It's Daddy Warbucks."

My stomach twists a little. Not into MPE territory yet, though. I hold up a finger to delay my dad.

"How's all that going?" McKenna asks.

"I haven't seen him since we've been back from New York." I guess it's hard to tell your daughter she can't spend extra time with her ailing mother, so Dad's been leaving me alone.

Dad waves me in.

"I guess I should go talk to him."

"You gonna be okay?" McKenna asks.

"Yeah," I say. "Can you give me just a minute?"

"We'll wait," Brendon says.

I approach my father's limo and lean into the open window. "Yeah?"

"You doing okay? You're not returning my texts."

I shrug. "Yeah, well . . . I've got plans right now, so how about we do this another time." Let's see how *he* likes being brushed off.

"Where are you and your friends going? I can give you a lift. We can talk on the way."

"I don't really know what there is to say. You know my mother has cancer. You know it's going to take every dime she has to fight it. But you're still being a jerk in court."

He closes his eyes briefly, shakes his head, like he can deny what I've said. "Maddy, I'm sorry about your mother, but she's going to get through this. And at the end of the day, the law is still the law, and the laws are pretty clear. There are certain ways the system is run, and I have every right to due diligence, here. I don't think you fully understand—"

"I understand that you're trying to drag things out until she doesn't have money to fight."

"That's an oversimplified version of what's happening." Dad leans out the window. "McKenna! Brendon! Come on, I'll give you a lift."

My friends look to me. This is why I love them. They don't make assumptions, they don't take advantage, they wait to see what I want.

After a moment, I give them a nod and invite them to join us.

I know what Dad's trying to do. He thinks I won't air our dirty laundry with the Weekes twins right here. He'll give me a wad of cash to cover our snacks and entertainment for the evening—so everyone will go on thinking he's this amazing, generous guy—and he'll expect me to forget about everything he's doing to ruin Mom again.

I can't blame him for trying. It's worked in the past. But it won't work this time.

The twins approach and follow me into the car.

"What's this I hear about plans?" Dad asks. "Where are you going?"

"Counter Offer," I say.

"Counter Offer it is," Giorgio says. "Address?"

McKenna rattles it off.

"It's a little café near the courthouse," I say. "You know the courthouse, right, Dad? It's where you're filing continuances until my mother runs out of money."

Brendon and McKenna are sharing an uncomfortable glance that says it all—this car isn't big enough for this type of discussion.

I feel a rush of guilt. I shouldn't have put them in this position. I didn't consider how Brendon and McKenna would feel about witnessing the whole thing. I send an apologetic look in their direction; I'll have to make it up to them.

"Maddy, this isn't the time or place," Dad says.

And just like that, my guilt is gone. "Now, of all times, is the time to be decent, Dad. You know my mother isn't extravagant. She asked for more money for *me*. Not for her. We already sold everything and moved in with Nana Adie. She hasn't had a lifetime of earning power like you have, because she was busy taking care of us, and now that she's sick, she can't work, she has practically no earning power, and you're doing just fine. I think you're selfish, if you want to know the truth."

"We should really discuss this some other time—"

"You can't even see how what you're doing hurts me, Dad. It hurts me. And I guess it hurts Mom to see me hurt, so if that's your goal, it's accomplished. I mean, don't you even care that my mother is battling cancer? *Again*? Are you going try to blame her for *that* too? Or do you just not give a shit?"

His jaw sets. "Giorgio, you can pull over up here and let the twins out."

"You can't just drop them on the side of the road," I say.

"You insist on talking about private business," Dad retorts. "You're making our guests uncomfortable."

"If they get out, I get out."

There's a long pause. "To Counter Offer, then," Dad says.

It's a small victory—the first I've won against my father. I've never challenged him this way before, and I'm not sure *anyone* talks to him the way I just did. I can't quite believe it worked.

No one says another word until Giorgio pulls over at the café.

I get out of the car and watch it pull away.

"Wow," McKenna says, putting an arm around me. "So that's what a high-stakes negotiation with a top manager looks like."

"I'm sorry you two had to hear all that." I sigh. "I almost wish I hadn't agreed to talk to him at all. It's like it couldn't have gone well unless I'd agreed with everything he said."

Suddenly I can imagine what it must have been like divorcing him . . . and I get why Mom may have agreed to things she shouldn't have agreed to. Played nice to avoid being on his bad side, even if she must have known he was going to turn on her in the end anyway. Maybe he hemmed her in, and she had no choice but to let him do it.

The afterburn of the realization settles in my gut, a little like the way I feel when I know an audition hasn't gone well, like I wish I could rewind time and do something different.

There are going to be consequences for what I've done. But I have to get through to him somehow. I need to stand up for my mom . . . and myself.

"Hey, it's gonna be okay," Brendon says, as if he can read my thoughts. "He's your dad. He *has* to love you."

I'm not so sure about that.

CHAPTER 32

I'm on the L, headed home. It's crowded. There must be a ball-game of some sort today, or maybe one of Chicago's famous summer fests is going on.

The crowd starts to thin the farther we travel from the Loop. I switch trains to cut across to Wicker Park.

No sooner do I sit down than I see a familiar figure—this time wearing dark gray. No one can convince me he isn't the same man I've seen several times before.

He's looking at me, but pretending not to see me.

My heart starts beating fast.

Maybe it's nothing. Maybe he lives in my neighborhood. He got off the train at my stop once before, when the Sophias were trying to finagle coffee with me at the Factory. He has every right to ride the L.

I click a picture and text it to Hayley with a one-word caption: scared.

If he's just a patron riding the train at the same odd times I ride it, he'll get off at my usual stop.

Or he could be getting off at my stop because *I'm* getting off at my stop, in which case . . .

I have no idea what to do if he's actually stalking me.

Frozen with fear, I stay glued to my seat, even as the train approaches the stop closest to our place.

The man watching me doesn't budge. Which means he doesn't live in my neighborhood.

Me: Last time he got off at my stop. He didn't do
    that this time.
Hayley: Phew. So you're good.
Me: No.
Me: I didn't get off at my stop either.
Hayley: Are you sure it's not related to Dylan
    Thomas?

I think about it. I did message Dylan on Lyrically and ask him to meet the Weekes twins and me. So I did tell him where I was going to be.

And he obviously knows where I live. If he's a Chicago native—as he claims to be—it wouldn't be too tough to figure out which trains I'd take to get home. Shit.

Me: Maybe you're right.
Hayley: STOP TALKING TO HIM. PLEASE.
Me: That's beside the point right now!
Me: I now have a long walk home if I get off at
    the next stop.
Me: What do I do if this guy follows me?
Hayley: Ella probably can't meet you.
Me: No, she had treatment this afternoon.
Me: She's probably sleeping.
Hayley: Call Dad?

I can't do that, either. Not after our last interaction.

Me: I'm going to get off at Milwaukee and go to the
     Factory.
Hayley: Good plan.
Hayley: Stay around people.
Me: And I'm going to see if Ted can meet me.

I don't want to make a call on the L, so I text.
Please, Ted. Please, please, please answer.
When my phone chimes with Ted's text tone, I nearly cry
with relief.

Ted: Be careful.
Ted: I'll get there ASAP.

I gather my things and prepare to exit at Milwaukee.
Not surprisingly, the stranger rises, too.
I walk quickly down the stairs at the platform. He's not far
behind me . . . just a few, maybe five or so steps.
Now I'm practically jogging. I glance over my shoulder.
He's walking in long strides at a clipped pace.
He *is* following me. There's no other explanation.
I see the Factory up ahead.
He's gaining on me.
All I have to do is cross the street—

CHAPTER 33

I allow myself to exhale as I step into the coffee shop.

Safe.

Someone's onstage performing a poem. I keep an eye on the performer, even though my ears are ringing and I can't really concentrate on anything he's saying. Everyone's underwater. I inch my way to the register to order something. I don't want anything, per se, but I can't just loiter until Ted shows up, so I get my usual mocha roast, and a chai with soymilk for Ted.

That's good. It'll look like I'm not alone.

I snag a seat not far from where I found the original origami moon.

I was here.

I try to fade into the woodwork. I want to be as anonymous as possible.

"Lainey?"

I flinch. But instantly, I feel my shoulders fall.

I throw my arms around Ted, and—I can't help it—suddenly I'm crying and I just can't stop.

As if Mom's illness weren't enough. As if the court case weren't enough. "He's following me."

"Which one?" Ted brushes my hair from my forehead and

kisses me there. "Guy in the gray cap?"

"Yeah."

"I'll take care of it." Ted practically has to pry my hands off him, but he manages to do it. He runs a hand from the crown of my head to the base of my cheek. "You okay now?"

"I . . . yeah. Yeah, I'm good. I'm just so glad you're here." I don't know if I've ever been as scared as I was on the short walk here. Worse than any burst of panic I've ever felt: a deep, all-consuming fear.

"Are you going to be okay if I go have a word with him?"

I don't necessarily want him to leave me, but I take another deep breath. "I'm okay."

Ted cuts his way through the crowd toward the guy who's been stalking me. There aren't enough chairs in this place today to hold all its patrons, so it's not like Ted can simply corner the guy and sit him down.

I overhear: "Dylan Thomas, I presume?"

My would-be perpetrator backs against a thick structural column with flyers pinned to it. "Get lost, man."

"Are you Dylan Thomas?"

I hear the man who was following me: "You have me confused with someone else."

"I don't think so. You've taken an interest in my daughter?"

Daughter.

Now a police officer is making his way over to Ted and the mystery man; Ted talks to him quietly.

The poet on stage finishes his performance, and the place erupts in the traditional finger snapping for a job well done.

I take a deep breath. The snapping sounds like raindrops on a tin roof. A calming timbre. A welcome, musical sound.

I close my eyes for a second, imagine my mother twirling

and bourrée-ing in delicate little steps from one place to another.

And lyrics flash in my mind:

Run, run, run to the ends of the earth
Run in silent rage
To break you, they must catch you first
Upon an empty stage.

My eyes snap open.

I take in every detail of the room around me. I feel the room in my bones, in my nerves, in my teeth, like tiny grains of sand.

Oh. My. God.

I did it. I actually wrote lyrics.

I open the diary app on my phone and jot them down.

And just that quickly, the panic is gone.

I take a cleansing breath and look up. Ted's on his way back to me. The police officer is leading the guy in gray toward the door.

"You won't have any more trouble with that guy," Ted says. "I called the cops right when I got your text. They're going to need a statement from you, and we'll file a report, but in the meantime, they're asking him some questions."

"Who was he?"

"No one important." Ted picks up his tea, thanks me for it, and takes a sip. "Walk you home?"

"Thanks," I say.

After a few strides, I have to ask: "Did he admit to being Dylan Thomas?"

"No."

"Okay. Because . . . Ted? I sort of *like* Dylan Thomas. And

I don't want to believe he's a bad guy. But if there's any chance that guy was him . . ."

"Unfortunately, he might be."

"I felt so at home with him." My voice comes out small and wobbly. "He seemed to get me."

Ted nods. "It's easy through a screen. You don't have to be real online. Plenty of predators know what to say to make sure you do like them. Then when you trust them, they pounce."

I take deep breaths, fight back tears. "Did the guy tell you *anything*?"

"He said he was just doing his job."

"Following me was his job? I didn't realize stalker positions paid all that well."

"Maybe he wasn't a stalker. Maybe he was hired."

"Hired? By Dylan?"

"Let's let the police figure that out. Once we file a report, we'll have the report number. We can check for updates."

And to think I sought Dylan out. I pursued a relationship with him—for the sake of a song, but still. "God, I'm an idiot."

"You're not an idiot for trusting people."

Sheesh. If I make twenty more terrible decisions about whom to trust, I'll tie my mother's record.

"I'm glad you texted," Ted says. "Don't hesitate, okay? Ever."

"Thanks."

We sip our beverages.

"Thanks for the tea," Ted says.

"Thanks for calling me your daughter."

"You heard that, huh? Well . . . I know I'm not your father. But I call 'em like I see 'em." He tips his cup of tea to my cup of coffee.

"How's Vinny?" I ask.

"He misses you."

I look down at his shoes. Penny loafers. With nickels.

Predictable.

Dependable.

Whimsical.

Soooo nice.

"Ted?"

"Yeah?"

"We *all* miss you."

CHAPTER 34

I open Lyrically to see that Dylan has been messaging on and off all day.

> Dylan: What's up?
> Dylan: Madelaine?
> Dylan: Anybody home??
> Dylan: Is everything ok with your mom?
> Dylan: Miss talking to you.

Part of me thinks I shouldn't even reply. If there's even a smidgen of a chance that he's not really a teenage guy, and that he was the one following me, I should block him and never look back. But there's a bigger part of me that wants to know for sure that it was him before taking action.

It's like what happened in New York. Dad just made an assumption about Brendon and me and ran with it. It felt awful.

> Me: Do you have something to tell me?

There's a long pause. The ellipses appears, showing me he's writing, but after a minute it stops. I hold my breath.

Me: Are you who you say you are?
Me: Why won't you answer?
Me: Do you know where I live?
Dylan: Yes.

My fingertips go numb.

Me: Are you following me?
Dylan: I see you sometimes.
Dylan: I don't always talk to you when I see you.
Dylan: And you don't always see me.

Oh my God, he *is* the one following me. He's probably not even seventeen. He's—

Dylan: But I'm not stalking you.
Me: Why should I believe you?

The little dots appear again. A minute goes by. Another minute.

Dylan: I'm sorry.
Dylan: You have every right to be upset.
Dylan: I screwed up.
Dylan: But I'm trying be honest with you now.
Dylan: Because I like you.
Dylan: Because in a world where we don't fit, we
        fit together.

I don't want to do it, but I have to.
I block Dylan Thomas on every social media site.

CHAPTER 35
Saturday, June 10

It's been strange not communicating with Dylan Thomas. It's hard. I really got used to talking to him.

Even though we don't know for sure that he was the guy who followed me, odds are he was. Who else could it have been?

Funny how someone you don't know, have never known, and never will know can become so addictive, such an important part of your life.

And while the origami moons sort of freaked me out at first, I also really enjoyed finding them. Or rather, I enjoyed what finding them led to.

They were a crucial stepping-stone on my path to producing my own music. And while there's no way I'm going to collaborate with Dylan Thomas now, I did learn something from him.

I learned that I can put myself out there, I can create beautiful things, and creativity can be contagious.

It's hard not being able to bounce ideas off him.

Brendon and McKenna help fill the loneliness. And we share in a great production, which will open at the end of the month. My name will be in a program at the Chicago Theater. God, I'm still in awe.

And soon, if I do what I know I can do, I'll be on Broadway.

"Are you still awake, Mom?"

We're FaceTiming. Her blood counts were low this morning, so Ted brought her to the hospital. They're going to keep her overnight at least, but I wish they'd let her come home so I can sing to her in person.

"Play it again," my mother says. "You sing so beautifully."

For a second, I stare at the screen—my beautiful mother. Even with a scarf where her hair used to be. Even with her face drawn and hollow. Her eyes are the same . . . and they're the same as mine.

I take a screenshot, crop it close to her eyes, and post her image to my Instagram: A hint of chocolate, evergreen rims, and golden slivers of wisdom . . . the windows to my mother's soul. The most beautiful eyes a story ever told.

I play and sing for her. The song still needs work, but it's close.

Soon Ted's looking into the camera, placing a finger on his lips.

"She's sleeping?" I whisper.

He nods.

"I'll come see her soon," I promise. "But I want her to sleep."

She used to sing me to sleep all the time. Now I've returned the favor. And the song I just sang . . . It's her song. I wrote it for her.

And someday, we'll be onstage together. We promised each other.

Ted gives me the bye sign, and we terminate FaceTime.

Five minutes later, while I'm recording the song, my phone won't shut up.

I go to turn my ringer off, but I see a message from my sister.

Hayley: Been thinking about what u said.

Hayley: We have to fix this between u and Dad.

Hayley: Maybe we should stop by Dad's for
 lunch today.

Me: . . .

Hayley: You have to move past this.

Hayley: He's our dad.

Me: He's probably busy today.

Me: That's why I'm in the city instead of in Kenilworth
 with him.

Me: It's his weekend.

Hayley: He's so crushed that you're angry at him that
 I'm not surprised he's stopped trying to see you.

Me: I have no interest in going there right now.

Hayley: You have to talk to him sometime.

Me: I want to stop in to see my mom today.

Hayley: Go to the hospital after.

Hayley: I'll go with you.

Me: Really?

Hayley: Yeah.

Hayley: She's my mom, too.

Me: <3

Hayley: We'll take the Metra.

Hayley: I'll be in the third car.

Hayley: Get on at Clybourn.

Hayley: I'll be looking for you.

CHAPTER 36

"Sister!" Hayley stands and waves when I slide open the door leading to the third car.

I wish I'd worn something other than dance shorts and a tank top, because Hayley looks awesome from her messy bun to her open-toed sandals. She's wearing a cute blue sundress, which makes her eyes look positively cerulean. I assume she made the dress herself. The girl can teach herself virtually any sort of craft after watching even half a video on YouTube. She and Nana used to paint and sew and create together all the time. Once they even took a pottery class together.

But once the divorce was final, she and Nana stopped doing that sort of thing.

I try to put myself in Hayley's shoes. Would I suddenly shy away from someone I used to love simply because my dad decided he wanted out? Like, if I get to know Miss Karissa and her kids, and we get along and become family, and in a few years, she and Dad break up, would I decide they're not my family anymore?

I don't know. I miss the days when things were simple, when I had a mom and a dad and a sister—and we were all part of the same family.

I let her hug me. Her apple-scented shampoo mingles with her cinnamon-flavored gum. She smells like a late September orchard and looks like she just stepped off the pages of a magazine.

My gorgeous sister.

She moves an elegantly wrapped present from the bench to her lap to make room for me next to her. The train lurches forward.

I sit. "What's with the gift?"

"It's a wedding present."

"Oh. Show-off. I didn't get them anything."

"Yes you did. *We* got them this cookie jar. I signed your name on the card."

"Thanks."

"So I figure we'll stop for a snack. Maybe some ice cream at Homer's, then we'll cut down Woodstock and have a nice leisurely walk to Dad's place."

Dad's place. It used to be home. We all lived there.

"Sound good?"

"Sounds good." I hand an earbud to my sister. Together we listen to my favorites on shuffle: Nirvana, Prince, the Beatles, the *Thoroughly Modern Millie* soundtrack. And when "Forget About the Boy" comes on, we sing. Or rather, *I* sing, and Hayley tries to.

The only other person still in the train car by the time we reach Kenilworth, a man in his fifties, smiles and claps when the song is over. "Bravo."

"My sister," Hayley indicates me, as if I'm a prize on a game show. "See her in *Annie* at the one, the only, Chicago Theater!"

We get off the train and walk a few blocks to Homer's, which is crowded, so we get our ice cream to go. We take turns carrying the present and eating as we walk down Woodstock. It's a nice summer day: blue skies, the same color as the crayon boasting the name, and it's pushing eighty degrees. But the closer we get to the lake, the cooler the wind.

"I'm still not sure this is a good idea," I say. "Just dropping in like this."

"If we told him we were coming," Hayley says, "he'd tell us not to. He'd make other arrangements, which you would likely blow off. He'd meet us in the city weeks from now, and nothing would get accomplished. Besides, this way, we'll get to jump-start the blending process. He can't keep us separated from Karissa and the kids if we're all in the same house together."

"Maybe we should have at least texted so he'd know we're on our way."

"Lainey, you're missing the whole point of this."

"Maybe you should tell me what the point is, then."

"I want to see him in his element, you know? I want to catch him off guard, so he doesn't have a chance to prepare for our visit. I want to see these kids when their mom doesn't have time to sit them down and remind them of their manners."

I shrug. It's a good plan, I guess.

But the jagged remnants of what used to be our family are spinning in my gut right now. Something tells me this is not going to go well.

When we're about a block away, with Dad's house in sight, that spinning sensation kicks into high gear. The gate is closed across the driveway. "We're going to have to call," I say. "He's going to have to buzz us in."

Hayley waves away my concerns and opens the keypad. "It's our house, too, isn't it?"

"I don't think so. When was the last time you were here?"

Hayley's fingers fly over the keypad.

"Do you have the code since he changed it?" I ask.

The light on the keypad flashes red, denying our entry and punctuating my point. "Why would he change it?"

"He said he didn't trust that Mom wouldn't stop in." And he didn't share the new code with me because I'd covered up Mom's cohabitating with Ted. He was afraid what I knew, my mother would know.

"We'll climb through the hedge," Hayley decides. She shoves the present into my arms and leads the way. When she's made it past the hedges, I shove the present at her. The branches snag on the shiny wrapping paper.

"Well, it used to look nice," Hayley says.

I come through after her, and together we follow the winding driveway to where the house sits on a bluff overlooking the lake.

Dad's on the large, circular driveway steadying a bike while one of Miss Karissa's sons rides it.

Miss Karissa is standing in the doorway, smiling at the whole scene. A proud mom. A satisfied wife. "Okay, a few more minutes," she says. "But then lunch, okay?"

The other boy is directing a remote-control car.

And a little girl, who must be Jennica, wiggles and spins a Hula-Hoop around her waist near the sidewalk.

I stop in my tracks.

I recognize her. She's the little girl in the Gap commercial. The little girl jumping rope. That means . . .

My dad probably manages her career.

He's probably running her all over the city for auditions, which is why he's been sending Giorgio to shuttle me.

He never was present for me. He left it to Mom to run me

from casting call to casting call. And now . . .

Hayley looks at me over her shoulder. "Come on, Lainey."

But I can't move. I gaze at these ordinary, humdrum events taking place along the lakeshore, the secret lives woven beneath the surface.

There's no reason Hayley and I can't be here for this. No reason we can't be part of it. Yet we're never invited. Dad surely can chisel out some time for us amidst this mundane idyll—more time than a rushed dinner at insert-name-of-a-downtown-steakhouse.

"No." I turn and decided to head back before he notices our presence. "I changed my mind."

The next inbound train won't leave for another hour, but I don't care. I'd rather sit at the station than watch this life of his unfold without regard for Hayley and me—not to mention my mom, who's battling for her life again.

"Where are you going?" Hayley's suddenly in step beside me, whispering as we round the bend in the drive.

"Don't you get it? *He doesn't want us here!*"

"Lainey, wait."

"Look at them! Does it look like he needs his *old* daughters interfering? Does it look like he's missing us at all?"

Hayley grabs my wrist. "Hang on. I want to follow through with this. I need him to come clean. He owes it to us to welcome us into his life here."

"You say that as if he's actually going to do it!"

"Who are they?" The voice of a small child echoes across the vast motor court.

"Girls?"

Simultaneously, we turn to see our father, one hand on the handlebars of Boy 1's bike and the other at the base of the bike seat.

Boy 1—I don't even know his name—stares up at us with mouth agape.

"What are you doing here?" Dad asks. "How did you—"

"Daddy!" Jennica yells from the porch. "Watch!"

Dad swallows hard. His Adam's apple noticeably bobs in his throat.

"She calls you daddy?" Hayley asks. "Doesn't she have a dad of her own?"

"Who are they?" Boy 1 asks again.

"Tell you what." Dad kicks down the kickstand, pulls the kid from the bike, and crouches at the kid's side. "If you run all the way up to the door and back, I'll let you stay up ten minutes past your bedtime tonight."

"Promise?"

"I promise." Dad tousles the kid's hair.

"Okay, Daddy." The kid takes off.

"Why are they calling you Daddy?" I ask. A tornado of inadequacy slams into me. He didn't care enough about Hayley and me to stick around. But he's playing with these kids. And they call him *Daddy*.

"Is Jennica your daughter?" I force the words out. "Are the boys . . . what are their names?"

"Daniel and Karl."

"Are they your sons?"

When he looks at me, his eyes are wide, his expression somber. He doesn't say anything.

I could take this to mean that I have a half-sister and half-brothers. That I'm no longer the littlest sister. But I didn't come here to make assumptions. I want him to tell me in his own words.

"Well?" My voice is shrill. "Are they yours?"

His jaw clenches. He finds his voice—not the Fun Dad voice, the Stern Dad voice. "This isn't the place for this conversation, Madelaine."

"What does that even mean? It's your weekend. I'm supposed to be here—"

"I deposited an extra hundred and fifty into your mother's account for your expenses this weekend."

"Dad, I don't want you to pay someone so you don't have to see me—"

"And you haven't been returning my texts, which tells me you don't want to see me." Dad says. "The last time I tried to see you, you embarrassed me in front of your friends—"

"Oh for God's sake." Hayley shoves the present into our father's arms. "Congratulations on your recent nuptials, jackass."

Dad looks from me to my sister and back. "You told Hayley about the wedding, when I specifically asked you not to—"

"Of *course* she told me!" Hayley cuts in. "Because you chose not to!"

"I was going to tell you when the time felt right . . ."

"How long were you going to wait, Dad? It's been over a month."

"You were busy with finals and interviews for your internship."

"I don't want to hear it," Hayley says.

Jennica's staring at us inquisitively. While Dad and Hayley snipe at each other, I pull up the browser on my phone and search *Jennica Gap commercial.*

Dad sighs. "I'll come to the city tomorrow, and we can talk about this. Over lunch. What do you say? We can hit the aquarium, maybe. You used to like the belugas."

Within seconds, pages of links load onto my screen. I click on one of them, and the little darling's face fills my screen. Her name: Jennica Joseph.

CHAPTER 37

"I'd like to go inside before we leave." Hayley plants her hands on her hips and doesn't budge.

Dad looks nervous.

"What? I can't go in? I used to live here, but you don't want me in your house?"

"It's not that," Dad says. "It's just that the kids have had a busy morning, and—"

"What are you hiding? Kitchen remodel? Prized artwork? Assets Ella can't know about?"

"Lunch!" Miss Karissa appears in the doorway again. This time, she sees Hayley and me. And the color flushes from her cheeks. "Jennica, boys. Come inside."

No one moves.

"*Inside*," Karissa says again. "Now."

This time, the little minions jump to it. Karissa takes a step toward us, but Dad holds up a hand to keep her in her place. "A minute, Kari?"

"For Crissake, Jesse." Karissa folds her arms across her chest. "Let the girls come in."

"A minute, okay?"

She shakes her head but disappears along with her children.

"Why don't you want us inside?" Hayley asks. "Maybe you don't want us to see the pictures of the wedding in Italy. In a mansion on the Isle of Capri, I'm guessing. During your trip in March. Am I right?"

"Hawaii." Dad says, dangling the gift in one hand, pinches the bridge of his nose with the other. "Early April."

"And you're calling Mom's three-day visit to Mayo Clinic a vacation?" I ask. "You think *Mom's* spending irrationally?"

"We wanted to have another ceremony, one that would include all of you, but then Ella's court case came, and—"

"So you lied to us," I say.

"I didn't want you to feel the way you're feeling right now," Dad says. "As if I didn't make the effort to involve you."

"Then maybe you should have *involved us!*" Hayley's eyes are even bluer now, with tears swimming in them. "But we're just burdens to you, aren't we? If my mom had her shit together, if she'd been capable of taking care of me, you would've turned your back on me a long time ago."

"No. You're my daughter. Nothing can change that."

"And yet my mother lives in a one-bedroom apartment in Waukegan. And Lainey and Ella are crammed into Nana Adie's three-flat, while you're spreading out in a house that Ella made a home, playing family with someone else." Hayley shakes her head in disbelief. "You're casting us out."

Dad shakes his head. There might be a bit of helplessness creeping into his eyes, but maybe that's just wishful thinking on my part. "You're older. You have your own lives to live. I do want to continue to be part of your lives—"

"But you don't want us to be part of yours," I say.

"Maddy, that's not true."

"Don't you dare." Hayley wipes away a tear. "Don't talk to

us like we're stupid. Like we're *overreacting*. Hell, I can't believe I defended you for so long. Come on, Madelaine. We don't have to listen to this." My sister takes my hand, and we walk back down the driveway.

✳✳✳

I aim my phone at the floor of the Metra car and snap a picture—my Chuck Taylors and Hayley's sandals, side by side.

I'm about to caption it and post it to my Instagram, but nothing comes to mind.

I delete the post. I have nothing clever to say, no color to assign to my feelings.

I flip back to Jennica Joseph's bio. "You know, it could just be a stage name," I say to Hayley.

She gives me her gimme-a-break look. "It's possible," I say. "I mean, every time I walk into an audition, and someone makes the connection between me and Jesse Joseph, it's another bridge, another bonus. Maybe he just gave the kids his last name. Maybe their dad's not involved, and he's adopted them."

Hayley shrugs. "Possible. But probable? They call him *Daddy*. In fact . . ."

Hayley pulls a small notebook from her purse and flips past notes about great works of literature, symbolism, and a hundred other things professors over-emphasize to suck the life right out of a story. On a blank page, she draws a horizontal line and begins marking it with little Xs, one of which she labels *Leaves Ella*, another *Divorces Ella*, and one at the end, which she coins *Today*. Ah. It's a timeline.

"Think about it," she continues. "We have a roughly ten-year timeline. At the beginning, we have the day he decided he was done being married to Ella. Five years later, we have the divorce being final. And five years after *that*, we have today. Jennica, who's . . . how old?"

"Eight."

"When's her birthday?"

"I don't know."

Hayley rolls her eyes.

"What?" I say. "Like that's something Dad would've mentioned to me?"

"No, I know. It's just ridiculous that there's so much we don't know. We don't know *anything* about these kids."

"Duh. What do you think I've been trying to tell you for the past . . . forever?"

"Let's assume she's not newly eight. Let's assume she's somewhere between eight and nine. Eight and a half."

"Wait." I again check her bio on my phone. "Yeah, she'll be nine in October."

"That means she was born around here." Hayley marks the line with another X—this one just past *leaves Ella*, and about five years before the divorce was final.

"That means," Hayley says, "she was conceived around here." The final *X* lands right before *leaves Ella*.

I look up at her. "He left us for them?"

"Well . . . come on. You had to have known he was involved with Miss Karissa before he left your mom. You're not *that* naïve."

"So we weren't enough for him." I mentally tumble backwards in time over all my aspirations. Every audition. Every role I didn't get. But Jennica . . . she's in a Gap commercial. Daddy's shining star. I'm just a girl who's been tossed a few pity roles, probably to appease my manager father. "We weren't good enough."

"I'm starting to wonder if *anything* would be good enough for him."

I feel strange, like I'm in a foreign country and don't speak the language but suddenly catch onto the fact that everyone's making fun of me. Jennica is almost nine years old. My father is the same man today that he was yesterday, and every day for the past nine years. Yet suddenly, I feel differently about him.

I stare at my phone. He's not calling. Not texting.

Hayley and I just walked out of his life, and he's not even trying to explain himself. Not even trying to get us back.

It's like the bottom of the world is dropping out from under me, and he's simply watching me flush my way out of the solar system.

No hand reaches out to catch me. No voice at my back begs me to hang on.

"I stood up for him all this time," says Hayley wearily. "I made so many excuses for him. I believed the best of him even when he gave me no reason to. God, this sucks."

"But we have each other." I lean my head against her shoulder. "We have each other. And Mom and Nana."

"Always, sister." Her cheek rests against the crown of my head. "Always."

I cue up one of my new tracks and pop in an earbud. The other, I hand to Hayley, and together we listen.

I hear the words no one's singing, in accompaniment to my notes:

Cloves of a new day
Cloaked in a new wave
Loved on a Tuesday
Lost on blue day

But I wouldn't change it for the moon
I wouldn't change it, for it's doom
I would've sung it on the last day
of a rose blooming in June.

It's a song about me, about what I'm feeling. But it's also about more than that. It's about losses that are bigger than just me.

With my mom so sick and fighting. With my dad recently carved out of my life. I think I know now that losing isn't about not getting the role I had my heart set on. It's not about missing an opportunity.

It's about sorrow.

But it's not about who hurt you or how or why.

It's about hope and the will to survive.

I open my diary app and jot down these thoughts. They make a nice couplet.

Without thinking, I open Lyrically to share the two lines with Dylan Thomas. I stop myself, of course. "You don't still talk to him, do you?" Hayley asks.

She's obviously looking over my shoulder and knows I'm on Lyrically.

"No. I blocked him." But a longing pulls at my heartstrings.

"Good," my sister says.

"But I do miss talking to him."

And the things that transpired today are exactly the types of things I would talk to him about. I'd get his perspective. He had a way of calming me down.

"Trust me, Lainey. There will be other guys. Real guys, who are who they say they are."

We ride in silence to the hospital.

CHAPTER 38
Wednesday, June 14

Over the next few days I run myself into the ground, going from rehearsal to the hospital to the apartment, where the chores never seem to end.

Now I'm riding home on the L with Ted. My phone chimes.

> Hayley: Any change in Ella's prognosis?
> Me: If anything I think she's worse.
> Me: It's breaking my heart.
> Hayley: She's going to be ok
> Me: I'm not sure this time.
> Hayley: Has Dad been in to see her?
> Me: No. I don't expect him to.
> Me: I've hardly talked to him.

Even when my paychecks hit and he usually sends me a "good job, kiddo," my phone has been silent. Total freeze-out.

> Me: If he'd admit what he did was wrong, and if he wanted to be different, things between us might change.

Me: But until he does that I don't have anything to
    say to him.
Hayley: I wish he would.
Hayley: But I'm starting to think he's just incapable.
Hayley: No one says no to him.
Hayley: He always has everything just as he likes it.
Hayley: But we shook him up.

And this is what happens when things don't go his way. He pouts in a proverbial corner and makes life hell for the rest of us. And usually, I scramble around, try to make him talk to me, try to get him to tell me whatever it was I did wrong, whatever it was I did to deserve the cold shoulder.

I don't care this time.

This time, I *know* I'm not wrong.

However, if I'm getting paid, and he's taking a cut as my manager, and he's not in contact with me . . .

How do I know I'm paying him the right amount?

I never thought I'd come to a place where I didn't trust my own father to not swindle me, but after everything he's lied about . . .

It's not that I think he's actually cheating me. But I no longer think he's the type of person who wouldn't.

"Hey, Ted?"

"Yeah." He looks up from the book he's reading.

"Is there a way to ask to see my pay stubs?"

"Well . . ." He tucks a thumb into the novel to bookmark his page. "It's my understanding that that's part of the court case. Full disclosure as to your earnings, his percentage of your earnings . . . and the determination of whether your father should continue to act as your manager."

Wait. The court case is dealing with that directly? "I thought it was about child support and maintenance. And Mom being compensated for everything she's done for me."

"It is, but I think it's more about gaining control of information. I know your mom had been trying to get the records for months, if not years. She seemed to think your father didn't have enough time on his hands anymore to do justice to you and your career."

Because he was busy getting gigs for Jennica.

"She said *she* wanted to manage me."

"Mmhmm."

The cancer sits in the air between us. "But even if she can't now, Dad should've been paying her all along for taking me to auditions and rehearsals. I hope she at least gets some compensation out of the court case."

"Well, it looks like your dad found a way to prove you didn't need the escort to your auditions anymore." He looks at me for a bit too long. "He hired a firm to record your movements, and he proved that you're pretty self-sufficient and city savvy."

"Wait. Hired someone." It hits me: "It wasn't Dylan Thomas following me?"

"I checked in this afternoon for an update, and the cops said that guy turned out to be a private investigator working for your dad."

"My dad was having me followed?"

Ted nods.

"Tracking me to prove I went places all alone?"

"Looks that way."

"But he knows I can do that *now*. That's not the point Mom's trying to make! The point is that I never used to do that when I was younger."

"That's what your mom is trying to prove."

I picture the guy who followed me. I think about every hitch in my breath, every faltering heartbeat, all the time and energy I spent trying to figure out if he was really tailing me. All because my dad had wanted to score some points against my mom.

"God, I'm clueless, aren't I? I didn't know the first thing about who my dad really is . . . and then there's the whole Dylan Thomas debacle. I mean, what kind of a girl becomes addicted to talking to a guy who isn't who he says he is? Only to block him because I think he's someone else?"

"Listen, Lainey. Don't beat yourself up."

"This stuff doesn't happen to Hayley. She's socially adept. She knows how to talk to people face to face. She has good judgment." Although, until recently, she's also been Dad's staunchest defender.

"You'll get there. And anyone can be fooled by a skilled liar." He slips the glasses from his face and chews on one of the arms. Then, just when I think he's going to say something, he leans back, slips his glasses back onto his face and goes back to his book.

"Ted? Do you think—I mean, since Dylan wasn't actually stalking me—I mean, he's shy, and I understand shy—maybe I should give Dylan another chance?"

He sighs heavily and turns a page. "Whether or not Dylan Thomas was stalking you, I still don't think he was being completely honest with you."

But I wonder . . .

My mother is giving Ted a second chance. Or he's giving it to her.

Maybe that's the right thing to do.

Or maybe it's time to admit that I sort of fell for Dylan Thomas.

Okay, not sort of.

Did.

***

Later, I'm on my bio page on Lyrically.

My mouse hovers over the UNBLOCK button next to Dylan Thomas's profile picture.

Should I?

Shouldn't I?

CHAPTER 39
Saturday, July 8

"You'll be home by next week," I tell my mom. "You have to be."

I'm supposed to be onstage for open mic at the Factory, and I really want my mother to hear me sing the song I call "Warrior" for the first time in public. I squeeze her hand.

She weakly tightens her fingers, as best she can, around mine. "Whether I'm there or not," she says in a breathy, wheezing voice, "you have to go on."

"Mom. No."

"The show goes on, baby girl. Promise me. If I'm there, or if I'm not, you'll sing that beautiful song."

"I promise." I climb into the tiny hospital bed with her.

It doesn't take a rocket scientist to see that she isn't getting better. She isn't responding to treatment the way the doctors hoped she would. And it feels like there's a lot more room in this hospital bed than there used to be.

The doctors and nurses say all the right things when I talk to them.

And she's still witty and she still smiles.

But yesterday, I caught Nana Adie all-out bawling in the waiting room. She sees it, too. We both hear what the doctors won't say.

My mother is slowly dying. My beautiful, graceful mother. She's fading away.

"Let's get a picture," I say. "I won't post it if you don't want."

"I don't mind," Mom whispers.

"You're beautiful," I tell her. I kiss her cheek and think of all the times I pulled away when she used to peck mine. Tears prick my eyes, but I will them away. I don't want her to see me cry.

I snap a selfie of the two of us and post it to my Instagram: *My #mauvelous mother. #PinkStrong.*

I stay with her until she falls asleep. Eventually I carefully climb out of the bed, contain my sadness until I reach the family waiting area, and burst into tears.

I sit against the wall and bury my head in my hands, sobbing violently. I want to scream.

After what feels like an hour, I pull in a long, difficult breath and dare myself to hold my head up.

The first thing I see: A pink-and-gold swirled origami moon, just sitting there on a side table where people usually perch their Styrofoam coffee cups.

I peel myself up from the floor and grasp it. Eagerly, I unfold it.

Afraid of what the future holds
Afraid my story will never be told
Well, my life's always on-air
My life's always a bear
But I reach high for the gold
I seek only the bold
I fight because I care
I live because I dare.

"Lainey?"

"Ted."

"You okay, kid?" He folds me into his arms.

"She's dying," I say between sobs. "I don't know how to live without her."

Ted squeezes me. "You've got to hang in there. She's still fighting. You can't give up while she's still fighting."

I nod against his shoulder, and finally back away, wiping tears from my cheeks.

"You need a break. Want to walk Vinny? Nana's here. And we'll come right back."

***

It's almost two in the morning, but I can't sleep. Even Nana has turned in by now.

I log into Lyrically. I find Dylan Thomas's page.

Unblock.

Me: Hi.

Within a few minutes, he responds.

Dylan: Hey!

Me: Why are you up?

Dylan: I'm not entirely. The message alert on Lyrically
    woke me.

Dylan: I've been trying to reach you.

Me: I've been confused.

Dylan: About?

Me: Us.

Me: You and me.

Me: What we are. What we aren't.

Me: Why I feel I can tell you everything

Me: but you hide behind a screen.

Dylan: So do you.

Me: But I don't watch you from a distance.

Dylan: I know. That sucked, didn't it?

Dylan: I really am sorry.

Dylan: If I'd been more confident, I wouldn't
    have done it.

Dylan: But every time I tried to tell you who I am

Dylan: I froze.

Dylan: Not that that's an excuse.

Dylan: I'm sorry I hurt you.

Me: You SCARED me.

Dylan: I'm sorry about that, too.

I don't know what to say, and he must not either because for long minutes, I stare at a quiet screen. Finally, he starts typing again.

Dylan: Is there any way we can start over?

I'm not sure I believe in starting over. I've never seen anyone succeed at it. And yet I find myself typing . . .

Me: Next week.

Me: Open mic.

Me: The Factory.

Me: I'll be singing a song I wrote entirely on my own.

Me: Notes, lyrics, the whole shebang.

Me: No screen.

Me: I'll be getting real.

Me: Maybe you can, too.

Dylan: You want me there?

Me: Yes.

Dylan: Then I'll be there.

Me: It's time we meet face to face.

Me: I sing in front of the whole world.

Me: And you shake my hand and let me know
the real you.

Dylan: Madelaine?

Me: ?

Dylan: These past few weeks without our chats
have been AWFUL.

✳✳✳

Later, when I'm finally dozing off, my phone buzzes again with a message from my sister:

Hayley: The Vagabonds site!

Hayley: There's a rumor that they're about to
release a new song.

Hayley: This is a sign.

Hayley: Good things are coming.

CHAPTER 40
Friday, July 14

I wish I shared in my sister's optimism.

Sure, it looks like Vagabonds are back in business and that thrills me. After a year-long hiatus, they're back on social media and rumor has it they'll be releasing a song by tomorrow morning. There's also talk of an upcoming album and even a tour. Nothing is official yet, but Dad texted me to ask if I wanted to see the show when they come to Chicago in October. United Center, Concert Club . . . the whole shebang.

I haven't replied to Dad.

"So you're not going to go?" McKenna asks as we sit talking before the open mic starts.

"I don't know," I say. I mean, of course I want to go, but not at the expense of something else. It's hard to juggle professional productions and school as it is, and if I'm starting at the academy soon, I'll be even busier than usual. Plus I don't know what Mom's going to be going through by the time the mythical tour kicks off.

Besides, I have an inkling Dad offered as a way to bridge the gap between us without having to change anything.

Still, I can't wait to see what snippet of genius the band will be dropping.

As for what I'm about to drop . . . groan.

The Lyrically community seems to like it. But now I'm about to sing in front of a crowd, and there's just too much that can go wrong.

Everyone who cares about me is here to see me perform tonight: McKenna, Brendon, Hayley, Nana, Ted . . . everyone but Mom, who's not well enough to leave the hospital. Even the Sophias are at the next table. Probably getting ready to heckle the hell out of me.

When Dylan Thomas shows up—he promised he'd be here, too—I'm sure he'll remind me that I'm a pessimist for assuming I'm going to bomb.

"Dad's here," Hayley says.

"What?" I look toward the Milwaukee Avenue entrance. My father and his wife are paying cover at the door. "Did you tell him about this?" I ask.

Hayley shakes her head. "I haven't spoken to him since we were in Kenilworth."

"So how'd he know to come here?"

She shrugs.

Karissa smiles when she sees me. Dad makes eye contact, but quickly looks away.

I wave. Karissa waves back.

But I don't beckon them over, and they don't come without an invitation.

The emcee takes the stage and welcomes the crowd. "So, here's how it works. We'll hear from twenty performers tonight. Each has a time limit of three minutes . . ."

I zone out as panic sets in.

I won't be July out there, or Jane Banks, or Thoroughly Modern Millie. Tonight I'm taking the stage as *me*.

" . . . so I'll put my hand in the hat, here," the emcee is saying. "And I'll put out our first performer . . . Everyone, please welcome to the stage here at the Factory: Madelaine Joseph!"

The place erupts in applause, but I'm like a deer in headlights. I have to go first?

I'm numb as I grab hold of the handle on my guitar case.

Numb as I climb the stairs and lift my acoustic fender from its velvet bed.

Numb as I take a seat on the stool in the spotlight and strum.

I see Ted's phone go up. He's going to record my performance for my mom. He gives me a nod of encouragement.

I take a deep breath.

How am I going to play guitar with fingers that won't stop shaking?

And, God, I wish I hadn't worn a dress tonight. I'm certain I'm giving everyone a show of my underwear.

And there are so many people here, and more people coming in . . .

I can't do this.

Shut the world out. My mother's voice is crisp and clear. So vivid that I flinch when I hear it in my mind. It's like she's here. *Just perform. This isn't about anyone out there. It's about you . . . you and that stage. You love it. Share your time with it, your heart with it, your soul with it, and it will love you, too.*

I will.

You can do this.

"I can do this," I whisper to myself.

I pull the microphone closer.

"This . . ." I clear my throat and try again, speaking into the microphone. "This is a song I wrote . . . for the bravest woman I know. She can't be here. She's battling another round with breast cancer. But she's a survivor."

The crowd erupts in another round of applause.

"For my mom."

I strum the first chords, and a funny thing happens—the crowd really does fade away. I belt out the first words of my ballad: "Run, run, run to the ends of the earth . . . Run in silent rage . . ."

As I sing, I imagine my mother's feet, clad in pointe shoes: entrechat, *ronde de jamb* . . .

And she's really here with me. She's here in my heart.

I sing as if no one else is here, as if I'm on the empty stage I reference in my lyrics.

By the time I strum the last note, awareness of the crowd begins to filter back into my consciousness, bringing me back to reality.

I drop my pick. The crowd roars.

Nana is on her feet, as are Ted, the Weekes twins, and Hayley. Even the Sophias are screaming and clapping.

I look to Dad and Karissa. I think Karissa is actually crying. Dad's lips are in a thin line, as if he's holding back tears, himself. He gives me a nod.

"Thank you," I say. I don't know if I'm saying it to the crowd, to my mother, to myself, or to whatever force in the universe smiled on me to make this go right tonight.

The emcee: "Madelaine Joseph, everybody."

I picture the carving near my favorite seat at the cafe. Finally, it's true: I was here.

CHAPTER 41

Dylan: Who says I wasn't there?
Me: I didn't meet you. So . . .
Me: You reneged on the deal.
Me: You were supposed to come clean.

I'm still tingling with the reverberations of tonight's applause, but I can't help feeling a tinge of disappointment about Dylan standing me up, letting me down, yet again.

Dylan: I would never miss your open mic.
Dylan: You were wearing a pink dress.
Dylan: You don't usually wear pink. OR dresses.
Dylan: You dedicated the song to your mother, the
    toughest warrior in the world.
Dylan: You're a mezzo-soprano
Dylan: but you have incredible range.
Dylan: And you didn't know it, but you hugged me at
    the end of the night.
Dylan: I was there.
Dylan: And I'm pretty certain that I don't want to miss
    any performance from now on.

What the hell? I mean, I hugged a lot of people after I got offstage. There was kind of a swarm and I was still in a state of semi-shock. But still . . .

He was there, he hugged me, and he didn't introduce himself?

Dylan: But there's something I haven't told you.

Me: What?

Dylan: I told you I'm not a poet.

Me: 😕 All evidence to the contrary.

Dylan: I'm serious.

Dylan: All those lyrics that enthralled you . . .

Dylan: they weren't mine.

Dylan: Which is why I couldn't face you.

Dylan: You can't know who I really am because
    I know you won't forgive me after I tell you
    the truth.

Dylan: I wanted to confess in person, but I lost
    the nerve.

Dylan: And there's no point in it now.

Dylan: You just can't know.

Me: What are you talking about?

Dylan: The poems you're finding.

Dylan: I didn't write them.

Dylan: I'm not the one leaving them for you.

Dylan: I don't know who is.

Dylan: I just told you it was me so I'd have an excuse
    to talk to you.

Dylan: I should've been honest about that ages ago.

Dylan: But then it felt like we had this real connection

Dylan: that had nothing to do with the poems

Dylan: And I didn't want to lose that.

Dylan: You're all I think about.
Dylan: This can't be the end.

Worse than I imagined. The only reason I started talking to him at all was for access to the lyrics. This whatever-this-is-between-us is based on music and the truth woven throughout the art form.

And it's all been a lie.

CHAPTER 42
Saturday, July 15

"You really crushed it up on that stage," Ted says. We're sitting in his living room, sharing a large order of cheese fries.

"Thanks." I shrug. I'm still distracted by thoughts of Dylan Thomas, by the revelation that he deceived me, by the question of who really wrote those poems and left me those origami moons. I haven't had the heart to mention any of this to Ted yet.

"I noticed your father showed up."

I nod and grab a fry.

"Things any better there?"

"He's texted a few times."

"And?"

"And I don't know. I'm mad at him. For what he's been doing to Mom. For constantly trying to hurt her through me. For hiring a private investigator to follow me just so he can get a leg up on the court case. For hiding so much from me. It all seems—inexcusable."

Ted sighs. "I'll tell you what. If you were my client, I'd probably be counseling you to do whatever you can to reconcile with him, at least until you turn eighteen and gain control over your own assets. But hey. You're not my client. And I'm not your father. But like I've said—I'd be happy and honored to fill that role." He stands. "I'm gonna get some coffee. You want some?"

"Sure. Thanks."

While Ted's in the kitchen, I notice Vinny poking his nose into a box in the corner.

"Vin-vin," I say. "Come."

But he only digs deeper into the box, so I go to him.

"What are you getting into?" I slip an arm under Vinny's belly, and he squirms.

I let him go. He's not comfortable being held, I remember. Ted said he was probably abused as a puppy, and he's just getting to know me. He has to trust me fully before he'll let me pick him up.

"I understand," I tell him. "You want to be held on your own terms." I stroke him from ears to tail. "Me, too."

For a brief moment, he seems content, but a second later, his nose is back in the box. This time, I move the box instead of grabbing the dog. "Ted won't like you screwing up his stuff."

Wait a minute.

I peer into the box. It's filled with paper. Paper with pearlescent sheens, linen textures, subtle strips and plaids. Thick, quality stock.

Like the paper used to fold Dylan Thomas's origami moons.

And tucked under a few sheets of paper in the box is a how-to book . . . origami. I pick up the book. It falls open to a dog-eared page: how to make a moon.

Ted calls from the kitchen: "Want almond or coconut milk?"

I think about all the poetry slams Ted used to participate in. All the times he'd leave poetic little musings on the foyer mirror, scrawled in his artsy penmanship with dry-erase markers.

Have the words I've been gathering been the work of a guy who'd do those sorts of things?

I think about his abrupt exit from our lives, which never made sense to me. His leaving because he couldn't handle the reality of the situation.

I think of the times I was supposed to meet up with Dylan Thomas. All the times Dylan Thomas never showed. All the times Ted would coincidentally be there instead . . .

Is Ted Haggerty posing as a teenage guy online?

To get close to us—close to me—again?

These past few weeks without our chats have been AWFUL.

No. It can't be.

But why else would he have all this paper?

He knows my favorite seat at the Factory. He knows I go to Saint Mary's on the Mount. He knows where I live.

He's coincidentally been in the vicinity nearly every time I found an origami moon: the hospital, the front porch . . .

And he knows me . . . he knows what to say to calm me down, knows what I'm into, what types of things I like to talk about.

No wonder I clicked so quickly with Dylan Thomas. No wonder I was so comfortable talking to him.

Because Dylan was actually Ted.

Oh my God. It's beyond comprehension. It's so . . . *creepy.*

My heart starts racing, and my ears go cloudy for a second.

"Lainey?"

I shove the box back into the corner and scramble to my feet just as Ted appears in the doorway. "Almond? Or Coconut?"

"Um . . . actually . . . Thanks, Ted, but Nana Adie just texted, and I have to get home."

"Oh." He frowns a little. "Everything okay with your mom?"

"Yeah . . . I . . ." I force a little laugh. "She's nagging me about some chores I didn't do."

"Well, maybe you can come by some other time. Like we were saying before. Take Vinny for a walk."

Upon hearing the "W" word, Vinny jumps up and plants his little paws on my hip. "Or puppy sit from time to time," Ted suggests. "If you'd like."

I pet the dog that was supposed to be mine.

If my mother's pseudo-boyfriend is really doing what I think he's doing, I can never see Vinny again. I mean, engaging me in an online relationship? Trying to pass off Dad's private investigator as the culprit?

I take a deep breath. Maybe I'm wrong. Maybe I'm jumping to conclusions.

I look again to the paper in the box, the book. I don't know that there's another explanation.

I wish, wish, wish there were.

But for now I have to go.

I look into Vinny's dark brown eyes. He's looking at me as if he knows this is the last time. He pushes off and lands all four paws on the floor again.

"It would be good to see you more often," Ted continues. "Hell. Maybe soon, when your mother's feeling a little better, and she's got time to consider it, we can try living together again." He presses a hand to his heart. His brows slant slightly downward. "I love the hell out of both of you."

I can think of nothing other than getting the fuck out of here.

"Well, thanks for the fries." I'm already stuffing my feet back into my Chuck Taylors. "But I really should get going. I barely have enough time to get to rehearsal."

"Here's an idea."

I wish he'd shut up. Why, Ted? Why did you have to do it? Why couldn't you just be normal?

"Let's all go out to dinner on opening night. And maybe on your first day at the academy, too."

I physically feel my heart drop. That's right. The academy. He was supposed to pay my tuition.

I can't accept the offer now.

I see Ted's lips moving, but I can't hear him talk. My vision blackens at the periphery.

Dylan Thomas's words ring in my ears: *You're all I think about.*

"Lainey?"

"I have to go."

CHAPTER 43

Normally, when I find myself in an upsetting situation, I'd hightail it home to Mom and Nana.

But I know no one's at our place. Nana is spending the entire day at the hospital. She has meetings with Mom's team of doctors, and she spends as much time as she can at Mom's side—just like I know Mom wouldn't leave me if I were really sick.

If I didn't have rehearsal, I'd go to the hospital myself.

But I'm not sure how I would even begin to explain all this to them.

God, I'm such an idiot. I blindly believed in Dylan Thomas without knowing *anything* about him. How is anyone going to take me seriously when I've proven to be so stupid?

And secondly . . . there's the fact that it was Ted who duped me.

How can I burden my mother and Nana with this now? They have enough on their plates. I mean, of course they should know the truth about Ted. But if Mom is as sick as I think she is—I feel like she's weaker by the day—this news will only make things worse.

I block Ted on all social media and, of course, my phone, and that helps for a few beats.

But thirty seconds later, the feeling that I've been violated and manipulated churns in my gut again. I feel like I might hurl. I text Hayley.

Me: Have to talk to you.
Me: Important.

I stare at the screen, but no reply comes. She must be working at her internship, or maybe she's even out on a date.

In the absence of Nana, Mom, and my sister, I'd usually text Ted when I have a problem of this magnitude. Not that I'd tell him everything, but I'd share enough that he'd know what fortune cookie tidbits would suffice until Mom was available to dig into the issue. Just like he tried to do today.

But today, I saw through it.

From the L car, I stare out at the city blooming with summer. So much life. But I don't see the promise in it.

I feel alone and desperate—as if I'm out of options, as if Mom is, too. As if I'm going to be on my own.

I open my text thread with Dad.

I scroll all the way back at to the days when we were prepping for the New York trip and read up to the texts I received an hour ago. There's a huge gap in between, right after Hayley and I confronted him in Kenilworth.

But the messages slowly warm over time.

All set for the meet & greet has morphed over the months to *I was blown away to see you singing on stage.* Gradually followed by . . .

Dad: Proud dad over here.
Dad: Miss you, Madelaine.

Dad: I have some ideas about how we can get past
   this.
Dad: Willing to talk?

Part of me doesn't want to give him the satisfaction.

But another part of me wants to put everything aside just for now. At the moment, I'm just a girl who needs her dad.

I take a deep breath.

Me: Something bad happened.
Me: I don't know what to do.

I stare hopefully at my phone, willing it to light up with a message from my father. But the L is approaching my stop, and he's not texting back.

If I were in Dad's position, and I had been wanting to make things right with my daughters for weeks, I'd pounce on the message and reply instantly.

But that's not how my father works.

He wants me to sweat it out.

When a few minutes have passed without word, I rationalize that he could be on the phone, or in a meeting. He could be at an audition with Jennica—his star client.

I get off the train with my phone held firmly in my hand, so I can feel the vibration of an incoming text—but none comes.

The gasping starts a few steps toward the rehearsal hall. It's like I can't manage to inflate my lungs.

I'm dizzy, and the whole world is a blur. People come at me, rushing toward me on the sidewalk, like I'm the only one heading upstream, and I'm drowning in the crowd.

Just have to get there. Just have to make it to the next block.

But the closer I get to it, the farther it seems to be, as if it's at the end of a never-ending tunnel, an illusion.

Even as I climb the steps and yank open the door, the building feels ethereal and malleable, as if it might collapse around me. I'm going to be buried in the rubble. No one will find me.

"Madelaine."

Tears of relief sprout when I hear Brendon's voice.

"Honey."

I barrel into Brendon's arms, and soon McKenna's joined in, too.

"What happened?" McKenna asks. "Is it your mom?"

I shake my head, but I can't speak.

"Mom's okay?" Brendon confirms.

"Y-y-yes." For the time being. But I don't know how much longer she'll be with me, and on top of that I've inadvertently brought another shitty guy back into her orbit, and my relationship with my dad is broken, and I can't take it. I'm heaving over tears.

"Breathe, girl. Breathe." Brendon strokes my hair.

"What's going on?" McKenna asks.

The sound of our director's two sonic claps jars me.

"Shit. Go time," McKenna says. "We'll talk after?"

I eke out a nod. Brendon releases us. He hands me a tissue for my tears.

I close my eyes.

Time to let go of Madelaine.

Time to become July.

CHAPTER 44

"Madelaine, wait up," Brendon says.

I'm practically running out of rehearsal. It's not that I want to avoid the Weekes twins, but I don't have time to get into everything that's happened. And maybe I'm not ready to admit that I was so easily fooled by Dylan Thomas. It's hard to imagine that they won't lose respect for me when they find out the full story. "I'll text later," I call over my shoulder. "Gotta get to the hospital."

"Okay, but—"

McKenna's words are lost in the breeze.

A familiar limo is parked at the curb.

Emotion floods me again, cycling through gratitude at Dad's gesture, to annoyance that he didn't come himself, to relief that I don't have to be alone in this . . . running and repeating in the matter of seconds.

"Miss Madelaine." Giorgio opens a door for me. He remembered to use my full name.

I crawl into the car.

As soon as Giorgio closes the door, I burst into tears again. I can't help it. I'm raw and tired, and even rehearsal today was an emotional tirade—we ran the most heart-wrenching song of the production about a hundred times. I may have escaped into July for a few hours, but July went through hell today. Needless to say, I wholly identified with my character—a wanderer without a home base, without parents to rely on when the going gets rough.

"Maddy."

I look up. "Dad."

He's sitting across from me. Within reach.

And for the first time in a long time, I see him the way I used to, when I was a little girl. Something stirs in my heart. I feel as if I've been holding back, afraid to reach for him for years, but suddenly, the barrier between us has melted away.

His brows slant downward. He looks sad, as if he feels just as worn out as I do with the cold war we've been fighting. Slowly, hesitantly, he raises a hand for a high five and sort of shrugs, as if he doesn't know what else to do.

I look at his hand, then back to his face.

The periphery starts to darken and close in on me, as if I'm being swallowed by a black hole.

He starts to lower his hand and look away—*please, no . . . look at me*—and at the last minute before darkness encapsulates me, I catapult into his arms.

He startles, but quickly wraps one arm around me, then the other. "Madelaine."

I inhale all his scents—the cologne, the lingering aroma of fabric softener in his shirt—and try to remember if he ever held me like this when I was little. I don't know.

"Are you okay? Madelaine?" He takes my chin in his hand. "Honey, calm down."

As if I can do that on cue.

He's talking, but I can't concentrate on what he's saying,

but it doesn't matter. It's not as if my father knows how to be a calming influence these days.

An image pops into my head: Mom's feet in pointe shoes, dancing under the table.

And suddenly, my lungs inflate, and the black mist closing in on me turns to charcoal, then gray, then to a silvery glitter that quickly dissipates when I meet my father's gaze.

"Madelaine?"

"I'm okay." But the *shazam*s of panic still beat in my ears like a bass drum. I wipe a tear from my cheek, concentrate on my breathing, and blurt out everything. Finding the origami book and the paper at Ted's place, about his creepy hand over his heart and the *I love the hell out of both of you*. About the guy I all-out fell for online being none other than Ted. God, it's so gross.

Dad's brow is knit, and he's staring me down. I brace myself for his anger, his disgust, his disappointment that a daughter of his could be so incredibly stupid.

He bites on his lip. "You know this isn't your fault, right?" Oh.

"This is—" He shakes his head. "He's going to pay for this."

The darkness starts to close in again. "Dad. Mom doesn't know yet. And I don't know how to tell her . . ." How to tell her *Your pseudo-boyfriend pretended to be a guy my age. He's been luring me into a relationship with origami moons printed with poems.*

"Don't worry. We're on our way to the hospital. You can talk to her now. Nana's there too, right? Okay. You're okay now," Dad says. "Things are going to be better."

He calls Nana and asks her to meet us in the hospital lobby.

When we get there, Dad helps me get out of the car and walk through the sliding doors on my trembling legs. I practically collapse into Nana's arms.

"What's going on?" It sounds as if my grandmother is under water.

Nana strokes the hair from my face. "What happened?"

"Nothing," I say. "I'm okay." At least I think I am. I want to be. Dad just said I was, so I must be.

"She's having a panic attack, Adie," Dad says. He looks ashen, beaten, worn. "She's been through something. She needs help."

I start to shake my head, but I can't bring myself to form the words on the tip of my tongue. *I'm fine.*

I struggle to pull in a deep breath, but it feels as if the world is spinning, and I can't stop it.

CHAPTER 45

"Madelynn?"

When the static in my ears fades. A bright light practically blinds me. I flinch, and the physician crouching next to me lowers the penlight.

"There we go," says the doctor, smiling. "How about you sit up for me, Madelynn—slowly. Good."

Dad is crouching next to the doctor, and Nana is pacing just beyond them.

In a flash, it all comes back to me: Dylan Thomas, the moons, Ted. My breath catches in my throat again.

I don't remember fainting, but I guess if you're going to black out, a hospital is a prime place to do so. Plenty of people to take care of you there.

"Do you have a history of anxiety?" the doctor asks.

"No," I say, as Nana says, "Yes."

"No?" the doctor asks for confirmation.

"Undiagnosed," Nana says. "But I've suspected for some time."

"I mean . . ." I swallow hard. "I panic sometimes, but—"

"Cloudy vision?" The doctor asks. "Shortness of breath, shakiness, rapid heartbeat?"

"Yeah, but—"

"How often would you say that happens?"

"Um . . . I . . . a couple times a week, maybe?" Or more. Several times a day, when I'm stressed. I've always known that doesn't happen to everyone. Not to Hayley, not to my cast-mates. Which is exactly why I don't talk about it, why I try not to make a big deal of it.

"That's anxiety." The doctor looks over his shoulder at Dad—"It's treatable"—then back to me. "Would you like to talk to someone about it?"

I start to shake my head. *God, no.* The last thing I need is for someone to officially label me as screwed up, let alone some-one digging into my psyche to determine *why.*

But I look to Nana, to Dad, both of whom are nodding. Amazing: they agree on something for once.

"Maybe." I start to get to my feet.

"I think it's a good idea," Dad says. "You've been dealing with a lot. And I had no idea the—the anxiety attacks were this bad for you, that they happened this often. That's not your fault either. It's not a weakness. You know that, right?"

I shrug helplessly. I *feel* weak. I feel dumb.

"You don't have to brave this alone," Nana says. "I think it'll help you to talk."

"Okay," I say.

CHAPTER 46

My first therapy session is scheduled for tomorrow. Now that I have a semi-weekly appointment on my docket—in addition to rehearsals, voice lessons, dance class, and a strict cardio routine—my schedule is going to be even more packed. I'm dreading it, but I also know the panic isn't going to simply go away. Too much has happened. I need to find a way to cope.

With Ted. With Mom's cancer. With Dad's secret second family.

And the first step is to tell Nana what's been going on with Ted.

Dad insists on sticking around until I get through the whole story.

By the time I mention Vinny's nosing through the box of origami paper, Nana is gripping my hand, eyes wide.

"That rat bastard," Nana says when I'm finished.

"I blocked Ted on everything, so I don't expect to hear from him directly. But I'm scared, Nana. I'm scared that I'll have to see him again. Or that he'll use Vinny to get another girl to trust him, or . . ."

"Oh, honey, of course you're scared. You have every right to be. I can't believe he would do this to you—"

"But what if I'm wrong, and he *didn't* do this? What if there's another explanation? Accusing him of something like that . . . it would ruin any chance Mom has if she wants him back."

"The last thing your mother needs is a man like that!" Nana clears her throat. "And you're not wrong. All the pieces fit."

"I'd like to file a police report," Dad offers.

I stare at him. "Will he get arrested?"

"If we're pressing charges, then yes."

"Hold your horses, Jesse," says Nana. "Let me talk to Ella first. I'll text you."

"I appreciate it, Adie." Dad looks at me. "Want me to take you home, kiddo?"

I do, but I don't know if I'm ready to leave my mother's side. "I'll stay here for now," I say. It feels good to put her first for once. Dad can wait. I know he's never tried it before, but he can do it.

✳✳✳

A few hours later, Mom is awake. I'm sitting on her bed, with Nana Adie in the chair right next to me. Even though I've told the story to Dad and Nana already, the words stick in my throat now. So I fish a moon out of my backpack and hand it to her.

She unfolds the moon. Her eyes grow large and well with tears. "I don't understand," Mom says.

"I kept finding these," I try to explain. "At school. At my favorite seat at the Factory. Even on the front step."

"Madelaine." Mom irons the paper with her hands. "Someone left you these moons?"

"The words were just amazing. And the guy who wrote

them started talking to me online. I only found out today that it was—"

"Lainey," Mom says, "these words are mine. From poems I wrote, private poems. I should've said something when I first heard your song, but I was fuzzy-headed from the treatment and wasn't quite sure how to explain it. I don't understand how someone else could've—"

"It was Ted," Nana says.

"He had origami paper and instruction books in his house," I try to explain. "And he's one of the few people who would know when I was at all those places."

Mom goes back to staring at the paper. "Ted must've stolen the poetry from me. Copied it from my notebooks, back when we were together."

It's starting to sink in now. Ted wasn't the author of the words that touched me so deeply. My mother was.

It doesn't change anything that happened with Dylan Thomas, but it means something: Mom and I can finish the song. We'd always wanted to work together, and without either of us knowing it, we did.

"Well, plagiarism is the least of his faults," says Nana crisply. "Following Lainey around, leaving these moons for her to find—it's inappropriate. It's disturbing. Jesse's ready to press charges, but I don't know if we'd have grounds . . ."

"I'll send him a message," Mom says firmly. "I'll ask him not to contact any of us again. If he doesn't respect those boundaries, we'll look at our legal options."

I let out a long, shaky breath.

Mom's tearing up again. "I'm sorry, Lainey. I'm sorry I brought him into your life."

"It's okay. You didn't know."

"It's not okay. It's not."

"I was the one who was stupid enough to think Dylan Thomas was harmless, even when he was leaving stuff for me at school and at home . . ."

"You're not stupid," Nana says firmly. "Neither of you is to blame for this. Ted is responsible for his actions. Not you two."

"But I'm responsible for my actions," I say as my throat starts to close up. "And my actions were dumb." But I remember that even my dad, who's never afraid to be critical, told me this wasn't my fault.

Nana looks like she wants to hug me, but for now she just holds my hand. "If you're not making mistakes," Nana says, "you're not trying. Hang in there. We'll get through this."

CHAPTER 47
Sunday, July 16

I hug McKenna and Brendon once we're out of rehearsal.

"Coffee soon?" McKenna asks.

"Love to," I say. "Text me."

"Madelaine?" Brendon, hands in his pockets, head hanging slightly, chews on his lip for a second. "Is everything okay?"

They've been sort of tiptoeing around me all day, since I was a godawful mess at rehearsal yesterday, and unavailable for comment all night. But I don't want to get into it.

The truth is that *nothing* is okay at the moment. My dreams of attending the academy next year are circling the drain. My mother is really sick, my father is avoiding me, I've lost a friend and a father figure in one fell swoop, and I'll never see my dog again. I shrug. "It has to be, right?"

He cracks a smile.

"Keep on, sister," McKenna says. "Love you."

"Love you, too."

On the L, on the way to my therapy session, I open the text thread from my father. His last message came in last night: *Let me know when you're ready to talk again.*

I text my sister.

Me: I need Dad to come through for tuition for
    next year
Me: so I'm going to have to play his game.
Hayley: I thought Ted was paying your tuition???
Me: Not after yesterday.
Hayley: WHAT HAPPENED YESTERDAY?
Me: Long story.

I shudder with the thought of it. I'll explain it to her later, in person.

Me: I'm going to have to apologize to Dad for things
    I'm not sorry for.
Me: If I expect to go to the academy next year, I have
    to play by Dad's rules.
Me: I understand now how this world works.
Me: And it sucks.

I open my diary app and jot down how I'm feeling: bitter, cheated, but strong. Like Mom, a survivor. Ready to do what I have to do.

Hayley: Do you want to go see him?
Me: Because that went so well last time you
    suggested it.
Hayley: Maybe we can all meet in the city for lunch or
    coffee.
Hayley: I'll go with you.
Hayley: Strength in numbers.
Hayley: If we want to overcome this, we have to start
    somewhere.

Hayley: He's had enough time to think about things.

Hayley: Maybe he'll surprise us and have an actual conversation.

Me: I'll let you know how it goes after we talk.

Hayley: Love you BFFLS.

Me: Love you too BFFBS.

I swipe over to my dad's thread again.

Me: I need to talk to you.

I take a deep breath and send the message off.

✳✳✳

The therapist is fine. She treats me like an adult, like we have a professional relationship. Only now does it occur to me that if Nana guessed I had anxiety, and Dad recognized it the first time he saw me have a panic attack, Ted—a *psychiatrist*—must have figured it out. Yet instead of encouraging me to try therapy, to get help from someone who wasn't part of my personal life, he used my fears to his advantage. To get me to trust him. To get me to rely on him.

Suddenly I'm very, very tired.

I'll wait until I get to the hospital to sleep. I'll cuddle up with my mother, and for a few minutes, everything will be all right.

✳✳✳

Something feels different. I notice it the second I step out of the elevator at the hospital.

Maybe the scent in the air is stronger than usual. A combination of that antiseptic hospital smell and flowers. It smells like a funeral.

My phone chimes.

Dad: Come to the hospital.

Oh no.

There's only one reason he would be at the hospital: it's time to let Mom go.

No, no, no, no, no!

I'm sprinting through the halls toward my mother's room. My eyes are burning with tears. I round the corner and come to an abrupt halt outside her door. I'm afraid of what I'll see when I step inside.

Holding my breath, I enter the room.

The drape conceals her bed, but I see my father is there, sitting at her bedside, his fingers tented under his chin.

My knees are shaking. I take another step. And . . .

I hear her laugh.

"Mom!"

My father spins toward me, but I don't acknowledge him. I dart around him for a glimpse of my mom.

She's on her feet. In street clothing. She's packing her things. She still looks frail—sunken cheeks, dark rings under her eyes, a scarf wrapped around her balding head—but her smile brightens the room. "I'm coming home, baby girl."

I slip into her open arms. My tears are now happy and even more uncontrollable than they were yesterday. "How? You've been so sick."

"That's what chemo does. It kills you. But I passed the last round of tests. I'm coming home."

"You're getting better?"

"Cancer: zero. Ella Norini: two." She pumps her fists in the air.

I laugh and cry even harder.

"I'll, uh . . ." Dad rises. "I'll be downstairs. If you text when you're ready, I'll have Giorgio bring the car around."

"Thanks," Mom says.

Dad turns to me. "Talk soon, kid." He touches my shoulder. "Okay?"

I glance at his hand, and as politely as I can manage, step out of his reach. "Okay."

Once he's out of the room, I take Mom's hands and sit her down on the bed. "Okay, how is this happening?"

"He's been coming the past couple of weeks, and—"

"No, I mean . . . you're coming home!"

And at the moment, I don't care about how or why my father decided to be decent. I don't care that Ted decided to be creepy. I don't even care that I'll probably end up again at Saint Mary on the Mount High School with the Sophias next year.

All that I care about is that my mother has once again prevailed.

"I love you, Mom."

She cups my face in her hands. And it doesn't bother me.

"Back to your father, though. He told me what happened when you and Hayley went to Kenilworth. He feels awful about the way things played out with Karissa and the kids . . ."

"Does he also feel awful about hiring a private investigator to follow me around, so that he could make you look bad in court?"

She winces. "He does, actually, especially now that he knows about your anxiety."

"Mom, he's been a jerk on so many levels, for so long."

"Yes, and he wants things to be better."

"How does anyone expect me to believe that after the way he's acted?"

"You're pretty special, you know. He doesn't want to lose you. He's willing to change. I think he just didn't know how."

"Then why should I trust that he'll put in the effort?"

"Because we've had some good talks lately. About you, about our marriage, about how things went so wrong. Things are going to be better. More transparent. More respectful."

"I guess time will tell."

"It will. And luckily we've got it, baby girl. Time."

CHAPTER 48
Saturday, July 27

"Madelaine," Nana calls down the hallway. "Your father is downstairs."

"Coming." I hop down the hallway, as I shove a combat boot onto my left foot.

Mom's in her room, sleeping. Nana is in the kitchen, sorting through junk mail. "I don't care that your mom decided, for whatever reason, to forgive that rat bastard," Nana Adie says. "I'm still pissed at him."

"Me, too," I say. "But I have to talk to him."

"Be my guest, but I don't want him in my house right now." Nana sighs with closed eyes. "I'm sorry. He's your father. This is your home. Invite him up if you'd like."

I shake my head and kiss my Nana's cheek. "We'll go grab a coffee."

"I'm sorry," she says again.

"It's okay, Nana. It's all going to be okay. I can't believe Mom's home!" And my tears start all over again. She's been home for over a week now, but it still seems surreal.

"She's home, all right." Nana's grin is wide. "Hey, look at this. From the academy. Addressed to one amazing Madelaine Joseph." She tosses an envelope to the table.

I tear it open. "Oh. My. God." My eyes race over the words, then double back to read them again. "Nana, they're giving me a scholarship! A fifty percent credit toward tuition based on *merit*!"

We jump up and down, and Nana starts singing one of Madonna's girl-power songs. Off key, of course.

✳✳✳

Dad and I are at the café at the Factory. I trace the carving on the wood: I was here.

Neither of us has said much beyond small talk. I suppose neither of us is very good at admitting how we feel.

"How are Karissa and the kids?" I ask.

"They're good."

"Do the kids—know about me? Do they know they have two older sisters?"

"They do. They've always known."

"But they didn't know what we looked like. Or they would've recognized us when we showed up. So you must not keep photos of us in your house."

Guilty silence from Dad.

I cut to the chase: "I think I would've been happy to know I had a little sister and brothers. I mean, it would've taken some getting used to, but I think I would've been excited."

His head bobs, and he stares into his coffee. "It's been weighing on Karissa, as you can imagine. She never wanted things to be this way, and she's felt as if I were hiding her and the kids."

"You were. Finding out about them this way . . . it makes me feel like I wasn't important enough to know about big things happening in your life."

"No, Madelaine." He snaps his gaze to mine. "*No.* Don't ever think that."

"What am I supposed to think?"

"It was just the opposite, actually. I didn't want to minimalize what you are to me, what Hayley is to me. And we were going to tell you—Karissa wanted to tell you from the very beginning—but I thought your mother would use it against me. I thought it would make her angry—"

"It *should* make her angry. You didn't even leave us just for Karissa, which would have been bad enough. You left us for Jennica. And then you lied to us about it for *years!*"

I can tell Dad's having a hard time meeting my eyes, but he manages not to look away. "Have you ever lived a lie so long that the longer it goes on, the more impossible it seems to see the truth?"

I shake my head.

"Believe it or not," Dad says. "I did it because I thought it was best for you at the time. I didn't want you to feel pressured to accept Kari and the kids into your life. I didn't want you to think that you'd have to consider them family if you wanted a relationship with me."

"Dad, that's so messed up. You could've talked to us about it and given us a choice about whether we wanted to get to know them."

"I know. I just—I didn't want you to look at me the way you're looking at me right now. The way you looked at me at the house in Kenilworth. All I wanted to do right then was come clean, but the truth hurt you—"

"You hurt me."

"I wish I could go back and do things differently. The marriage really wasn't planned. It just felt right out there, and we were going to do it all again for you and Hayley. But then the court case came, and I was angry that your mother was able to put a halt to my plans."

"But she did it because she got cancer. She wanted to make sure I'd be taken care of. That she would be compensated for all the work she'd done for free over the years."

"I know that now. And I'm going to make it right."

"Dad, it's not that simple. It's going to take me a long time to get over all this. I'm still angry."

He stares at me, eyes wide. "I don't want to let you down." That's all he says.

I take a deep breath. "You have let me down sometimes. But you don't have to keep letting me down."

Dad nods slowly. "So where do we go from here?"

"You know what would be a good start? I need an education. I don't need a hundred pairs of shoes, and hats, and trips to Broadway, and tickets to see Vagabonds. I love shopping with you and going to all those awesome places, and I'm thankful that you can do all that for me, but when you refuse to acknowledge that what I really need is to go to the academy . . . it's wrong."

"You need to go to that school. I agree. I've had this mistaken impression that I was teaching you a valuable life lesson but talking to your mom the last couple of weeks has put things in a different light.

"I'm sorry I've been so stubborn, but I'm going to pay for your school."

"Dad, I'm going to need you to pay for half of it."

"No, one hundred percent. You're right. I have the means, I shouldn't hold it over your mother's head."

"Half at the academy will be fine," I say.

"Now who's being stubborn?"

"The same girl who got a fifty-percent merit scholarship."

"Maddy." His eyes light up when he smiles, and suddenly, I remember that he used to smile a lot when I was a little girl. "That's fantastic!"

"About NYU, though. I know the courts determined that you'd split it with Mom, but . . . Are you paying for Hayley's school?"

"Yes."

"One hundred percent?"

"Yes."

"You can afford it. Mom can't. So I'd like you to do for me what you're doing for Hayley, and what you'll do for Jennica and the boys. I want you give me the same financial support you're giving them. And while we're on the subject, I'd like you to work *with* Mom in managing my career. I know you don't like each other—"

"I can be civil." Dad sighs. "But your mom's not equipped for that career. No experience. No, there's too much on the line. I can't put your career in her hands."

"Dad, come on. I trust her, and I'm old enough to have a say in who manages my career. You have enough clients. You won't miss the commissions from my roles. You can get Mom started in the right direction, so she can have the same type of security you have. She made your life possible, and you make her life difficult. If you want me in your life, you're going to have to work with my mother."

"Okay, okay. You raise some good points."

"I have your word. You'll work with Mom."

"Consider it done."

Well. That went a lot better than I expected. "So are you

going to tell me why you were hanging out in my mother's hospital room?" I ask. "I didn't know you'd been visiting her until she mentioned it the day she left."

"It was Karissa's idea."

"Really?"

He gives me an uncomfortable half smile. "She had a feeling it would be good for me. This may seem strange to you, but I have a problem with anxiety sometimes."

"Maybe you should go to therapy, too."

"Strangely enough, talking to your mother was a little like therapy. I get anxious when I feel like someone is going to know I've done something wrong. And let's face it, I've done more than my fair share wrong. Your mom's the one who's borne the brunt of it, so nothing surprises her. She knows Karissa and I had an affair. And now she knows I've been keeping the children a secret from you. And I . . . I guess I just worry that you're not going to love me as much as you love your mom."

"Dad. No. In fact, opening night of my show, I want you all there. You, Karissa, Jennica, Daniel, and Karl. And I want to go out to dinner after. And I don't want to have to split my time—half with you, half with Mom. I want all of us to eat together."

"Really?"

"Yes, really. You can think about it, if you need to. But you need to get used to the idea fast. You told me you were upset that you didn't know what was going on in my life. So *be part of* my life."

"Deal." He smiles wryly. "You know, that Brendon kid gave me the finger at your open mic."

"He did?"

"It's okay. I deserved it."

"Agreed."

Dad lets out a little laugh.

"And there's one more thing. Can you stop calling me Maddy? I really prefer Lainey."

"Really?"

"Yeah."

"How did I not know that?"

"Dad, we just don't really talk about important things."

"Well, Lainey, I think we're going to have to start."

I smile.

He smiles.

CHAPTER 49

Dad drops me off at home. I wave goodbye and walk up.

And there, sitting on the landing, leaning against our door, is an origami moon.

Ted's been here.

I freeze for a second but ultimately pick it up, if only to throw it away once I'm inside.

I unlock the vestibule door. Classic Madonna drifts out to meet me, and Nana is getting into the groove.

Two steps past the threshold, I hear Ted's voice: "Hi, Lainey."

My heart starts to gallop when I see him sitting on the steps leading up to our third-floor apartment.

"What are you doing here?" I back toward the vestibule, but what can I do? If I run outside, he'll follow, and that'll be more dangerous than being in this tiny space with him. At least here, if I scream, someone might peek out a door to help me.

"You seemed upset the other day," Ted says. "I've tried to text . . . nothing delivers to you. But I thought we should clear the air."

"There's nothing to clear. You should just go home."

"Lainey, I believe in you. Always believed in you, and I

knew someday your mom would see the benefit of having me in your life." He's on his feet now, lingering on the steps.

"You're sick." My hands are shaking, and so is my voice. "You're pretending to be a teenaged guy online to get close to me."

"What?" He takes a step toward me.

I take a step back. "Dylan Thomas. That's the name you go by."

"Lainey . . . no." Ted says. "I'm not Dylan Thomas."

"I saw the origami book and all the paper at your place. Mom already told me she wrote the poems, and you're the only one who could have had access to them."

"I left you the moons. I did. But only because you mean so much to me." He's invading my personal space now, standing less than a foot from me."

Tears burn my eyes. "Please. Stop."

He's getting closer now.

"Nana!" I yell. "Mom!"

He chuckles. "The thing about Adie. She sure loves her Madonna, doesn't she?"

My back hits the vestibule door.

"You deserve to be a priority for someone," Ted says. I smell the coffee on his breath. "Jesse Joseph doesn't deserve to be your father."

"Mom! Please! Someone—"

"Shh." He moves, like he's going to wipe a tear from my cheek.

I flinch and scream again.

"Lainey, *shh*."

"That's quite enough, Ted." Nana's voice.

I look up to see Mom and Nana, and my patchouli-loving

neighbor with her phone aimed at the action, coming down the stairs from the apartments above.

The whir of a siren sounds in the distance.

"Get the hell away from my daughter," Mom says.

Ted shoves me aside and opens the door.

"Madelaine!" Mom is instantly at my side.

I look up from her embrace to find Giorgio lumbering up the steps and blocking Ted's exit. Ted takes a step back, but Giorgio catches and holds him with his arm twisted behind his back. "I saw the moon you picked up, Miss Madelaine," Giorgio says. "When I mentioned it to your dad, he called the police and we circled the block and came back."

I see him now: my father standing at the corner.

"Ella," Ted says. "Tell them . . . You understand why I did it, right? To be a father to her."

My mother straightens up and holds me a little tighter. "You crossed a line, Ted."

"And," I say, "I already have a father."

He's not perfect, and we have a lot of things to work through. But he's my father, and I love him, and he's working on earning my trust. Something Ted has lost forever.

I breathe steadily.

CHAPTER 50

I'm so tired. This day was *insane*.

And maybe I should just let a sleeping dog lie.

But Ted has been arrested, and the cops assured me he won't be arraigned until tomorrow morning. I know he's in the clink all night. I'm safe.

I open my laptop and surf to Lyrically.

I unblock Dylan Thomas.

Maybe this is crazy, but if Ted was lying—if he's really Dylan—he won't be able to reply to me tonight from a holding cell. And if Ted's telling the truth—if he's not Dylan—maybe I'll find out who is.

It's now or never.

Me: Who are you?

A few minutes pass with no reply. I hover over the block button, but a split second before I tap it, Dylan starts to type.

Dylan: You know me.
Me: WHO ARE YOU?
Dylan: You'll be mad.

Me: I'm already mad.

Dylan: Promise you'll listen?

Me: If you're legit my age, I need to know.

Dylan: FaceTime?

Me: Not giving you my number.

My phone starts to ring. I gasp when I see the name lighting up the screen.

No.

Maybe it's a coincidence.

Dylan: Answer please.

Dylan: We should talk about this.

I look again to my phone, at the invitation to FaceTime. I accept.

Brendon's face fills the screen. "Do you hate me?"

CHAPTER 51

I can't say anything for a full five seconds. It doesn't sound like a lot of time, but when you discover one of your best friends—one of the few genuine friends you have—has been deceiving you, five seconds could be a lifetime. Finally, I manage, "Why would you—"

"I saw you post the lyrics. I thought it would be a good way to get to know you."

"You know me already."

"Not like this. Like I told you in New York. You're legendary in my house ever since *Mary Poppins*. And then we worked together in *Peter Pan*, and you were amazing, but you were also so reserved. I don't think you said more than five words to me that whole time. I was hoping to find a way to get to know you."

I shake my head. I'm so confused. And I'm pissed. "Why wouldn't you just talk to me?"

"I was nervous. You should know what that's like. You're closely acquainted with insecurities."

"But you're you, and I'm me," I say. "You don't get anxious."

"Everyone is anxious sometimes. I know I give off this outgoing vibe, but when it comes to making small talk with cute, talented near-strangers I practically get hives. Communicating online bypassed all that awkwardness. It let us be ourselves with each other right away."

"But you weren't being yourself. You lied to me."

"From a certain point of view."

"From *all* points of view. You let me think you were the origami poet. You told me your name was Dylan Thomas."

"It is. Or *was*. I was born Dylan Thomas Weekes. I changed my name legally to my stage name after *Peter Pan*. My sister told you. I named myself after Brendon Urie."

I don't know what to say. This feels like a technicality, not like exonerating evidence. "This is so screwed up."

"I'm sorry I scared you—"

"You did more than scare me. You manipulated me. And you had so many chances to tell the truth, once we were actually friends in real life. With everything else going on, I really needed someone to be honest with me."

He sighs and leans back. "I know. I'm really sorry. It was dumb and it was cowardly. I was hiding behind Dylan for fear you wouldn't feel the same way about me, and then in New York, you all but told me—well, you didn't tell *me*, you told your dad—it was never going to happen. So how could I come clean after you'd said that, and face you every day?"

"I said that to my dad to get him off my back, not because I wasn't into you! Besides, you'd been dating a guy . . ."

"Yeah." He shrugs a shoulder. "Then a girl caught my eye. Like I said." There's a pause. "Is there a chance now? Now that you know?"

On the one hand, I can't believe he would even ask this. On the other hand, even now, I don't want to stop talking to him. Under all my confusion and frustration and anger, there's still this other feeling, this insistent sense that I can trust him, this sense that we understand each other in ways that go deeper than the lies. "I don't know."

He sighs. "You know what? Stupid question. I understand. I hope you can accept my apology. If you can't, I'll do my best to give you all the space you need onstage. But maybe at some point we can be friends again."

I feel like I should say something, but I'm totally at a loss for words.

"Goodnight, Madelaine."

"Goodnight, Brendon."

He sighs again before the screen goes black.

A few minutes later he texts me.

Dylan: I just wanted to say one more thing.

Dylan: Like I said, I get it if we can't be friends after this

Dylan: but I hope you'll remember that if you're feeling all alone and like no one understands you, I'm a few neighborhoods away

Dylan: and I'm wishing we could be alone together.

Dylan: Because I do understand you. And I love you for who you are.

CHAPTER 52

"Mom?" I stand outside her door. "Can I come in?"

"Of course, baby girl."

I lie down next to her on her bed just like she usually does on mine. I tell her about Brendon being Dylan Thomas. "In a way it's a relief to know that he was the one I bonded with online, not Ted. And at the same time, it feels awful. Because we were friends. And maybe we could've been more." I sigh and lean back on the pillows. "I think I inherited your bad judgment when it comes to men."

She laughs. "It's not hereditary."

"All evidence to the contrary."

Mom looks at me thoughtfully. "I know things have been especially rough lately, with your dad and then with Ted. And now this boy with his secret identity. A lot of people have let you down, in a lot of different ways."

She strokes my hair, and I find myself thinking about how I dyed it reddish brown to satisfy Dad. I've already decided that I'm going to tint it pink again, and this time it'll be doubly important.

"But I'm glad Brendon apologized," she says. "I'm not saying you have to accept that apology or pick up right where you left off with him like nothing's changed. But I don't want you to feel as if you can't give anyone a second chance. Some people are capable of righting their wrongs. Some people can grow and change for the better. I think we're starting to see that with your father. Maybe you'll see it with Brendon too."

I close my eyes. "I want to believe that. But it seems naive."

"Oh, honey, it's not naive to trust. It's not weak to have faith that people—certain people—can be better. Of course, I will *never* encourage you to settle for less than you deserve. But you should always believe in love."

"Even if it means getting your heart smashed to a million pieces?"

"Yes, because if you're lucky you learn from it and get stronger from it, and then when something truly wonderful comes along you can appreciate it more fully. You know, I've fallen for twenty idiots in my lifetime, but the twenty-first time . . ."

"I know," I say, rolling my eyes. "We've been over this. You loved Dad more than you imagined you could love another person."

"True. Until I had you. *You* are number twenty-one. I fell in love for the twenty-first time the moment I looked into your eyes. I knew at that moment, that nothing anyone could ever say or do would change the fact that I love you. And if I never love so completely again—on the stage performing, or even at home, with the next guy I decide is worth a chance—I am forever fulfilled being your mother. You are my twenty-first love."

She kisses my forehead.

I feel music in my bones. I see notes pop up on the staff in my mind.

✳✳✳

In the morning I text the Raspberry Beret crew.

Me: Counter Offer before rehearsal?
McKenna: You know it!
Brendon: Wouldn't miss it.
Brendon: :)

Maybe a full reboot on my friendship with Brendon won't be possible. But I want to at least try for a fresh start. For once, I want to not assume the worst. I want to leave the door open for trust.

And maybe for something more.

Me: <3

I open the diary app on my phone and record how I'm feeling. Celestial. Musical. Loved and accepted.

Like a song just waiting to be sung.

Acknowledgments

Thanks, as always, to my agent, Andrea Somberg, and to team Lerner, especially the amazing Amy Fitzgerald, for putting your heads together to make this book a reality. I appreciate your patience as I juggled deadlines, and I appreciate your spot-on advice as this plot took a few twists and turns none of us expected, not to mention my own struggles in the medical realm. Sasha = 2. Breast Cancer = 0. Thanks for hitting the pause button while I kicked some cancer ass.

To my cover designer, Kimberly Morales: I could not have imagined a better representation of my Madelaine. Bravo, from the mess in her head to her pink hair peeking out from beneath her beanie! It's almost as if you lived in my brain while you conjured her.

To my family: Thanks for your cheers and well-wishes. LOVE YOU ALL TO PIECES even though you're crazy. Nana, thanks for being proud of my Edgar nomination, even though you didn't know what it was. Then again, you'd be proud of me for unloading the dishwasher.

To Mary, for whom I wrote my first full-length manuscript at age fourteen: I have a great idea for a game with a hat and some laminated cards . . . I look forward to the days of the farmhouse and Swatch Talk.

Andrew Tomlinson, I know you're far too humble to have wanted your name in print, but your influence on both my daughters has been tremendous; forgive me, therefore, for slipping your name into this book. You are an incredible teacher, a brilliant choreographer, and an immeasurable sense of support. My girls will carry the lessons you've taught them far beyond the stage. "If you're on the run and bleeding, go to the vet. They have all the tools you'll find at a hospital. Just kidding. Turn yourself in."

To the rest of our Dance Connection family: you have supported generations of dancers throughout your many decades on Center Street. We both applaud you and are proud to be linked with you in our circle. You have provided the foundation from which many a dancer has twirled her way toward her forever—including two very close to my heart.

To the performers who lent their names to this tale— Madelaine, Emmah, Ella, Hayley, McKenna, Timothy, Daniel Karl, Kari, Jennica, Adie, Jess, and Jake-in-disguise: thank you for showing my youngest what true friendship means. I'm so pleased she found her people in you.

Joshua, as always, I appreciate your support in everything I do—even when I decide to bring home puppy No. 4. I couldn't help it . . . she's just so flippin' cute! Finishing this book with the crazy Daisy Maisy warming my feet was both challenging and rewarding. I love that we have sixteen paws in our house. No one is more determined than we are to fill our home with love—even at the risk of losing control. <3

Samantha Mary, I can hardly believe you're tap dancing your way onto college stages. You've grown so much since your name, and those of your friends, graced the pages of *Splinter*.

Thank you for being a supportive big sister to your own Madelaine, and for believing in all those around you, including your mama. You are a role model for dozens of little girls and boys in dance shoes, and I know you'll be a great teacher. Keep dancing. It's in your heart, your soul, your head, and I love that you spread the joy it brings you to all those to whom your light radiates. From the moment I knew you existed, I envisioned pink ballet shoes. And Miss Carlye is right: You're superhuman. <3

Madelaine Josephine, I know you'll touch the stars for which you're forever reaching. When you were a very little girl, you said, "I'm dancing because I hear music in my head." Not much has changed, has it? Your skills with the ukulele, guitar (rock that Fender, girl), piano, and (insert musical implement here) stun me to awed silence. Your voice is beautiful. Keep singing. Vienna waits for you—along with stages all over Chicago, New York, and LA, and anywhere else you shall roam. You only become more determined as you grow, and you pave your own paths to reach your destination. One of your first performances was to Madonna's "Holiday," which is why Nana Adie is obsessed with the QUEEN of the universe. See what I did there? QUEEN. :) <3

About the Author

Sasha Dawn creates tales of survival and terror, disasters and dreams. She has degrees in both history and writing, and she loves old buildings and new ideas. She fights traffic daily in the north suburbs of Chicago, where she lives with her husband, daughters, and puppies. Her debut YA novel, *Oblivion*, was an Illinois Reads selection and one of the New York Public Library's best books for teens. She is also the author of *Blink*, an Edgar Award nominee, and *Splinter*.

CHECK OUT ALL
SASHA DAWN'S NOVELS.

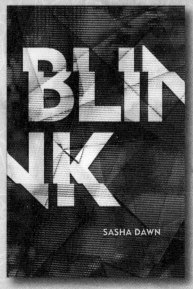

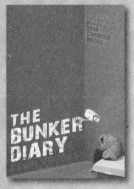